Given to So Edmeston Comm Church
in memory of Beatrice M. LAWRENCE

OCT 8, 1937 ——— Sept 25, 1996

THE SCENT OF
THE ROSES

A NOVEL BY ALEEN LESLIE

The Scent of
the Roses

You may break, you may shatter the vase if you will,
But the scent of the roses will hang round it still.
—*THOMAS MOORE*

PUBLISHED BY THE VIKING PRESS
NEW YORK

Set in Times, Scotch and Bank Script types and
printed in the U.S.A.

To Dorothy Ann Blank,

wherever she is

And to Muriel Roy Bolton,

Vera Caspary, and

Catherine Lynn-Thomas

And to my husband,

my daughter, Diane,

and my son, Jacques, Jr.

Contents

THE SCENT OF
THE ROSES

1

Saint Valentine's Day

IN A WAY my life began all over again the snowy night I became a member of the Weber family. Everything that had happened before, all remembrance of my mother and father, even of the murder, had left my conscious mind as though none of it had ever been. My lapse was not involuntary amnesia; I willed to forget with all the fervor of my ten-year-old heart, and I did. But the past was all there, hidden in my nerve cells, waiting, and when the second trouble came, as it eventually did, bringing the police and reporters trailing through the house of my beloved Webers, I remembered everything so clearly that, in spite of the long delay, I was shaken to bits.

Until then even the part about Sophie's bringing me from New York was blanked out. How we got off the train at Pittsburgh, Sophie carrying her big suitcase and my little one, our streetcar ride to Squirrel Hill, how I walked from the car line behind her, shielded from the wind and fitting my small feet into her larger prints, reaching the house on Wilkins Avenue at last, her rap on the stained glass of the huge front door—all that was lost. It was not until we stepped over the threshold and I saw Sophie's family for the first time that, tired though I was, I came to life. And then all my senses absorbed the warmth of open fires and loving hearts. I savored the drama of my unexpected presence there, watched the expressions on the faces, noticed every detail.

It was February 14, 1908. There were a few valentines propped up against some books on the hall table. One was large and lacy, one comic with a picture of a lady in a large hat drinking beer, the others little and insignificant.

Perhaps it was because I had been moving in oblivion that, when my rebirth occurred, I was able to see so acutely, and hear and smell. I took in everything, the wide hall with the great staircase ascending at the right, the parlor looming in shadows at the left, the dining room brilliantly lit by gas jets at the far end of the hall, and beyond it the conservatory. I saw the people, the lively little old lady who opened the door, Sophie's sisters and brothers interrupted at a late supper coming toward us from the dining room, and heard the surprise in their voices. I smelled good food, crackling logs in the fireplace, yellow chrysanthemums forced into bloom in the conservatory.

I went back to the house recently when I was in Pittsburgh and somebody told me it was about to be torn down. It looked shabby and small, as though shrunken by the years. I could hardly believe it had contained all the things that happened in it, the celebrations, the happy times, the funny events, and then the cataclysm and all its reverberations. But at the time I was ten years old the house seemed mammoth, shining with cleanliness and life, beautiful, even grand.

"Sophie!"

"Yes, Mama, I'm home."

Until I heard it spoken I did not even know Sophie's name. I glanced up at her. She set down the suitcases and took my hand. Her mother stared at me in amazement. Did she wonder who I was and why I was there? If she had asked me I would have been unable to answer. I knew nothing except that Sophie's hand had a familiar feel. I squeezed it tightly and listened to the exclamations from the other people: "For heaven's sake, where did you drop from?" and "We had no idea you were coming tonight— we would have met you at the station!" and "You wrote it wouldn't be for another few days."

"Yes, I got away sooner than I expected," Sophie said.

Her mother, vibrant blue eyes still glaring at me, asked, "And who's your friend?"

"This is Jane." Sophie bent over and smiled at me. "It's all right, dear. Nothing to worry about. We're home. This is where I live, and these are two of my sisters and two of my brothers and my mother." She threw her muff on a console table and lifted me onto a chair. "Jane's going to stay here with us." She stripped off her gloves and began to remove my overshoes and my hat and coat, continuing, "She's going to have the little room next to mine. I'm going to take all the files out, fix it up with a nice little bed, and paper the walls with roses. I think she'll like wallpaper with roses."

Then one of the sisters, a pretty girl with wavy black hair, said tartly, "Dandy, but who is she?"

Sophie ignored the question. "I'm going to get her to bed right away. She's very tired. She can sleep in my room to-night."

The other sister had the grace to exclaim, "My, isn't she sweet!" I glanced at her gratefully, for I felt a little as though I were on probation before so many inquiring eyes.

Sophie took off her own coat, which had a collar to match the muff. Her hat was of the same fur, gray caracul, thick and warm and curly. I thought her very stylish. Her skin was very white, and from under her hat there peeped hair of brilliant glorious red. Oh, she was wonderful! She said, "I'll put you in bed and then I'll bring you up something to eat—on a tray. Won't that be nice, Jane? Something to eat on a tray? In bed like a fine lady?"

I nodded. She picked up my suitcase and led me toward

the staircase. I looked back at Sophie's family, at the two brothers, so similar in height and coloring, at the two sisters, one dark-haired, one light, and at Mrs. Weber, tiny and alert, who pointed her finger and ordered, "Stay here, Sophie!"

"I'll be down as soon as I—"

"I want to talk to you."

"I know, but first—"

"Ich will mit dir sprechen!"

Sophie hesitated but after a second continued up the stairs with me. One of the brothers, amused, said to his mother, "Doesn't she know when you speak German it's a command?"

"Shush, Seymour. Elise, take the tureen in the kitchen and heat up what's left of the soup." The younger sister rolled her eyes heavenward and moved off down the hall.

I loved Sophie's room the instant I saw it. There were two white wicker chairs with curlicue backs and pillowed seats of green and white stripes. The bedstead was brass, and the spread was heavy white linen with lace insertions. The carpeting was green, faintly flowered, and the pattern of the wallpaper was lilies-of-the-valley.

In no time at all I was undressed, washed in a huge white bathroom, and tucked into bed. The light was left on when Sophie went away, for she was to bring me back my tray. I lay there for a few minutes, looking at the picture on the wall, a lithograph titled at the bottom "Ruth in the Fields of Boaz," and at the dresser, which had on it so many things I would come to know in time as intimately as I knew the lines in my palms—the buttonhook and the shoe-horn and the hair receiver.

I could not rest. I was too curious about myself. I got out of bed and went to look in the bureau mirror. If I hoped to see a familiar face I was disappointed. I saw a little girl in a nightgown with a ruffled yoke, but I did not know her. Light brown hair, long and straight, fell over her shoulders and was cut into bangs across her wide forehead. She was not very tall, but perhaps at her age, whatever it was, she was not supposed to be. "This is me," I told myself. But who was I and where had I come from?

I moved closer to the looking-glass and saw that my eyes were neither pure blue nor pure green but a mixture of both. My features were regularly formed, and my teeth, I saw when I tried smiling at myself, were white and even. But my image looked so frightened that I turned away from it to avoid contagion.

I was nervous and had to go to the bathroom again. I went out into the upstairs hall. It was dim and scary, lit only by the light that came from the half-open door of Sophie's room. I saw my own shadow on the wall, larger than life, and in trying to get away from it I grew panicky and became lost. I opened a door which led not to the bathroom but to a dark back staircase. Though it was black as a tunnel, I was impelled to descend it—for the same reason that a child will crawl into a hayrick or push through a thicket. I went down slowly, feeling my way, my hand clenched tight on a wall-rail. The stairs spiraled gently, like the path of a worm through wood.

I emerged finally in a kitchen filled with wonderful smells. Flame flickered on the gas range under a huge pot. For a moment I thought of going back upstairs the way I had come down, but I dreaded darkness so soon again, and, hearing voices, I went toward them.

That effort took me into a pantry, and there I stopped, for just on the other side of it the members of the family had gathered in the dining room and I was caught at once by what they were saying. They were talking about me.

"How terrible! What a dreadful tragedy!"

"How awful for the child."

"You had the hotel room right next door, Sophie?"

"Yes, that's how I heard Jane scream."

"That was the first time you saw her?"

"No, no, we were friends already. I knew her from the

lobby, and sometimes she came to my room to visit. We played ticktacktoe."

"And they don't know who the murderer is for sure?"

"No," Sophie said, "not for sure."

"But they suspect *him?*"

"Yes, but I hope they're wrong. Oh, how I hope they're wrong!"

"That would be even worse for the little girl if it was him, wouldn't it?"

"Terrible," Sophie said.

Mrs. Weber's voice came to me loud and clear. "He did it!"

"Mama, make up a story for the nickelodeon," Sophie cried, "but don't make up this. Maybe he did and maybe he didn't."

"I don't understand," Mrs. Weber said. "The little girl was there. She saw what happened. Why don't they ask her?"

"That's it—they've asked her again and again, but she doesn't remember a thing. Her memory is completely blotted out—everything that happened in connection with the murder and everything that went before. She's like a newborn baby with no recollection at all, except that she can talk, of course, and read, and knows how to behave. But everything else—gone."

"Impossible," said Mrs. Weber. "You can't forget like that."

"Yes, Mama. It's shock. Shock does it."

"Then something's wrong with her."

"Of course something's wrong with her! She witnessed something that was such an earthquake to her that her mind wouldn't accept it. I took her to a doctor and that's what he said. The mind has to forget, sometimes, what is too painful to remember."

"My, my!"

My feet were cold, bare as they were on the wooden

pantry floor. I wanted to get back to the warmth of bed, but I was rooted to the spot by the voices now raised in compassion over my plight. Sophie's sisters and brothers were sorry for me! I felt important. I had not the slightest sense of self-pity from within, but only as it came to me indirectly, bestowed through others, from without. If my feet were cold, my heart was warmed by the waves of commiseration that wafted from the dining room.

"I don't know if it will always be this way," Sophie said. "Sometimes I hope, for the child's sake, she never remembers."

So far, I had listened without any more pain than I would have felt for a character in a book, Snow White when she ate the poisoned apple, or Robinson Crusoe when he found the cannibal's footprints. But all changed the moment Mrs. Weber was moved to say, "Poor little orphan!" That I had won her sympathy, after she had looked at me with such coldness and suspicion, seemed almost a miracle. My misfortune must be of extreme gravity. Suddenly misery so overwhelmed me that I nearly sobbed aloud.

For a few minutes I lost all track of the conversation, and when I was able to come back to it the whole tenor of it had changed. Sophie and her mother were angry at each other.

"You're crazy, Sophie! How can you adopt a child?"

"I don't know that she *is* adoptable, but I will if I can get her. And until that's settled, whenever that may be, I'm keeping her. She needs me and—well, I need her."

"But you're not married. How can . . . ?"

"That's just it. I'm not married and I never will be."

"Crazy!"

"I won't be, Mama. But that doesn't mean I have to be denied the privilege of bringing up a child. I have just as much right to it as any other woman."

"A single girl with an adopted child! What will people think?"

"An old maid with an adopted child, that's what they'll think," Sophie said. "But I don't care. I can support her—as well as any man. I may not have a husband, but—"

"What's her name?"

"Jane Carlyle."

"How old is she?"

"Ten."

"Who let you bring her back to Pittsburgh? Doesn't she have any other relatives?"

"Only a grandmother, her father's mother."

"Well, why doesn't she bring up Jane?"

"Because she's old and sick and heartbroken. I went to see her."

"She gave you permission?"

"Yes, when she saw how Jane liked me. Jane didn't even remember *her*."

"Her own grandmother?"

"Mama, I *told* you—"

"*Ja, ja*, shock."

"We talked it all over, Mrs. Carlyle and I. She accepted me, she trusted me. She understood what I wanted and said she would help me when the time came, when things were settled, to make it legal."

"I won't let you make it legal!"

"You have nothing to say about it, Mama. I've been with Jane day and night for a week, through the hearings, through everything. I didn't even finish the Easter buying, that's how she needed me. I'm all she's got and I'm going to keep her. If you don't want her here I'll move out."

"Out of your own house?"

"If I have to. Do I?"

"*Lieber Gott!* Don't you dare!"

"All right, but remember, Mama. And now I've got to get something to eat up to the poor baby. She's hardly taken a bite all day. I wonder if she'd like a soft-boiled egg?"

"I'll take care of it," Mrs. Weber said. "What do you know about a child eating? Soft-boiled egg! She needs something that sticks to the walls of her stomach."

"And I know just what that will be," said one of the daughters. "Soup!"

"Shush, Elise. What do you know either?"

I scooted out through the kitchen just as Mrs. Weber and Elise came into the pantry. Making my way slowly up the back stairs, groping in the pitch dark, I heard the rattle of the pot lid below and Mrs. Weber saying, "Get the big tray, Elise."

"Sure. Who else is mother's little helper?"

"Adopting a child. Imagine!"

"She's one of those emancipated women you read about. She can do anything she has a mind to. I'd like to be one too."

"I can't get over it!"

"If anybody ever needed emancipating, it's me. Lincoln should have made a special proclamation for youngest daughters. Mama, not all that! I couldn't eat that much in a week, and I'm twenty years old."

"The child has to have something on her stomach. So skinny!"

"If she eats everything on that tray she'll be fat by morning."

The thought of so much food made me queasy, and I sat down halfway up the steps.

"This settles it!" I heard Mrs. Weber say firmly. "Sophie must get married!"

"Oh, Mama!"

"I never said a word before, never in all these years, but when my sister Yohanna was a girl, she was going to have a child, and my mother made her get married."

"So?" Elise cried. "What does Tante Yohanna have to do with Sophie adopting a child?"

"Shush, Elise, I've made up my mind."

"But it's not the same thing at all."

Then they must have gone back to the dining room, for I did not hear them any more. But how interesting they had been! I think at that moment, sitting on a step, I became an inveterate eavesdropper. From then on I listened to grownups whenever I could, openly if possible, covertly if necessary. I sensed that they would not like a child to do this, but I did not know it was actually wrong and felt no guilt. It was simply that I had learned that adults said fascinating things after children went to bed, and I had to know what these were.

I made my way back to Sophie's room, crawled into bed, and closed my eyes.

I smelled the food even before Sophie came into the room with the tray, and I wanted nothing to do with it. I shook my head when she sat down on the bed and tried to feed me.

"Please, Jane."

"No. Sophie, who am I?"

"Why, you're a pretty little girl who needs to eat."

"No, I mean, am I an orphan? What happened to me, Sophie?"

She hesitated, but she only answered, "Nothing so important that we have to talk about it tonight. Please eat, dear."

"I can't!" I cried.

"Too tired?"

I nodded and closed my eyes. I felt the bed spring back when she stood up. I pretended to be asleep. I knew she stood holding the tray and looking at me, wondering what to do, and I longed to put out my arms to her and have her kiss me, but I was afraid she might try again to make me eat.

A minute after she went away I heard the water closet gurgle and flush in the bathroom. Sophie was disposing of the food down the toilet! She was not going to be able to face her mother with the untouched tray.

She no sooner returned to the hall when Mrs. Weber came upstairs. "Well, how did the little girl do?"

"Fine, Mama."

"That's all she ate? She didn't touch the knackwurst?"

"She ate the soup, Mama." So soup was all Sophie had had the nerve to get rid of!

"Give me that tray! I'll make her eat."

"No, Mama. She's so tired, poor thing, she could hardly keep her eyes open for the soup."

"Nobody is going to bed hungry in my house!"

"She's too tired to be hungry. She's been through too much. But I'm hungry, and I wish you'd let me have *my* supper."

They went downstairs. Voices reached me faintly from the dining room. I pictured Sophie eating. My taste buds began to work, and I was sorry I had spurned the tray. I tried to go to sleep, but I was too stimulated by what had occurred to relax.

I reviewed the things I knew about myself now. My name, my age. Not much. Oh, and I had a blue coat and a blue hat and a suitcase from which Sophie had taken my nightgown. But where had I been until now? In New York, of course, but what had happened there? I tried to think back in time, to remember. But I could go no farther than the front door of the house in which I now was.

I got out of bed again and looked through the things in my valise. Among the dresses and underwear I found a doll, dainty and beautiful, though worn, as if someone had played with her very hard. She had a pale, blurry porcelain face, a blond tousled wig, and a white dress, very wrinkled; one of her little black shoes was missing. I wondered what her name was. I liked her very much and put her back in the suitcase reluctantly and only because I still had not gone to the bathroom.

This time I found it.

On my way back I heard the voices downstairs. I dis-

covered that, by lying very quietly on the floor in the hall
and sticking my head out between the posts of the balcony
rail, I could hear what was being said in the dining room.
Sometimes a word or a phrase would be lost, but most of it
drifted up to me.

Sophie was saying, "No hats at all. But I did get coats.
Berkhart and Mitchell wanted too much, so I got them from
Feiber Brothers."

"You did?"

"Believe me, I'm through with Berkhart and Mitchell. I
want my hundred-per-cent mark-up."

"Get wallets?"

"Yes, and I bought a gross of ladies' handbags. Sixteen
dollars per dozen. From Waxman. And three gross of *cheap*
bags from Shuster and Hess."

"How'd you do with boys' pants?"

"Fine. But christening dresses! Something else again. I
had to chase all over Eighth Avenue. Very scarce. I told
them they'd better start making more of them. A store in
Braddock, Pennsylvania, has to have christening dresses."

"Believe me! There's a christening every three seconds
in Braddock."

"So that's how we're set for Easter. I got some nice fancy
handkerchiefs, though. You need them for Easter."

"Yes, in Braddock they only blow their noses on Easter."

I would have gone on listening, but weariness overtook
me suddenly, so I got to my feet and returned to Sophie's
room. I didn't know when she came upstairs and slipped
into bed beside me.

When I woke up the next morning she was gone, but
the feeling that she had been there during the night remained with me. I still knew the touch of her arm against
mine, the warmth of her body, the scent of her hair. There
was a note on the dresser: "Dearest Jane: Just a word to
tell you that I've gone to the store. Though I will not be

home till night, try to enjoy your day with Elise and my mother. I will be thinking of you all the time and hoping you are happy. Love, Sophie."

I was appalled that I must spend the whole day without her and dressed myself slowly and fearfully, not knowing what lay ahead of me. Before I left the room I put her note in my pinafore pocket and clutched it for courage as I went downstairs. The black-haired sister was in the lower hall, dusting. She must be Elise. When she heard me on the stairs she said, without looking up, "Good morning, or should I say good afternoon?"

I did not know what she meant and murmured, "Why?"

"Because it's nearly ten o'clock. I won't ask you how you slept. It must have been good if it lasted so long. Well, would you like some breakfast, or would milady prefer lunch?"

Her voice was not unkind. She seemed more amused than critical. I felt brave enough to ask what I had to know. "Elise?"

"Yes?"

"What's the store?"

She laughed. "First question—the store! Already you know it's the most important thing there is to the Weber family. Well, it's called Weber's Dry Goods and it's in Braddock, which is a mill town on the edge of Pittsburgh."

"Why is Sophie going to stay there all day?"

"Because she owns it. Commander-in-chief. She's there every day but Sunday. All the Webers work there nearly —except me. I stay home with Mama. Well, go in the kitchen and report to the local commander-in-chief that you're in the land of the living."

I found Mrs. Weber in the kitchen. At first I felt with her like a stray kitten she didn't want but which she hesitated to put out in the snow. However, she was so pleased when I ate all my breakfast, not leaving a crumb, that she warmed to me and let me help her bake a plum torte.

I see her still as she used to be, a tiny woman, not five feet tall, but wiry and strong. I suppose she was about sixty then. Her hair had been red like Sophie's but was now faded into pink on the way to white. Her face was always animated, her eyes those of a young girl. Though she spoke sharply, there was something so endearing about her that nobody minded. She had come from Germany only ten years before and talked with a strong accent which I loved and was soon able to imitate. She wore glasses when she could find them. She lost them so frequently that a lot of everybody's time was spent searching for them. She wore black always but was so neat and glowingly clean that I never thought of her as being dressed in black, especially since she wore a white apron which she whipped off and on as company came and went.

When the torte was finished I wandered through the house, examining all the rooms and counting them. On the ground floor were the kitchen, the dining room, the parlor, and the music room. Elise told me the music room was by accident, for none of the family was musical. It began with the gift of a mandolin which no one could play, but which was considered ornamental and was hung on the wall. Then when Sophie bought the player piano because it could be operated mechanically and didn't entail frustrating lessons, the room got its name. There were also tiny uncomfortable gilt chairs and two love seats to match, a case of music rolls that came with the piano, and, on the walls, gold-framed scenes of Venice painted in sepia. I studied those pictures so frequently while I lived with the Webers that I was surprised much later, when I actually went to Venice, to find it was not sepia-colored at all but a city of marvelous mauves and purples and pinks and a thousand shades of blue and green.

The music room was separated from the parlor by a row of Ionic pillars rising from floor to ceiling, with only space for a not too stout human being to move between them.

The girls in the family entertained their callers in the music room because it could be approached only from the parlor, which meant that they had ample warning of an intrusion, but it must have been unmercifully comfortless to sit on those stiff little chairs and love seats.

In the parlor a great palm grew in a jardiniere. There were chairs tufted in velvet, long green portieres with little velvet balls at the bottom, a marble bust on a pedestal. I played for a while with the things in the curio cabinet, ivory elephants, miniature musical instruments, a tiny china cup marked "Souvenir of Atlantic City," seashells, a sprig of edelweiss.

In the dining room there was a ledge which ran high up all along the walls, upon which sat steins of all sizes with metal lids and handles and pictures in relief brilliantly colored. The room opened upon a little conservatory with a glass roof, and I went into it to look at the ferns and flowers all smelling of earth, rich and moist.

On the second floor of the house were four bedrooms, the little office which was to be converted for me, and a sitting room so pleasant I could scarcely bear to leave it. Because the day was cold the fire was lit. Little jets of red and blue flame spurted from the asbestos, fed by gas. Facing the fireplace was a sofa, stuffed, and covered with plush, not wine-colored as so many things were then, but patterned in blue and yellow, faded but warm-looking. I remember still how that plush felt against my cheek because of the many times I snuggled there, reading or daydreaming.

Behind the sofa was a large heavy-legged oak table on which were books and magazines and a globe of the world. I read a verse in a book and looked at a picture of a cannibal in a magazine. I opened drawers and found packs of cards and travel folders. I gaped at the huge shaggy bearskin with sprawling limbs and a fierce head that lay under the table.

One of the windows looked out at the back of the house

across the block, past a tennis court to a field and a red brick building beyond on the next street. I did not know it was a schoolhouse until the children returned from lunch. Then I watched them play, wondering if I would ever be one of them going there to school.

On the third floor were three bedrooms full of lovely carved furniture, chests and dressers with marble tops, beds with giant headboards.

I had no trouble filling most of the day by exploring the house.

In the afternoon Elise played dominoes and parchesi with me. She explained that these games were kept in a house in which there were no children because her elder brother, Hugo, lived a few blocks away and had four girls and boys who often came to visit. She had to teach me the games, but I learned so rapidly she said she was sure I must have played them before, though I couldn't remember. How many other abilities were there tucked in my mind, unknown to me? I wondered. Could I play the mandolin if I tried? Could I say a poem? Could I do a dance?

I expected Sophie home for supper, but Elise and Mrs. Weber and I ate alone. The store, they told me, stayed open on Saturday nights until eleven, and this was Saturday. I learned with dismay that there were other nights too that kept Sophie and Charlotte and Seymour and Sylvester there preparing for a sale, at the ledgers, or at other tasks that went into the running of a retail establishment. When would I be with Sophie?

I was sent to bed at eight. At ten I woke and she was still not home. I left my room, leaned over the balustrade, and looked down into the hall below. Mrs. Weber came out of the dining room calling, "Elise, Elise, come here!"

Elise emerged from the parlor. "What do you want, Mama?"

"Is your beau still here?"

"Shhh," Elise whispered. "He'll hear you."

"So?"

"So this is the first time he's called, and I don't want him to hear you calling him my beau."

"For such a new friend he's a late stayer."

"Oh, Mama!"

"I thought, if he'd left, you'd help me set the table. They'll be home soon."

"Well, Mr. Hermansdorfer is still here."

"I want to meet him, And you set the table."

"Oh, Mama," Elise cried, half in amusement and half in outrage, "if you meet him I know exactly what you'll do. You'll try to marry him off to Sophie."

Mrs. Weber looked at her youngest daughter with sudden interest. "He's old enough for Sophie?"

"Does it matter? In an emergency like hers, won't anyone do?"

"Shush! He'll hear you!"

"Oh, Mama, give up. Sophie's thirty years old."

"Don't talk that way about your sister!" Mrs. Weber commanded.

Elise shrugged her shoulders helplessly and went to get Mr. Hermansdorfer with a sigh of exasperation. Her mother took off her apron, waited expectantly, and looked pleased when Mr. Hermansdorfer came into the hall, for he was a serious-looking man, and, if not thirty, he was very close to it. He wore a high stiff collar and had not only sideburns but a fastidiously trimmed mustache. He was tall and well proportioned. Mrs. Weber gripped his hand with an enthusiastic shake when Elise said, "This is Mr. Hermansdorfer. Mr. Hermansdorfer, my mother."

Mrs. Weber repeated his name with a good deal of pleasure and lapsed into German. "*Deutsch, nicht wahr?*"

"*Ja,*" Mr. Hermansdorfer said, smiling.

Elise, annoyed because German was being spoken, snapped, "He's been in this country since he was a little boy, Mama."

Mrs. Weber ignored her. "What part of Germany did you come from?"

"Coblenz."

Mrs. Weber greeted this answer as though she had just been informed he was the son of the Kaiser, whom she admired at the time (she turned bitterly against him six years later when the war broke out). "The Rhineland! I, too. *Landsmann!* We're from Andernach! Next-door neighbors!"

When the miracle of the coincidence had been explored and at last exhausted, with Elise standing by Mr. Hermansdorfer as though to shield him from her mother, he remarked that the house was very handsome.

"My daughter Sophie bought it. Thirteen rooms," Mrs. Weber said grandly. "And a tennis court behind the house." I was proud of Sophie. "Elise, set the table."

The guest looked perplexed. "You're going to eat now, so late?"

"It's for my children who are working late," Mrs. Weber explained. "With a store it's always something. What business are you in, Mr. Hermansdorfer?"

"I'm a musician."

Mrs. Weber looked so disappointed that Elise felt impelled to supply hastily the additional information that he was a member of the Pittsburgh Symphony Orchestra.

"You make a living from that?"

"Of course he does, Mama, a very good living."

Mrs. Weber assumed a more cheerful expression and nodded. "There's business and there's business. Music is merchandise too." And, studying the guest with absorption, she reminded Elise again that the table needed setting.

Her daughter, knowing just what was coming but unable to fight off the inevitable any longer, did as she was ordered. Though I could not see her, I knew she was in the dining room, moving to and from the sideboard, putting out silver and plates and little individual salt dishes I had seen that day, each with its own miniature spoon.

Meanwhile, Mrs. Weber got Mr. Hermansdorfer seated on the hall sofa and leaned toward him confidentially. "You should meet my daughter Sophie." Then, noting that he seemed to have no reluctance to do so, she went on to tell how Sophie had first come to this country with her elder brother, Hugo, and how they had worked downtown as salespeople in Kaufmann's Department Store. When they had saved enough money to send for the rest of the family, and they had all come to America, Sophie had opened a store of her own in Braddock, the mill town beyond the outskirts of the city. "Mills, mining, steel, blast furnaces— *Schmutz*. But a nice store. My son, Hugo, an artist—not a businessman—went to work on the German newspaper, the *Volksblatt*. My other sons, Seymour and Sylvester, went in with Sophie in the store. Good hard-working boys, but Sophie"—tapping her head with her finger—"is the *Kopf*. She's a good girl, smart, and so sweet. You don't know what people think of my Sophie. She could have had twenty husbands."

Elise came out of the dining room just in time to hear the last extravagant remark. Mrs. Weber looked up at her daughter guiltily. "I was just telling Mr. Hermansdorfer about Sophie."

"Oh, I knew just who you were talking about."

"All the men like her so much, don't they, Elise?"

"She has to carry a policeman's club to keep them off the porch."

Mrs. Weber made a rapid decision to change the subject and did so by inquiring the first name of the caller. He told her it was Max.

"A good name! My *Grosspapa* in Frankfurt—Max. Max Hoffman. My maiden name—Hoffman."

"Is that so? My mother's name was Hoff*meyer*."

"Is that so?" Mrs. Weber said, beaming.

"What a coincidence," Elise remarked.

And just then there came a knocking on the stained-glass pane of the front door. "They're here, they're here!" Mrs. Weber jumped up and ran as she always did whenever a bell rang or when anyone called her name, as though she would be struck dead if she kept anyone waiting even for a second.

I never knew any of the family to carry a key, for the door was either unlocked or Mrs. Weber was there to open it. Now she turned the heavy brass knob and let in Sophie and Charlotte and Seymour and Sylvester. The men were in their middle twenties. They were good-natured fellows, neither of them very tall, not very colorful, but demonstrative in their affections, hugging and kissing at every arrival or departure. They both had light curly hair parted in the middle, and at first I could only tell them apart because Seymour had a brown birthmark on his cheek and Sylvester didn't. But I soon saw their differences. Seymour, who was the elder of the two, had a lean face, and Sylvester's was round and shiny. Charlotte was twenty-two, a placid, happy girl with a flawless disposition. She wore her fair hair in a fringe on her forehead and up in the back. She had lovely eyes set well apart with blue irises flecked with brown. Though her heart wasn't in it, she agreeably went to the store every day and did all that was expected of her. She was a romantic and lived for the day she would be married to the young man with whom she had been keeping company for a long time.

"*Guten Abend*," Mrs. Weber cried and lifted her head to receive her children's kisses. Snow had already been stomped from shoes on the doormat outside, but now came the time-consuming business of removing overcoats, tassel caps, earmuffs, and woolen mittens.

"It's starting to snow again," Charlotte said, storing overshoes in the great hall chest and hanging coats on the rack above it.

"How was business?" Mrs. Weber asked with a mind for more realistic things.

"Bum," replied Sylvester.

"Not that bad, Mama," said Charlotte, who always tried to make things seem better than they were. "Anyhow, it was only that there weren't many people out shopping because of the slush."

"Now that Sophie's back," Mrs. Weber said firmly, "business will be better—snow or no snow." And then she remembered Mr. Hermansdorfer and brought him forward to be introduced. He shook hands gravely with the men and smiled at the women. "I heard about Miss Sophie, but I didn't know there was still another daughter."

"Don't look at her! She's engaged!" Mrs. Weber put in quickly.

"Oh, Mama!" Charlotte said, laughing. "He can *look* at me."

Elise said, "There are four daughters altogether, and nobody knows what to do with them but Mama. She knows, all right."

Sophie said, "I must go to Jane. Excuse me, Mr. Hermansdorfer." And then she looked up and saw me at the balustrade and waved and smiled. She ran up to me and I let her think I had just come out into the hall, awakened by the voices. So she told me I could come downstairs as soon as I had put on my kimono and slippers.

When I went down the stairs she was in the parlor talking to the others. "What did you do today, Mama?" I heard her ask.

"Nothing."

Sophie said, "That means she scrubbed the cellar floor again."

"*And* the kitchen," Elise added.

"What are we going to do with Mama?" Seymour shook his head sadly.

"Don't we pay the colored lady to come and scrub?" Sylvester asked.

"Didn't she come?"

"Oh, she came," Elise informed them, "and scrubbed, but not good enough for Mama. Mama had to do it all over again."

"Go put the soup in the tureen, Elise!" Mrs. Weber cried sharply, banishing her, hating to be told on.

Sophie introduced me to Mr. Hermansdorfer simply as "Jane," and when he asked if I was a grandchild she said, "Yes."

"By adoption," Mrs. Weber added, and Sophie frowned at her and put her arm around me.

Mr. Hermansdorfer looked puzzled.

"Did you have a good time today?" Sophie asked me. "Did you miss me?"

"Oh, yes!"

We all sat down, and I squeezed as close to Sophie as I could.

"No nickelodeon today?" Seymour asked Mrs. Weber.

"No, not since yesterday."

"Yesterday? How did you get there?" Sophie asked.

"Huckster," Mrs. Weber answered.

"I beg your pardon?" inquired Mr. Hermansdorfer.

So Sylvester had to explain that his mother was a nickelodeon fiend and went nearly every day, bumming rides downtown or to East Liberty with anyone who came along in a wagon. Sometimes it was the old-clothes man, sometimes the iceman, the milkman, even the chauffeur of Mr. Andrew Mellon, the great financier who lived in the neighborhood. She took her rides from anyone, and the day before it had been the huckster.

"My mother leads a wild life, Mr. Hermansdorfer," Charlotte said.

"What was on the bill?" Sophie asked her mother.

"*Rescued from an Eagle's Nest.*"

"Good?"

"*Wunderbar.*"

"What was it about?"

"A little child. This big bird, the eagle, came swooping down and stole the child, picked her right up in its claws. The things that can happen!"

"Good thing we haven't any children to worry about," Sylvester said. "Except Jane," he added, winking at me.

"Then it flew away with the little girl," Mrs. Weber went on, "and took her to its nest way up on a mountain."

"Sounds exciting," Charlotte said.

"Dropped her right in the nest along with the eggs," went on Mrs. Weber, contemplating the miracles of the nickelodeon.

The eggs reminded Seymour that he was hungry, and his mother, brought back to reality, went off to the kitchen to help Elise. There was a moment's silence after she had left and then Mr. Hermansdorfer said, "I played the piano in a nickelodeon once."

"Is that so?"

"I didn't like it much, though. Very tedious work."

"It's wonderful what's happened in three years," said Sylvester. "Three years ago the first nickelodeon. Now over eighty in Pittsburgh alone."

"I hear the saloons are complaining," Seymour said.

"Well, look at the business it takes away from them," his brother pointed out.

"Yes," said Charlotte, "Mama hasn't been in a saloon since the nickelodeon started."

Everybody laughed, and then Sylvester asked, "In what way did you find piano-playing tedious work, Mr. Hermansdorfer?"

"Well, it's the keeping up with the picture, if you know what I mean. You have to play certain pieces according to what goes on up there on the screen. For instance, when the heroine comes in, you play 'Hearts and Flowers,' but you no sooner get started on it than the picture switches to something else and you have to change your piece because then they show the bad men, maybe, and then—I could tell you better on the piano."

"Oh, please do," cried Charlotte, jumping up and making the others enter the music room.

Immediately Mr. Hermansdorfer noticed the half-finished roll in the window of the upright section. "Oh, this is one of those player pianos."

"Yes, that's why we have it. It's the only way any of us can play," Charlotte explained.

"They make very nice music rolls nowadays," commented Sylvester.

"My favorite is 'The Blue Danube,'" Charlotte said.

Sylvester bent over Mr. Hermansdorfer and pushed a little key. "This turns off the automatic. Now you can go ahead."

We gathered around Mr. Hermansdorfer as he poised his hands over the keys. "Well, this is for the bad men"—and then he gave his audience the appropriate sinister music. "But you only see them a flicker or two and you're back with the heroine." Abruptly he changed the tune to suit. "Now you see the bad men again"—back to sinister music. "Now the girl again"—girl music. "She's on a train"—train music. "Another train, collision, smash"—smashing chords. "Confusion. The bad men have the girl. They take her to a mountain shack. They tie her up with ropes. They're going to kill her. Now comes True Blue Harold"—music for True Blue Harold. "He rescues her. He ties up the bad men. He takes the girl outside in a field of daisies"—change to pastoral music. "He makes love to her."

"Tell Grandma to come here," Sophie whispered to me.

I hated to leave the excitement, especially as Mr. Hermansdorfer was saying, "Now a fire breaks out in the

woods—big forest fire. The heroine and True Blue Harold
are in danger." But I went to fetch Mrs. Weber.

She was in the dining room with Elise, stacking soup
plates beside a steaming tureen. "But it isn't fair," Elise was
saying. "Not that I'm interested in Mr. Hermansdorfer,
heaven knows. But if I have to wait till Sophie gets married,
I'll never get married."

"You forgot the soup spoons."

Elise went to the sideboard for them. "What about
Charlotte?"

Her mother took the spoons from Elise's hand and set
them out one by one on the table. "Charlotte's not going to
get married till her Leon saves a thousand dollars. *She's*
safe." Mrs. Weber looked up and saw me, but she was listening to the fire music, which reached us indistinctly in
the dining room. Before I could say anything she cried out,
"Fire! Fire!" and, to Elise's amazement, bolted down the
hall and plunged through the parlor into the music room.
I ran after her and found her already among her children,
listening avidly to the magic that surged from the piano.

"Saved again," said Mr. Hermansdorfer. "Fire's out"—
transition from fire music to pastoral. "Love. Kisses"—
love-kiss music. Crescendo. Giant chord. "The end." His
hands dropped away from the keys and he stood up.

Mrs. Weber regarded him with undisguised admiration.
"Wonderful! Just like the nickelodeon!"

"You're a fine musician," Seymour said appreciatively.

Mr. Hermansdorfer thanked them but said it was really
nothing. He hoped his work for the symphony orchestra
was a better indication of his worth.

Mrs. Weber found that hard to believe. Nothing could
be better than what she had just heard.

But the soup was on the table and could no longer be
ignored. Mr. Hermansdorfer was offered supper, but said
he'd eaten at six, his regular time. However, he would sit
at the table and keep the family company.

We were no sooner seated than there was a sharp rapping on the front door, as though someone's finger ring was striking against the stained glass. Seymour was first on his feet, though some of the others rose and spilled out into the hall to see who had come so late. The door was opened, revealing falling snow and a man and a woman. He was of medium height and gave the impression of being mostly pince-nez and high collar. She was enveloped in a huge gray cape and wore a mammoth hat trimmed with stuffed birds iridescent-winged.

Even before Seymour could get the door closed, the woman cried, "Mama!" and moved swiftly, though laboriously, toward Mrs. Weber, who asked in alarm, "*Was ist los?*" Then the woman fell into Mrs. Weber's arms and burst into tears.

This seemed very odd to me, a woman of that age crying. I wondered who she was. A few days later, after a great deal of questioning about ages, I was able to write a list of Mrs. Weber's children that went as follows:

> Hugo, 32
> Sophie, 30
> Seymour, 26
> Sylvester, 25
> Ermanie, 23
> Charlotte, 22
> Elise, 20

And this was Ermanie, twenty-three, with her husband, Theodore, married over all Mrs. Weber's protests. "What's wrong?" Sophie sensibly asked Theodore instead of her hysterical sister.

"She insisted on coming home to have the baby."

"She's having it tonight?"

"No, but she absolutely refuses to have it any place else but here in her mother's house."

"But she's not going to have it until March."

"I know." Theodore sighed.

"*Warum*, Ermanie?" Mrs. Weber asked.

Ermanie managed to tell why through the sobs. "I won't have it any place else! I just won't!"

"I did everything I could to get her to stay home," Theodore said, shaking snow from his hat.

"If I can't have the baby here, I won't have it!" Ermanie wept.

"Ha!" said Elise.

Mrs. Weber looked sternly at Ermanie. "A wife should have her baby in her husband's house."

"I won't! I won't!"

"Aw, let her have it here," Seymour said to his mother.

Then I heard Mr. Hermansdorfer say, in hushed tones appropriate to the crisis, that he must leave. Elise gave him his hat and coat, and he went quickly.

"All right," Mrs. Weber said, "Ermanie can stay."

"Now what'll I do?" Elise asked. "The soup's on the table."

"Put it back in the pot!" cried Mrs. Weber imperiously. "I'm going to get Ermanie to bed."

Feeling better already, Ermanie started to go upstairs with her mother, then changed her mind. "Don't I smell sausage? I think I'll have something to eat first."

Mrs. Weber nodded. "Never mind the soup, Elise."

When Ermanie's snow-sprinkled cape was removed, I saw that she was rather fat in front. Smiling now, she went into the dining room with the others, all but her husband and Seymour and Elise, who stayed in the hall. Her husband took off his overcoat and sank wearily onto the bench. "I wish it were over. All day yesterday I kept thinking how nice it would be for the baby to be born on Valentine's Day."

"Oh, wouldn't that have been *romantic?*" cried Elise, not really meaning it.

He took off his pince-nez and wiped the mist from it.

"When I woke up yesterday morning I thought if only it would arrive."

"I'm afraid you're going to have to wait till next Valentine's Day."

"God forbid!"

Ermanie and her husband were given what had been known until then as "the guest room." Now there was someone else at home during the days. I was to start to school at the beginning of the coming week, but meanwhile I found little time to miss Sophie. Ermanie was making clothes for her baby, and I helped her. She showed me how to crochet, and I made an edging for a little jacket. She was good company. We thought of hundreds of names, boys' and girls'. I liked three so much that we decided to give them all to my doll. That was how she became Nancy Myrtle May.

The store closed early for a few days, and one evening we were all in the upstairs sitting room when we heard a pounding on the front door. Elise went to open it, and I looked down from the top of the staircase to see who had come.

This time it was a fine-looking man with a handsome mustache. He had four children with him, two boys and two girls.

"Hugo!" Elise cried.

Mrs. Weber heard her, rose, and went swiftly down the stairs, followed by the rest of the family. "Hugo! *Was ist los?*"

"Mama and Papa had a fight," said the smaller of the two boys.

"The same old thing!" Hugo exploded. "Daisy wants me to give up my job on the *Volksblatt* and go into business with her father. I won't do it! I've told her time and time again I won't do it."

"You walked out on her?" Sophie asked.

"No, she walked out on me. She's done it before. She goes home, and the next day she comes back. But this is the last time! Now there won't be anything to come back to. I closed the house, fired the hired girl, and here I am. I thought we could use the third-floor rooms here for a while."

"I want to go to bed," the littler girl said.

"Oh, the poor baby!" Charlotte cried. "Getting her up in the middle of the night and dragging her over here in the cold! Oh, the poor baby."

"It's only nine o'clock," Elise said.

But Hugo was still expounding. "I make enough money on the *Volksblatt*. Nobody's starving. I don't have to be a millionaire. I *won't* become her father's slave boy! It's too much to ask."

"Enough! Enough!" shouted Mrs. Weber. "Trixie must go to bed."

Hugo looked sorry for his outburst. "Of course." And instantly everyone was busy taking off the children's coats and overshoes.

"What a week!" said Elise. "Sophie comes home with an adopted daughter, Ermanie comes home to have a baby, and now Hugo comes home with his four children. What does that leave for me to do?"

Her mother pointed to the dining room and told her. "Warm up some soup!"

I had been in Pittsburgh only a few days when we had a visit from a policeman, a Mr. Flynn. He had been talking to Sophie in the parlor for some time before I was sent for. When I came in he was saying, "Well, since she's the key to the whole case if she remembered anything, we were hoping. Also we wanted to know what sort of life she was having here." He smiled as he said, "Let me assure you we don't let a ward of the court just walk away, without knowing something about the people she's staying with."

"You had me investigated?" Sophie asked, surprised.

"We had a report on you before you ever left New York with her."

"That was mighty rapid."

"The policeman on your beat is very friendly with your mother, Miss Weber."

Sophie laughed. "I suppose so. She's stuffed him with cake and coffee often enough."

"Now! Let me get it from the horse's mouth." He turned to me. "Do you recall anything that happened in New York?"

"No, sir."

"Anything before that? When you were with your parents?"

"No."

He seemed satisfied. "Now what about school?"

"I'm going to enter her next week," Sophie told him.

"Fine, fine. Well, I'll be dropping in from time to time, say about once a month." We went with him to the door, and he looked hard at me. "Are you happy here, Jane?"

I nodded emphatically, but I did not know whether I did it because I was really happy or because I thought it was expected of me.

That night in bed beside Sophie I asked, "Why did the policeman come to see us, Sophie?"

She was quiet so long I wondered if she'd heard me, but at last she said, "There was an unsolved murder in the hotel you and I were staying at in New York, and naturally people are curious to know if we can shed any light upon it."

"Can we?"

"I'm afraid I can't, and as for you, you don't remember anything, so you can't."

"Who was murdered, Sophie?"

"Someone. But I don't want you troubling your head about it. Some day you'll recall, but until then just think about now and enjoy yourself. Think about living here and being my little girl."

"Am I your little girl because I'm an orphan?"

"You're only half an orphan, dear."

"On which side am I an orphan?"

"Your mother is dead, dear, but your father is living."

"Does he love me, Sophie?"

"Of course he does."

"Where is he?"

"Well, he can't tell us right now."

"Why?"

"Because he's far away."

"If he loved me, he'd tell us."

"He will when he can."

"Why can't I remember anything about my father and mother, Sophie?"

"Because you were ill."

"I read in the newspaper that President Roosevelt's little boy was sick. Did he forget his father and mother?"

"No."

"It would be terrible to forget your father if he were President."

"It only happens sometimes."

"What was I sick from, Sophie?"

"Why, pneumonia, dear."

I realized she was telling an untruth, for I had heard her remark to her mother that the doctor had said I had lost my memory because of shock. I wanted to see the expression on her face, but it was too dark in the room. Then I wondered what sort of a disease shock was. Perhaps it was like pneumonia, and so Sophie had not meant to lie to me. I hoped so.

"Sophie, why must I have a room of my own?"

"Because you're a big girl, and I think you should."

"I like it here with you."

"I like it here with you too, but I wake you up when I

come to bed and disturb the sleep a growing child should have."

"I want you to! I don't care!"

"Also I like to read in bed, but I can't when you're here."

"Why must you read in bed?"

"Because it's the only time I have for it, and I have to read or die."

"Die, Sophie?" I asked, alarmed.

"It was just an expression, dear. What I mean is I can't live just going to work and coming home, without contact with other worlds. And how can I reach those other worlds except by reading? Who are my friends? The men and women who write the books, who tell me so much of other eras, other climes. I want to know what's happened in the universe so far, and what is happening now. I have to have my friends."

"I'd let you read in bed, Sophie."

"We'll see. But for heaven's sake go to sleep now, Jane."

I closed my eyes and thought of what the policeman had asked me when he was leaving. Was I happy? I didn't know.

2

Easter

IN THE DAYS that followed so much occurred that I had no
time to decide whether I was happy or not. I was too
busy getting used to the Webers, too caught up in their
activities, to think about myself much. Only now and then
did I puzzle over my past, what had happened in New
York, how I came to be living in a house in Pittsburgh, the
meaning of the policeman's call. When I thought of it at all,
I tried putting together bits and pieces of conversations I had
heard, but the more I tried to make sense of them the more
confused I became. Then frightening words jabbed at me,
"murder," "shock," "investigation." Nobody had explained
them or how they pertained to me. I had asked questions
and received baffling answers. Childlike, I feared to ask
more. It was better to shut the words out of my head, to
live as I did, each day filled to the brim.

I would dress quickly in the mornings, savoring the life
of the house that came to me in sounds, an argument between two of Hugo's children, the carpet-sweeper at work,
pots clanging in the kitchen, a gust of laughter, a shout. I
would go down to an enormous breakfast—hard-boiled
eggs, broiled chicken livers, oatmeal, Apfel Pfannkuchen,
jams, and pickled melon rind—the whole family present

and talking away. I learned to call Seymour and Sylvester "the boys" as the others did, and Mrs. Weber "Grandma," as Hugo's children did. It was wonderful for me having four playmates in the house, and I hoped Hugo would never make up with his wife so that they would never have to go home. I had them on my list as:

> Pauline, 12
> Ernest, 10
> Walter, 8
> Trixie, 6

Ernest and Walter were known as "the little boys," to distinguish them from Seymour and Sylvester, while Pauline, Trixie, and I were "the little girls." Pauline wore two long brown braids looped back at each side of her head and tied with ribbons. Trixie's blond hair was straight and short, with bangs over her baby face. The boys were dark and freckled even in winter. Their white shirts were clean in the morning but got spottier and spottier as the day wore on, and the bands on their knee pants frequently slipped, so they went around with one pant leg up and one down.

The five of us traveled as a pack, migrating from room to room of the overflowing house. Sometimes we would all be on the third floor, where they lived with their father. Sometimes we were in Elise's and Charlotte's room. The young ladies' quarters doubled as a sewing room. It was here the dressmaker's dummy stood, here that clothes for the whole family were altered or patched or darned, here that we made up endless games to be played with buttons or spools, here that the women of the family tried on dresses brought home from the store, to be returned the next day if something was wrong. Seymour and Sylvester had a room together, the least interesting in the house, nothing of note in it but racks full of pipes and stamp albums for which they had long ago lost enthusiasm. Ermanie's and

Theodore's room was stacked with items for the layette. Sophie's room was the prettiest and the most interesting, filled as it was with lovely things and hundreds of books, from Aeschylus to Zola. But it was Grandma's room we liked best.

We would find her there in the evenings when she did not have to wait up for anyone from the store. She would be in her nightgown, standing before her dresser, carrying out her beauty ceremonials, an Irish linen towel edged in crocheting over her shoulders. She was very vain. Her face had to be creamed, then wiped with soft muslin. Her wrists and elbows had to be massaged with an oily preparation from a little brown vial. Her rings must be taken off and hung on the little ring tree on her bureau, her nails filed, her cuticles pushed back. Basked by waves of heat from the fireplace and fanned by drafts from the chinks in the window frame, she stood making swift movements with her arms as she picked up the various objects from her tortoise-shell dresser set and put them back. We watched everything, but what we waited for most eagerly was the miracle of her hair when the pins were taken out. It would fall nearly to her waist; then she would take up her brush and stroke it fifty times, no more no less. Next, very deftly, hand over hand, she twisted it into a single long, thick braid. Then she would find a few loose hairs stuck in her brush. These she would wind around the end of the braid a couple of inches from the tip. Now the miracle! She picked up her scissors and cut off that tip, at least an inch of it every night! And yet each time the braid was the same length. No matter how hard we pondered, we could never figure out how she could grow a whole inch of hair every day. We talked about it again and again and marveled, but she would only shrug her shoulders and say, "*Il n'y a pas de quoi,*" a bit of French she had picked up as a girl, the only bit, I believe.

I envied the Weber children their father, who returned
at five every day to kiss them and ask about runny noses or
sore thumbs. Only when Sophie was home, and that was late
or on Sunday, did I have someone who was particularly
mine. Then I glowed with contentment if she brushed my
long brown hair, telling me I looked like Alice in Wonder-
land, or if she picked out a dress I was to wear the next day,
or if she told me a story alone in our room.

But occasionally something happened which shattered
my outer calm. One afternoon, very late, when supper was
being fixed, it was suddenly discovered there was no more
flour in the house, and Pauline had to be sent to the grocer's
so the gravy could be made. Pauline returned all excited.
"There was a man outside," she told Elise. "I saw him on the
way to the store and when I came back he stopped me and
talked to me."

"What'd he want?"

He had asked questions—did she live there, did a little
girl named Jane live there too? Did Jane speak of New York
often? "I said no, and he asked didn't Jane remember anything? I said no, did he know Jane? He said no, he was just a
reporter from the *Pittsburgh Gazette*." Had Jane heard
from her father? "I said I didn't think so, but would he like
to come in the house and talk to Jane, and he said it wasn't
necessary, and he went away very fast and that's all. But
wasn't that peculiar?"

Sophie thought it was very peculiar when she heard about
it. "What did this man look like?" she asked Pauline.

"I don't know. His hat was pulled down and his scarf
covered his chin, and besides it was very dark out. But he
had a black patch over one eye."

"A black patch!"

"Yes, like somebody with only one eye. He was nice,
though. He was very polite."

I could see Sophie was upset. Before she would eat her dinner she put her coat back on and walked up to the Walkers' house to use their telephone. When she came back she said she had called downtown to the *Gazette* and told one of the editors that any inquiries should be made to herself and that the children in the family should not be disturbed. The editor said he'd sent no one out on such an assignment, and when Sophie described the man as having a patch over one eye she was told there was no such reporter working on the *Gazette*.

"Maybe Pauline had it wrong and it was some other paper," Sylvester said.

"No, I didn't!" Pauline exclaimed indignantly. "I had it right."

"My God!" Seymour cried. "You don't suppose it was the—"

"Never mind!" Sophie interrupted. "Let's not talk of it now. Jane, run upstairs and get me a handkerchief, please. I think I'm going to sneeze."

Numb with apprehension, I got the handkerchief as quickly as I could and came down the back stairs. They were still in conversation in the hall. "Will we have to keep an eye on the child constantly now?" Seymour was asking.

"Pooh!" Grandma said. "Would a father harm his own child?"

"Now don't start that, Mama!" Sophie said severely. "You don't know anything about what happened."

"Well, where is he, then?"

"We'll all find out in due time," Sophie replied. "Well, here's Jane."

That night I was glad for once she was late in coming to bed. I could cry unseen. I wept not from sorrow but from fear of the unknown, of danger hanging over me waiting to pounce, of, most of all, my ignorance. For the first time my implicit faith in Sophie wavered. Why had she changed the subject when I came back with the handkerchief? If only she would tell me everything she knew! Then I would be able to stop groping for realities, for my own and for that of the world in which I lived. Or did I do her an injustice? Did she grope too, not knowing all the truth? Oh, it was all too much to figure out! What was the use of trying?

I was careful to hide the evidence of my tears, to turn over the wet pillow, to bury my face before she came into the room. If she was secretive, so was I.

True to her word, she entered me in school, staying home from work one morning to do so. She led me by the hand to the principal's office and then to the classroom assigned to me. I was glad for her presence before what seemed like a sea of strange, hostile faces and before such a tall, know-it-all teacher. I felt lost and small. Sophie did not leave until I was given a seat and the girl in front of me had turned around and smiled and I had smiled back.

Though the semester had begun weeks ago, I was soon caught up and able to get grades of "Fair" at first, and then "Good" and "Excellent."

After the first day I had the companionship of the Weber children on the way to school. We left the house by the back door, stopped sometimes to run up and down the slanted cellar doors, trailed along the garden path covered with fresh or trampled snow, passing the tennis court, traversed the great field that lay behind the house, emerged on the other side of the block, and crossed the street. There stood the schoolhouse, and, next to it, the fire-engine house. Since there were so many children about, the firemen took great precautions when there was an alarm, sounded louder bells and longer peals than was usual before the horses pulled the engines swiftly into the street and away.

While it was still cold we played running games at recess, and, when the weather grew warmer, hopscotch and jacks. The school could be seen perfectly from the upstairs windows at the back of our house, and once when I had to stay home with a cold I watched the children go inside in the morning and waited a hundred years until they came out at recess. I imagined myself there with them and wondered which one I was, the little girl with the red muffler on the swing, or the child in a tassel cap sitting on the steps. I was really Jane Carlyle, made to stay in a warm room with a mustard plaster on my chest, but I was lonely and enjoyed pretending.

Theater-minded Grandma often took us young ones to a nickelodeon on Saturday afternoon, or, even lovelier, to the Harris Theatre to see vaudeville, where we sat in a box at reduced prices because she knew Mr. Harris. A box of chocolate-covered cherries would pass from one to another. We never knew how many we ate, so rapt were we at the happenings on the stage. Sometimes we went to the Carnegie Museum and trooped past the dozens and dozens of plaster statues, copies of Greek and Roman sculptures (modified by the Puritan proprieties of the Museum's Board of Directors) on our way to the great room which held our favorite object, a marvel to be gaped at and speculated upon—the skeleton of a dinosaur. Though I didn't realize it then, the statues made a greater impression on me than the dinosaur did, because for years afterward I thought the male anatomy looked like a fig leaf in one particular place. It was quite a surprise to me when I learned later on that it did not.

It was a full life, and there was only one trouble with it. I saw too little of Sophie. Her family took her, the store took her, and there was hardly anything left for me. She went away early in the morning six days a week and often returned late at night when I was already in bed. On Sundays she slept until ten, and after that there would be people about all the time. I wanted her to myself and I was never alone with her. All I could do was look at her hungrily across a room, while everyone else nibbled away at her.

At first, when I still shared her room, she was mine at night. I was with her when she hung up her clothes and brushed her hair and smoothed the bedclothes that I'd mussed in my restlessness. I tugged at her attention in any way I could, complaining of feeling giddy so she would put her hand on my forehead and make me stick out my tongue while I asked useless questions, clinging fiercely to her in bed.

"Do you like me very, very much, Sophie?"

"Very, very much."

"Because I'm a poor child?"

"A poor child!" Sophie scoffed. "No, I love you because you're lovable."

I did not really believe I would have to leave her, but all too soon my room was ready and I actually found myself alone in it. Then anger at Sophie welled up in me; I was furious at her. I was an eaglet put out of its nest, a patriot sent into exile. That night I made up my mind I would no longer tag after her and vie with the others for her affection. But the next morning I was hers all over again, admiring and loving.

My little room! Before I had been in it a week I loved it. I can still see it, lace curtains at the window, a cherrywood night stand beside my bed, the high carved chifforobe which held my clothes. How often I counted the roses marching up and down the walls and watched the gaslight flicker in the incandescent mantle. Sophie, in a dressing gown, would come to kiss me good night. She would whisper, "Sleep tight," turn off the flame, and close the door. As soon as she left I would open it a trifle, pop back into my bed, and lie there listening to the adults, who gathered in the upstairs sitting room in the evenings when they were at home, sometimes making plans for the store, sometimes talking of John Philip Sousa, Olga Nethersole, John Drew, or Schumann-Heink. Sophie went to everything good that came to Pittsburgh, taking one of her brothers or sisters with her, concerts and the theater and occasionally a prize fight. Grandma told the plots of the day's nickelodeon, or there would be a discussion of some story Hugo was covering for the *Volksblatt.* Ermanie would complain of her discomfort, and her husband would hope, for the thousandth time, that the baby would come soon. Charlotte and Leon, her fiancé, who called nearly every evening, would come and go, searching in walks around the neighborhood for hard-to-come-by privacy. Sometimes there was a game of whist and I would listen drowsily to the slap of the cards, feeling safe in my bed, knowing there were people near, all of them ready to come to my rescue should anything happen to me.

How secure those nights were, with the happy sounds, the low complaining of the flames emerging from the rows of dots in the asbestos of the fireplaces, the voices, the wind outside where it could do no harm, the scarcely heard rattle of newspapers, the discussions of the Pittsburgh Pirates or the coming election.

I heard so much about myself through that slightly opened door of my room that I seldom asked Sophie questions any more. I had come from show people. My father's name was Edwin Carlyle, and he was a baritone. Grandma remembered seeing his act at the Harris Theatre and said she was amazed that a man with such a voice could have done what he had done if he had done it. My mother's name was Lily, and before she was married she had been on the stage too. Afterward she had traveled with my father and I had been born "almost out of a trunk," as Hugo remarked, though I didn't know what that meant. My mother was a well-educated woman who had studied voice abroad. I had never gone to school except in the spring (and I wondered where), when my father took a lay-off for my sake. The rest of the time I had been tutored by my mother. Sophie was in correspondence with my grandmother, who was

still ill and who worried about my welfare in spite of all
Sophie's reassuring letters.

I enjoyed hearing of my previous life and was curious
about it, but after several futile attempts I no longer attempted to remember any of it.

So the days went by, each one crammed with excitement
and fresh knowledge of the Webers. Time passed in rich-
ness, slowly as it does when one is very young. How fast
a morning goes now, gone in a flash! But then, on school-
less days, it was lived through leisurely, divided by dozens
of lovely *divertissements*, each one of which consumed only
a very little of my great hoard of time.

When I had first come to the house there was snow on
the window sill, and there were designs in frost on the pane
when I slipped out of bed to close my window, but now,
with the advance of spring, I left the window open and lingered in bed watching the curtains bulge and contract lazily
in the breeze. I knew the answer to the policeman's question at last—I was happy! I fitted into existence with the
Webers as though I had never known any other. I liked
them all, big and little.

And then it was the day before Easter.

I had heard so much about the store that I could hardly
wait until I was taken there. On that Saturday morning,
about ten o'clock, Elise got the five of us children onto the
streetcar for the long ride to Braddock. Braddock seemed
to me a foreign place. During the short walk after getting
off the trolley I heard alien languages spoken everywhere
on the street. The sun shone but wanly through the pall
that overhung the mill town. The shoppers, Poles, Hungar-
ians, people from other Middle-European and Baltic coun-
tries, all lumped together as "Hunkies," went about with
full pay envelopes in their pockets. Friday was payday at
the mills, and on Saturday the wives settled old bills and
spent what was left. They came out on Saturdays, the wives

with their children, and spent and spent, saving little, banking hardly ever. That was why Sophie had chosen to go into business in Braddock.

We went a block, and there, at a busy corner of the next block, stood the store. The door was at the angle, and the windows, trimmed for Easter, ran along both streets. Stuffed bunnies played on artificial grass among spring dresses, aprons, corsets and handkerchiefs. I was numb with admiration. Our store, I thought proudly—our store.

The inside bustled. Women fought over articles on the bargain tables set up in the middle of the aisles; little wooden money cups traveled on whistling wires overhead to the cubicle where change was made. The ground floor offered all the small articles, from stockings to beads. Here Charlotte reigned, directing the other salespeople in her gentle voice, making decisions, settling everything. To buy coats, suits or dresses, one had to walk upstairs, passing on the landing the little office where the bookkeeping was done. The second floor was Sophie's domain. Although she did the buying for the whole store and all policy originated with her, it was here she sold personally, and supervised the second-floor salesgirls.

But it was the basement that I loved the best. While it had in it the boys' and men's wear supervised by Seymour, the toy section supervised by Sylvester, it also had the workroom where they painted the signs and made the window decorations. Seymour designed the window displays, and Sylvester must be the greatest sign-maker in the world, I thought. "Ladies' Fine Handkerchiefs—2 for 5¢" he limned out so beautifully, or "Boys' Stylish Caps—49¢." That workroom was heaven to me. I longed to be loose in it, to block in letters on the posters, to dabble with the paints, to rummage among the decorations left over from other holidays —little Santa Clauses and cardboard firecrackers and flags and bells and artificial flowers.

We stayed all day and until the store closed at eleven

o'clock that night. We helped where we could, running errands, bringing replenishments from the stockroom, getting change from the bank across the street, rounding up the children of a customer who fainted, even waiting on the trade. Pauline helped to sell stockings, and I was put in handkerchiefs. Ernest, with Walter for an assistant, demonstrated toys. Trixie was in the way most of the time, though not willfully, for she tried very hard to be good and give no trouble.

Once when there was a lull in the toy department Sylvester told us each to pick out anything we wanted, a toy apiece. It was a wondrous delirium of choosing. Ernest and Walter settled on trains at once. Pauline, big as she was, took a doll, and so did I, though *which* doll, out of all the beauties there, was a long puzzlement. Trixie, to everybody's surprise, picked the ugliest object in the toy department, a black felt scarecrow of a man-doll with long skinny arms and legs and a pointed head, wearing nothing but a loin cloth. When I asked her why, she told me a strange story. At her house, whenever she broke a doll, it was put into a closet in the hall, waiting for the day her father could mend it—put the wig on again, or cram back the stuffing, or return an arm to its socket—a day which never came. So the closet was filled with "dead dolls," as Trixie thought of them, with holes in their heads, and smelling sickeningly of glue, and leaking sawdust, and whenever the door was opened, by mistake or otherwise, she went into a panic of fright, cried and kicked and broke into a sweat. She had nightmares about this mausoleum of the dolls, and would wake up sometimes in the middle of the night screaming. So now that she had a chance to choose a doll, she picked the ugliest one she could find because when it died, she said, she would not care so much.

We had lunch out of shoeboxes brought from home, in a little room on the store's second floor. A window there looked out on a courtyard, a grim, cheerless place, but with

one lovely budding tree growing in the middle of it. Even
now my sensations in that lunchroom come flooding back
to me. I see again the dirty window and the bits of paper
driven by the breeze around the courtyard. I smell the
hard-boiled eggs and the cheese sandwiches and the coffee
that was boiled on a gas ring. I feel the closeness of the room
and the friendliness of it. So many members of the family
went in and out of it, a nephew of Grandma's, an uncle on
Grandpa's side, Ermanie's husband, Charlotte's intended, second cousins I had never seen before, for everyone helped
Sophie out before Easter. Pauline said that her mother had
helped out before she had a fight with her in-laws years
ago and stopped talking to Hugo's side of the family, and
so had Tante Yohanna, Grandma's sister, before she broke
her hip.

In the afternoon Trixie took a nap in the workroom
while the rest of us kept to our chores. Although our energy diminished, our fascination never flagged. Sylvester
took us out to Ward's Restaurant for supper at six o'clock,
when there was a lull in the rush. By the time the store
closed at eleven we were dead tired, but watched, still interested, the dustcloths put over the counters, the receipts
put into the safe, the doors locked, and, best of all, the
janitor sprinkling sawdust over the floors and then sweep-
ing it all away again, along with slips of paper, bits of cardboard, lost hairpins, and the other debris of the day.

It had been a long time since we'd started out that morning, but it was meant to be, for it taught us how our elders
earned their bread, gave us a healthy respect for the work
they did, and made us see that our small complaints were
beneath contempt, scarcely worth uttering.

I learned that day what made the Webers a family, how
they helped one another as fiercely as they fought one another. If Hugo was not speaking to his wife, if Grandma
sometimes spoke cruelly of Tante Yohanna, it was not hate
that made them so adamant—it was simply that they could

not understand a member of the kin who did not give of self completely.

On Easter morning we slept late, and when we came down Sophie was already in the cellar, beginning the ritual of the Easter eggs. To the other children it was an old story; to me it was all new.

First a huge caldron of water was set to boil on the old iron stove in the cellar. (On Mondays the laundress boiled the white wash there; I often saw her before I went to school, filling the stomach of the stove with faggots from the woodpile and lighting them with a burning coil of paper.) Then Sophie put the eggs, dozens and dozens of them, one by one, delicately, into the seething water.

Meanwhile we children set up the chipped, cracked, or earless cups, saved for just this occasion. We drowned our pellets of dye, a different color for each cup, with steaming water from a kettle. We waved our tin spoons, danced, and complained in impatience until the eggs were boiled to Sophie's satisfaction.

Then what release from waiting it was to select an egg, dip it into one's favorite color, baste it with a spoon as its hue deepened, until it could be set out to dry, admired for a second, then forgotten for a new egg.

Sophie had a special technique. With steady hand she held an egg suspended part way in a cup until the lower portion was dyed, then turned it about and dipped the other end into a different color.

Once, as I tried to emulate her, my egg slipped from my hand and cracked on the cement floor. I was appalled, but Pauline said, "Don't worry, you won't have to wipe it up—it's hard-boiled."

"The rule is," Sophie put in, "anybody who drops an egg gets to eat it."

"Really? Right now?"

"Really."

Nothing had ever tasted so good, and nothing was as much fun as this Sunday morning, all of us busy as the people on a Brueghel canvas. "I'd rather dye Easter eggs than do anything else in the world," I said.

"I'd rather play baseball on the Pirates with Honus Wagner," said Ernest.

"I'm glad I belong in a family that dyes," confided Trixie, then added as an afterthought, "I'm also glad I'm in the first grade."

"Everybody who's six years old is in the first grade," Pauline said haughtily.

"I know somebody who isn't," Trixie retorted. "Kathleen Hackett. She's eight years old and she didn't even start to school yet." There was never any getting around Trixie, even though she was the youngest.

When the last egg had been dyed there were further embellishments with decalcomanias or with brush and water colors as we painted pictures or our names or "Happy Easter," "For Bowser, in Memory of a Good Dog," or "To be eaten only by Grandma."

While the arguments raged about which was the most beautiful egg, the last step was taken, the wiping of each one with a rag soaked in vinegar, to give a gleam. Even today when I smell vinegar I think of that wonderful Easter of 1908 and all its delights.

Right after lunch the hunts in the garden began and continued until Sophie and Seymour and Sylvester were exhausted from hiding the eggs. Then there was some excitement in the house, and the adults and Pauline left us. After that we hid eggs for one another. I was dimly aware that the grown-ups were concerned with the coming of Ermanie's baby, but I was too interested in the hunts to be inquisitive.

At three o'clock even we were tired. We went around to the front of the house and flopped into wicker chairs on the front porch. Trixie's piquant little face, in the center of her Dutch bob, sagged with weariness. Our dresses were rumpled, stained by grass and dye, and so were the boys' shirts and knee breeches.

Pauline came out, banging the screen door behind her, just as Mr. Hermansdorfer turned up the walk. He was dressed in his Easter best and carried a foot-square box, beautifully wrapped. We were glad to see him because whenever he called on Elise we asked him to play the nickelodeon music and he always complied. He had become a family favorite, admired most of all by Grandma.

"Hello, Mr. Hermansdorfer," Pauline said.

"Good afternoon. And a happy Easter. Is your Aunt Elise at home?"

"No, she isn't," Pauline answered. "She went to a whist party."

"A whist party?"

"Yes, but it's only a few blocks away, and anyhow she'll be home any minute because Uncle Sylvester just went to get her."

Mr. Hermansdorfer consulted the watch that hung from a chain over his vest. "The party is over so soon?"

"No, it's right in the middle."

"Then . . . ?"

"Aunt Ermanie is having her baby today. That's why Aunt Elise is sent for."

"Is that so?"

"At last."

Mr. Hermansdorfer looked at the box. "I wonder what I should do."

"Well, since Aunt Elise will be right home, why don't you wait?"

"I guess I wouldn't be in the way if I sat here for a little while?"

"No," said Pauline.

He took a chair and we stared at him in silence. He

cleared his throat and asked, to make conversation, "Is the doctor here?"

"No," Pauline said, "he hasn't come yet. My father went to get him. And Uncle Sylvester went to get Aunt Elise, and Uncle Seymour went to get Grandma. Grandma's at a nickelodeon."

"On Easter?"

"Oh, it isn't a regular nickelodeon. It's a private showing. Mr. Harry Davis is having it at Carnegie Hall by special invitation. Grandma got a special invitation. It's a three-reel Pathé picture in color called *The Passion Play*."

"In color!" cried Mr. Hermansdorfer, impressed.

"Hand-painted." Pauline nodded.

"So! I wonder who's playing the piano," he murmured with professional interest.

"There's to be an organ."

"An organ! Is that so?"

Aunt Charlotte appeared in the doorway, looking distraught. She nodded to Mr. Hermansdorfer and asked, "Any sign of the doctor yet?"

"No, not yet," said Pauline calmly.

"Oh, dear!"

"Hello, Charlotte, I . . ." Mr. Hermansdorfer began, but subsided because she had already vanished.

The silence was then so thick that even little Walter felt the need of talk. "My mother isn't on speaking terms with anybody in this house," he said.

Mr. Hermansdorfer moved restlessly in his chair. "Is that so?"

"She speaks to us. And she *did* speak to Papa until the fight," Pauline protested.

"But not to anybody else who lives here," Walter politely explained to Mr. Hermansdorfer. "It's on account of what Grandpa, when he was living, said once to Tante Yohanna."

"What was that?" I asked.

"Oh, Grandpa said that my mother wasn't good enough for my father."

"Isn't she good enough for him?" I wanted to know.

"*I* think she is," said Trixie.

"Grandpa swore up and down," Pauline interjected, "he never said any such thing. But Tante Yohanna swore he had."

"Anyhow," Walter said proudly, "my mother hasn't spoken to anybody in this house for *five* years."

"It's a record, all right," Mr. Hermansdorfer said.

"Grandpa was Grandma's husband, wasn't he?" Trixie asked.

"Of course, silly! He died three years ago," Pauline said. "I went to the funeral. I was nine then. I'm twelve now. He couldn't speak English. He couldn't speak anything but German."

"Why couldn't he?" I asked.

"He wouldn't learn. He was stubborn. He said anybody could understand German if they wanted to. If they couldn't understand his German the first time, he repeated it—louder. He couldn't see why anybody didn't understand *loud* German. He died at a quarter after eleven Christmas Eve. He wouldn't die till the store closed."

"Why?"

"On account of the Christmas rush. He put off dying for two weeks. He didn't want the store to have to close in honor of his death till the Christmas rush was over. He wanted Aunt Sophie to squeeze out every penny that was coming to her, my mama says."

Sophie had pushed the screen door open while Pauline was talking, and remarked dryly, "I bet your mother says a *lot* of interesting things."

Mr. Hermansdorfer rose. "Hello, Sophie."

"Oh, hello, Max." Then she turned to Pauline. "Any sign of the doctor yet?"

"No."

"May I inquire after the little mother?" Elise's caller asked.

"Doing fine," Sophie answered absently, looking worried. "As soon as the doctor gets here, hustle him upstairs as fast as his legs will carry him."

"Is the baby really coming?" Walter called out after her as she started back into the house.

"On greased lightning." And she was gone.

Mr. Hermansdorfer sat down again and there was quiet until Walter spoke up. "We had a false alarm in March."

Mr. Hermansdorfer looked at him. "I beg your pardon?"

"We thought Aunt Ermanie was going to have the baby then, but she didn't. She started to, but she stopped."

"And Grandma had to come home from the nickelodeon that time too," said Trixie. "And it was for nothing."

"She was terribly mad," Walter said.

I wondered aloud if the baby would stop again this time. Ernest didn't think so. This time, he said, it was going to go right ahead and get it over with.

"I wonder why it stopped the last time. Maybe it doesn't want to be born."

"It *has* to get born," Pauline said. "Everybody has to get born. It's Fate."

Elise and Sylvester came down the street and hurried toward the porch. Mr. Hermansdorfer stood up again, and as soon as Elise saw him she cried, "Max! Well, for goodness' sakes, what are you doing here?"

"I came to say good-by to you, but I realize it's at an unpropitious time and—"

"Oh, you're leaving on the symphony tour?" Elise asked. "When?"

"Tomorrow."

Sylvester was more interested in the baby and asked if the doctor had come yet. We told him no.

Mr. Hermansdorfer, looking a little ashamed, held out his box to Elise. "I brought you—well, a little Easter token."

"How sweet of you, Max."

We were on our feet now. "Open it, Aunt Elise! Open it."

"I suppose I really ought to be getting upstairs, but . . ." She started to open the box. "Well, I just can't resist looking."

We gathered around her as she pulled off the wrappings and took out of the box a large chocolate Easter egg decorated with white frosting.

"Chocolate! It's beautiful."

"It's got a little window you can look into," Mr. Hermansdorfer said, and showed her how to peep through.

"I want to see!" cried Trixie.

"You'll all get your turns," Elise said, and when it was mine I looked and saw a little pastoral scene inside, trees and tiny lambs gamboling on the green.

"Be careful," Elise kept saying, as Mr. Hermansdorfer looked proudly on.

"Uncle Seymour isn't home with Grandma yet?" Sylvester asked us.

"No," Ernest replied.

"Funny."

Elise put the egg back in the box. "Now I've *really* got to go upstairs and see if I can help."

"Yes," Mr. Hermansdorfer said. "Well, Elise, good-by till July."

Elise took his hand and shook it. "Max, maybe—well, when Mama and the doctor get here—well, they may not need me at all. Stick around a while."

"No, I feel rather—well, a family probably prefers to be alone at a sacred time like this."

Elise laughed. "Alone? A mob like this?"

Mr. Hermansdorfer had a sudden idea. "I'll come back tonight?"

"That'll be fine."

"Then good-by. Or rather, *auf Wiedersehen.*"

We watched Mr. Hermansdorfer leave and then we all followed Elise inside. The father-to-be was coming down the stairs. His eyes, behind the pince-nez, were blurry, as though he hadn't slept in weeks.

"Well, *wie geht's,* Theodore?" Sylvester asked.

"I don't know, I don't know." Theodore groaned and sat down on the hall chest. We all studied him.

"You look bad," Elise said.

He shook his head in bewilderment. "The baby seems to have taken a long time in coming, but now that it's here, I'm not ready."

"You'd better get ready," Elise said.

"You mean the baby's already here?" Walter asked.

"No, it's not here. What I meant was—now that its birth is here . . ." Theodore put his head in his hands. "I don't know what I mean."

"You'd better pull yourself together," Sylvester suggested.

"If the doctor'd only come. What takes him so long?"

"He'll be here, he'll be here."

"But in the meantime," Theodore protested, "poor Ermanie, up there at the mercy of Sophie and Charlotte—two spinsters. Neither of them's ever had a baby."

"I hope not," Elise said. "Well, cheer up. I'm going upstairs, and that'll make three spinsters."

When she'd left, Sylvester tried to console Theodore. "It isn't so bad. Look around you. Millions of people. And every one of them was born."

"Remarkable!"

"Mothers gave birth to every one of them."

"I don't know how they do it."

Sylvester lost interest in Theodore and turned to us children. He helped himself to an egg from a basket Trixie was carrying. "Let me eat one."

"Not that one, Uncle Sylvester. That's too pretty. Eat this one. Walter smeared it."

"I did not!" cried Walter.

Sylvester took the proffered egg and read what was written on it. " 'The Weber family.' Well, that's me."

While he was eating, the door opened and Grandma, followed by Seymour, came bounding into the house, a dynamo, small but powerful. "Well, *wie steht's? Wie steht's?*" She sounded angry.

Theodore leaped to his feet. "Mama Weber! Thank God you're here!"

"Yes, I'm here. Halfway through the show"—pointing to Seymour furiously—"he comes and tells me!"

"The doctor isn't here yet, Mama," Sylvester informed her.

She turned and glared at him. "No? He can stay to the end of the show! Me, I had to walk out!"

Theodore looked from Grandma to Sylvester and back in confusion. "The doctor's at the show?"

"No, no, he's not there. Mama's sore, that's all," Seymour said.

Then Elise appeared suddenly at the top of the stairs and called down to us all, "Hallelujah! The baby's born!"

There was an outburst of questions: "*Ja?*" from Grandma; "Honestly?" from Sylvester; "Truly? Oh, goody!" from Trixie.

"Yep, it's here, all right," Elise said, coming down a few steps.

Theodore had grown white as a sheet. "But it can't be. The doctor isn't here yet."

Elise laughed. "What do you want me to do? Put it back till he comes?"

Grandma had no time for Theodore and his troubles. "So it's born! Without me! I could have seen the end of the show!"

"I'm sorry, Mama," Seymour apologized.

"I'll never know how it ended."

"*The Passion Play?*"

"I'll go and see Harry Davis and ask him," Elise offered.

"How's Ermanie?" Theodore gasped.

"Oh, she's perfectly all right," Elise told him. "Well," she said to the rest of us, "you've got to hand it to Sophie. There isn't *anything* she can't do."

Theodore started for the stairs. "I'm going up to Ermanie."

"No," Grandma commanded. "You stay here. *I'm* going up. I came home, so I'll go up."

When she had stomped up the steps and disappeared from view, Seymour laughed and said, "She's mad again."

His brother smiled. "Well, it's pretty inconsiderate of Ermanie—always waiting till Mama is at the show."

Elise said, "You didn't hear me complaining about leaving the whist party. It was going to be awful anyhow. All she had for prizes were sachet bags. I can just see myself playing whist like crazy all afternoon to win a sachet bag."

"What is it, a boy or a girl?" Sylvester asked suddenly.

"Didn't I tell you? A girl."

"My God! I forgot to ask!" cried Theodore.

Sylvester gripped the father's hand. "Well, congratulations!"

"Have a stogie!" Seymour declared, pulling one out of his vest pocket and pushing it at Theodore.

The new father turned his head away from it in revulsion. "Take it away. It's making me sick."

"Look," Seymour said, "you've just had a baby. You're a father. You should feel great."

Theodore answered dismally, "I will when I get used to it. It's been so sudden."

"Sudden?" Elise repeated. "I bet Ermanie took ten months. I bet it was the longest time ever taken in history."

"Shhh. Not in front of the children," Seymour said.

Grandma came flying down the steps, speaking with such urgency in her tone that we all stared at her. "Seymour! Sylvester! Did the doctor come yet?"

"Why? Is something wrong?" Theodore asked, frightened.

"*Nein, nein,* nothing wrong! But he didn't come yet?"

"No, Mama."

"Good! Then listen. When he comes tell him to go away!"

"Go away?"

"We'll save the twenty-five dollars."

"Oh," Seymour said.

"Well," Elise commented, "that's the second twenty-five dollars we've saved. We sent him away for the false alarm too."

Sylvester came over and put his arm around his mother. "How do you like having another grandchild, Mama?"

"A girl! For a girl I had to walk out in the middle of the show!"

"Is it a nice little girl?" I asked.

"Yes, what does it look like?" Seymour wanted to know.

Grandma shrugged her shoulders. "What does a baby look like, anyhow—a baby!"

"Can I go up now?" Theodore asked plaintively.

But before anyone could answer him, the screen door burst open and Hugo, all out of breath, rushed into the house, bringing what he thought was great news. "He's here! The doctor's here!"

We could see old Dr. Reichart huffing and puffing on the porch, his hand on the screen door. But Grandma moved so rapidly she was able to stop him before he got over the threshold. "Go away!" she cried.

Dr. Reichart's white mustache quivered. "What?"

"*Gehen Sie!*" Grandma commanded, a tigress protecting her lair.

Embarrassed, Seymour came up beside her and tried to explain through the screen Grandma was holding firmly shut. "Uh—Doctor Reichart, you see—uh—the baby's already been born."

Hugo was astonished. "Honestly?"

"*Heraus mit Ihnen!*" Grandma told the doctor.

He answered angrily, his nose flattened against the screen, "Now, see here, Mrs. Weber, I came all the way over here. I was playing pinochle and I left the game just to come here. And this is the second time this has happened. The same thing happened in March."

Grandma laughed scornfully. "He left a pinochle game!"

"I demand to see the mother."

"She doesn't need a doctor. An hour ago maybe she needed a doctor. Now she doesn't. Go away."

Hugo tried to smooth things over. "It wasn't his fault, Mama. It took me all this time to find him. He wasn't at home, he was at a friend's house. It wasn't his fault."

The doctor pushed at the screen from one side, and Grandma pushed back on the other. "I was called, and I'm going to attend the patient."

"Oh, no. Twenty-five dollars. For what?"

"I didn't make any price, Mrs. Weber."

"I know you robbers."

The doctor was offended and dropped his hands to his sides. "Now, Mrs. Weber!"

"I'll pay the fee," Theodore said, trying to make peace. "I'd just as leave pay and—"

Grandma didn't listen to him. "Twenty-five dollars is what Hugo paid—for Trixie. Hugo, you paid twenty-five dollars for Trixie, didn't you, Hugo?"

Hugo tried to reason with his mother. "Mama, it doesn't matter what—"

But she didn't let him. "Go away," she said to the doctor again.

He replied with ill-suppressed fury, "All right, Mrs. Weber! All right! But the next time a baby is born around here, don't call *me! I won't come!*"

"We don't need you!"

"As far as I'm concerned, no Weber will ever have a baby again!"

"We don't want any more!"

"From me you won't get any more, believe me!" exclaimed the doctor, and turned away.

But Grandma got in the last word anyhow, as he left the porch. "We have enough!"

She deserted her post at the door, looking a little sheepish now that he was gone. There was a long, accusing silence until Elise said, "Well, Mama, I guess you saved the money."

She seemed relieved when Walter changed the subject by exclaiming, "Let's all go see the baby!"—and she didn't stop us as we children charged up the stairs.

"Papa paid twenty-five dollars for me," Trixie said proudly, mounting.

We heard Hugo laugh in the hall below. "I wonder if she was worth it."

3

Memorial Day

————◆◆◆————

S HORTLY AFTER Easter, Sophie had to go to New York on
a brief buying trip and decided to take me with her.
When I heard we were going to visit my grandmother
there, I was very frightened. What if she kept me and I
could not return to Pittsburgh? That fear was always at
the back of my mind, and I enjoyed the train trip only
sporadically.

New York was so wonderful I nearly forgot to worry. I
did not mind going with Sophie to a police office, where
she reported on my progress, because we went in a subway.
I liked the crowded pavements, the street thick with carriages and occasional motor cars, the wholesale district
where Sophie bought by day, and the theater we went to
one night. Best of all I liked Fleisher Yarn's great electric
sign high above Broadway, showing a kitten playing with
a ball of wool. The sign was so bright and the kitten so dear
that my heart thumped.

Sophie had been corresponding with a vaudeville couple
who had been friends of my parents, and one of the first
things we did was go to Hammerstein's Victoria, where
they were playing. As soon as the final curtain came down,
while the audience was still applauding, we left our seats
and found our way backstage. It was exciting to be there,

to see people still in costume, to hear snatches of their conversation mingled with the shouts of the stagehands, and then to go into a dressing room to have a fuss made over me by performers I had just seen behind the footlights. "Jane, darling, how nice you look! What a pretty little hat! Oh, that long, lovely hair and those beautiful eyes. Come kiss me, dear. Now, tell Aunt Helen, do you still sing 'If a Table at Rector's Could Talk'?"

"No, I don't."

"No? It was so sweet the way you used to do it. And I'll never forget you taking off Irene Franklin singing 'Red Head,' or falling down like Leon Errol. Such a mimic, this child!"

Oh, they knew me so well! And I knew them not at all —except that they were billed as the Merry Merriweathers, and Mrs. Merriweather came on stage wheeling a baby carriage and was very funny, and Mr. Merriweather was a lamplighter who got into a conversation with her and was very funny. Funniest of all was the baby, which turned out to be a little dog and which, at the end of the act, jumped out of the carriage and did cartwheels across the stage and into the wings.

Sitting at their dressing tables, taking off their make-up, the Merry Merriweathers chatted of this and that, but never once did they mention my father or my mother or anything they must have thought would upset me. "What a shame you came tonight of all nights," Mr. Merriweather said, "when *we* had to replace the headliner."

"You were ever so good," Sophie said.

"But you missed Ray Beaumont!"

"Poor Ray," Mrs. Merriweather said. "He was so pleased when I told him you were going to be here tonight. Dying to see little Jane again, he said. Then half an hour later he had to leave the theater."

"Why? What happened?" Sophie asked.

"He got sick."

"I wondered, when it was announced he wouldn't appear. What was wrong?"

"He told the management acute indigestion, but—and this is confidential, don't repeat it—he has a bad heart. It happened once before. Well, let's hope this wasn't a serious attack, but it's such a pity you didn't see him. Of course Jane has seen his act half a dozen times, but have you, Miss Weber?"

"No, I haven't," Sophie replied, "and Jane wouldn't remember."

"Oh, excuse me!" Mrs. Merriweather cried, as though she'd said something terrible.

"It's all right," Sophie said. "Jane understands. We talk about her loss of memory freely."

Mrs. Merriweather turned in her chair and swooped me into her arms. "I'll tell you what, darling. We'll all go for a bite to eat at the Metropole and celebrate our reunion. It's a famous theatrical restaurant. All right, Miss Weber?"

I looked longingly at Sophie. "Could we? Oh, could we?"

"We certainly could," she answered gaily.

Yes, I liked New York. But I did not like my visit to Grandmother Carlyle.

We were ushered into a well-furnished little apartment on Riverside Drive by the lady who took care of her, and were helped out of our coats. The lady's name was Molly. She had sad eyes in a sad face and just before she opened the door to my grandmother's room she rolled them upward in a signal to us to expect the worst. My grandmother was in a bed in a room that was almost dark, though it was still afternoon. Her gray hair was perfectly coiffed, and she wore a lavender silk bed jacket. She held out a well-shaped thin hand, on which the veins showed even in the gloom. She would not let Molly turn on a lamp, and we sat down in chairs beside her bed after I had dutifully kissed her. She had once been very beautiful, I decided, and did not like us to see how she looked now. Once again I was asked if I was happy. I could have answered her with enthusiasm, but the atmosphere of the room restrained me and I only nodded. Then she wanted me to tell her about Pittsburgh, but before I could say very much she interrupted me, saying, "Why don't you go out in the sitting room, dear, and play with Pussy?" and then the next thing I knew, Molly had taken me away.

Molly brought Pussy from the kitchen, but I compared him with the Fleisher kitten and hated him. He was old and his coat was sparse, and instead of purring he seemed merely to complain. I turned my back on him, wishing he would stop making his petulant noise, and looked glumly out the window at the boats on the Hudson on the other side of the drive.

I knew why I had been sent out of the bedroom. My grandmother wanted to talk to Sophie alone. What were they saying to each other? "After all, I'm her father's mother." "Certainly, Mrs. Carlyle, it won't matter about school—it will be simple for her to switch to one here in New York." "She'll enjoy it so with me. After all, there will be Pussy to play with." Pussy! After Trixie and Walter and Ernest and Pauline?

I was sick with imagining.

Molly made tea, and when she took the tray into the bedroom I caught a glimpse of Sophie leaning confidentially toward my grandmother as they talked. Molly came back and brought me a cup too, but I did not drink it and nibbled at the cooky only because it was very, very good.

I thought about the Webers. I thought of the evening Sylvester had taken me to a spring festival gay with Japanese lanterns and crepe-paper-decorated booths. His round shiny face beamed. He enjoyed the punch and cupcakes and the puppet show as much as I did. I thought of the cradle for Nancy Myrtle May that Seymour had made. When I put her in it he smiled so hard the brown birthmark on his

cheek stretched and stretched. I thought of the dress Charlotte had embroidered for me with scallops all down the
front and along the hem, and of the coat Sophie had bought
me. It was a winter coat trimmed with white fur studded
with black ermine tails, bought at *especially* wholesale price
because it was left over from the past season. I would not be
able to wear it for a long time, but in the meantime I could
enjoy looking at it.

How good the Webers were to me! How much I loved
them! Oh, I belonged to them, not to my grandmother!

I thought of a day I had been at the player piano, pumping away, first one foot and then the other—not like the
treadle on the sewing machine, which had to be rocked
back and forth, both feet together. When the roll finished
I touched the quiet keys. Suddenly I was playing a piece.
There was nothing in my head, but my fingers knew the
notes. Pauline was familiar with the tune and sang the
words, verse after verse.

> *I wandered today to the hill, Maggie,*
> *To watch the scene below,*
> *The creek and the creaking old mill, Maggie,*
> *As we used to long, long ago.*

Sophie said when we finished, "I didn't know you played.
I wonder if your mother taught you, Jane."

"She plays beautifully!" Grandma cried, beaming with
approval. "She's so musical!"

"She's certainly not a Weber," Elise said.

After that I never touched the piano again.

At last the bedroom door opened and Sophie beckoned
to me. I came toward her, tense with fear, looking into her
face for a sign of what my future was to be. I could read
nothing there. It was not until I had spent at least five more
minutes being polite that Sophie said, "Well, Jane, say
good-by. It'll be a long time before you'll be in New York

again." Then I gave her what must have been the most radiant smile she had ever seen.

At the last moment my grandmother began to cry and clutched at me, pulling me so close I felt the bones at the base of her neck and smelled the talcum powder she used. "Darling," she said, sobbing, "you see how it is, don't you, with me bedridden for nearly a year now and nobody to help me but Molly?"

"Oh, yes," I said, "I see."

Then she let me go, except for my hand, which she kept kneading nervously. She stopped crying and spoke to me gravely, "Listen to me, Jane. No matter what's said or what happens, your father couldn't have done anything wrong. He's a good man. Always remember that."

I felt sorry for her, but I was relieved when she let go of my hand. And how glad I was to put on my coat, my spring coat that I would wear back to Pittsburgh!

On our last day in New York, Sophie and I went for a walk on Fifth Avenue. She pointed out Mr. Frick's house. He was a multimillionaire, she said, who had made his fortune in Pittsburgh in the coke industry. It was interesting, she told me, that his beautiful mansion, which was filled with world-famous paintings and sculptures, was bought with money made from the by-products of ugly soft coal. "You never know what loveliness comes from dirty old things," she said, laughing. "Take Braddock, for instance."

"It's not so bad," I said loyally.

"No, Braddock's not so bad."

"When I get old," I said suddenly, "I'm going to make a lot of money and buy you a house just like Mr. Frick's."

"That's nice of you. *Very* nice. But I think it's rather large for me."

"Oh, I'll be living with you, Sophie."

"Will you, dear? I'm glad."

"Just the two of us. We won't have anybody else living with us but Hugo's children," I said.

"They'll be grown up then."

"That's true. Well, if we don't want them, we'll get some other children."

"We could have dozens in a house like that and never know the difference."

"Maybe we could invite your whole family. I hate leaving any of them out."

"Then let's have them all."

"Won't it be fun, Sophie? Not that there's anything wrong with Wilkins Avenue."

"Not a thing."

"Of course not."

"Anyhow, a mansion like Mr. Frick's is a lovely present."

"It's just that I want to buy you something, Sophie."

She laughed, and then, right there on Fifth Avenue, leaned over and kissed me.

It was May and it seemed a long time since we had waded through snow on the way to school. Along our paths the verdure changed as the year progressed; buds appeared on bare branches and became leaves, grasses grew green and tall in the fields. The pussy willows had had their day; the trilliums and daffodils had come and gone. Now that the weather was really warm, the fields were thick with clover, tangy and bee-visited. Buttercups and daisies would soon be coming into their own. A pair of yellow butterflies, fluttering around each other, followed us across the field. Earlier there had been violets in the woods on the other side of Wilkins Avenue, and we had gone there to gather them and made leaf-ringed bouquets to sell for a nickel. Now we had lemonade stands, though there were very few customers. Sometimes Mr. Andrew Mellon appeared from Woodland Road on his morning constitutional and would buy from us. Rich though he was, living in an enormous ivy-covered mansion, he never bought more than one bunch of flowers or one cup of lemonade. But he seemed a very nice man.

We missed hunting for spring violets and May apples and jack-in-the-pulpits, but now there were lilacs in bloom near the tennis court, and we cut sprays heavy with a thousand tiny florets, each a four-branched star, each perfect.

Friends came on Sundays to play tennis, young ladies in long white linen dresses, half-dollar-sized pearl buttons all the way down the front, young men in white ducks. While I helped Trixie make mudpies, or lolled in the grass with Pauline, blowing on dandelion puffs which separated into myriads of tiny parachutes, the good cries, "Thirty love!" "Take two," "Fine rally!" drifted to us through the fragrant May air.

Sophie was a particularly good player, light on her feet and quick. I watched her with the friends of her brothers and sisters. How few friends of her own she had and how scant were her social pleasures! Ermanie was married, Charlotte engaged, Elise had half a dozen beaux, but Sophie's life was the store. No wonder Grandma fretted and sighed for a suitor for her.

Actually Grandma had taken things into her own hands, and, now that Ermanie and Theodore had gone home with their baby and there was an empty room in the house, she had put an ad in the paper for a male boarder.

The ad appeared on Friday, and all Memorial Day applicants came and went, interviewed personally by Grandma.

The store was closed, and the house bustled with people, but the day was a lonely one to me because Hugo's children spent it with their mother and her family. They left early in the morning, jabbering to one another in anticipation of an outing in Schenley Park, making me feel left out and abandoned. Sophie and her brothers played tennis. Elise entertained some friends. Grandma interviewed. In the afternoon, Hugo took me with him to the cemetery to visit Grandpa's grave. Though I enjoyed the flowers and wreaths and the little flags on the graves of Civil and Spanish-American War heroes, I felt bereft of companionship, truly an orphan in a world of grown-ups. I was delighted when the children came back that night, though they were tired and cranky and bragged about a wonderful picnic I had missed.

At nine we were sent to bed. I was restless. I lay wide awake, and the heavy, almost unbearably exquisite scent of roses filled the room. Why did I smell roses when the only flowers there were lilacs which I had picked that day? The scent of roses! What did it mean? I did not know, but I began to think of my mother, and of *temps perdu*, to me doubly lost. I wondered again where my father was and if he cared about me, and, if so, how he could have left me so abruptly to a life with strangers. Strangers? I knew the Webers as I knew the familiar things I had worn on my back that day and which now lay sprawled on a rush-seat chair—my Ferris waist with the bone buttons onto which my bloomers fastened, my long white lisle stockings, my petticoats, ruffled and ribbon-drawn.

I watched yellow light fall on one corner of my room and travel slowly across the ceiling to the other side as carriages went by in the street. I tried for a long time to go to sleep. At ten I gave up because I was hungry and because I wanted to know why the house was so quiet and what the family was doing. I slipped out of bed and down the back stairs. Before I got to the bottom I heard voices in the kitchen. I had learned that the law of the house was that children, once sent to bed, should not be caught in their nightgowns except on the way to or from the bathroom. Just once more I would break the law. I sat down on my familiar step. I tucked my nightgown around my feet and wrapped my arms around my knees expectantly.

I could smell the coffee Sophie was making and I could

hear Hugo, who was probably sitting at the kitchen table, rustling the pages of a newspaper as he turned them. "My," he said, "there've been a lot of robberies in the neighborhood lately."

"Yes, I read it," Sophie said. Then she put the coffeepot on the table, and the chair scraped as she sat down. "Where's Mama?" she asked.

"Out on the porch interviewing another boarder."

"They're *still* coming at this hour of the night?"

"Still coming."

"Some idea—a boarder! We need a boarder in this house like we need a kick in the pants."

"Well, you know Mama when she makes up her mind to something."

"You know what I think? I think she's trying to find me a husband."

"Sophie, you're crazy."

"No, I mean it. What's she being so particular for? If she just wants to rent a room she could have done it a dozen times over. But she's looking the applicants over with a fine-tooth comb. Do you realize she's stipulated single men only?"

"You saw the ad?"

"Yes, and that's what it says."

Hugo laughed, and then he asked, "There've been so many answers, what did she offer? Breakfast in bed and dancing girls on the chiffoniers?"

"The big attraction is price. Three dollars a week, room and board. Now don't tell me for three dollars a week Mama is going to all this trouble! No! That extra room is meant for a soulmate for Sophie Weber!"

Hugo laughed again. "Mama is some potatoes."

"Now she won't have to go on the outside. She'll have nice steady work with a man right here in the house to throw at me."

There was a long silence, and then Hugo asked, his voice very serious, "Sophie, did anybody ever ask you to marry him?"

"No." Another long pause, and then she added softly, "But I asked somebody to marry me once."

"Honest?"

"Yes, I was crazy about him. But he said, very kindly and regretfully, of course, he didn't want to marry a cash register."

Hugo exclaimed, his voice thick with compassion, "What a terrible thing for him to have said!"

"Oh, I don't blame him. My interests are more those of a man than a woman, I guess."

"Oh, Sophie."

"I'm not complaining. I have my excitement. Making the store out of nothing, buying, and gambling whether what I buy will sell or not—that's a romance too. And power, Hugo. I think I'm getting to like power. Seymour and Sylvester do whatever I say. Whatever I think, even about politics—if I say I think it, they think it too. Books, plays, baseball even—they wait till I have an opinion and then that's their opinion. Everybody looks to me, and I like it. I control my world."

"Except Mama."

"Yes, except her. I have everything I want, even a daughter. If Mama'd leave me alone about getting married, I'd be perfectly happy."

Then there was nothing but the sound of coffee cups on the saucers. If Hugo doubted Sophie's happiness, he didn't mention it. Presently Sophie spoke of his own situation. "Do you ever hear anything from Daisy, Hugo?"

"Not a word." He sighed. "I'm so disgusted. When is she going to give in?"

"When are *you* going to give in?"

"Never! It's up to her. At her folks' three blocks away

all this time, and does she ever so much as walk over here and say hello to me? No. The children have to stop in to see her every day, but she can't come here."

"Maybe you should make the first move."

"And go back to the same thing about going into business with her father? No. She has to see my point of view once and for all."

"Well, at least there's one good side. This gives me a chance to see something of you for a change."

"Yes." And then he said he thought he would have a cooky. I heard Sophie rise to get the cooky jar. He sighed and continued, "I think I'm doing the right thing, but—oh, if I weren't so crazy about her."

Sophie, her voice full of sympathy, said that she knew.

"Her ambition for me! What's wrong with working on the *Volksblatt*, Sophie?"

"Nothing. You're doing something imaginative, something you're fitted for, with your editorials and everything You're not fitted for taking orders from the Czar."

"I've told her that a thousand times. She won't admit her father is a czar, but all she has to do is look at her brothers. They've taken orders from the old man so long they can't even think for themselves."

"Like me—with Seymour and Sylvester?"

"Sophie, don't be silly."

"I know, I know, mine's an altruistic empire."

"Our boys are nice fellows, but not too smart. They learn from you, Sophie, that's all. But Daisy's brothers are completely cowed by the Grand Pasha. They're *Nichtsnütze!*"

"Well, don't you become one."

"I won't, but—oh, Sophie, it's tough without Daisy."

"She'll come around."

"If I can hold out long enough."

"Having gone this far, I suppose you can't give up now."

"If it only happens before I weaken."

"It will."

I think he must have reached over and taken her hand. "If it weren't for you, Sophie, I . . ." His voice trailed away in futility.

"And you've always helped me, Hugo. Actually, you're the only one in the family I can really talk to."

If she would only talk to me, I thought, I would be so happy to have her confidence. I would give her such good advice—well, perhaps not advice, because I didn't know very much, but I could give her understanding. Suddenly I was so sorry for her I longed to run to her and squeeze her hand, and Hugo's too.

I heard Grandma come in from the porch and shut the front door firmly. She came down the length of the hall to the kitchen, passing my dark perch on the back stairs. She poured herself a glass of water. She must have been thinking hard. She did not even speak to Hugo and Sophie. I moved down one more step so I could see what was happening. She took a piece of paper and a pencil out of her bosom, where she kept things in the top of her corset. She studied the paper, which we all knew was a list of potential boarders because she had been jotting notes on it all day.

"Well?" Hugo asked, watching her.

"Too fat," Grandma said.

"I like fat men," Sophie put in unexpectedly and boldly. "There's nothing I'd like to marry more than a fat man."

"Who's talking about marrying?" asked Grandma innocently, but she changed the subject. "Well, I think I'll go to bed. Tomorrow I'm going to take down all the curtains."

"Every day's a busy day for Mama," Sophie said.

Grandma moved away from the sink but stopped when Elise came in the back door, her dark curls in disarray and her tennis shoes in her hand. "Where were you?" her mother asked.

"No place important. Just sitting in the back yard with Charlotte and Leon." Leon Bauer was Charlotte's young man. Elise threw her shoes down and went to the stove to pour herself a cup of coffee. "Mama, I've got bad news for you. Your daughter Charlotte's fiancé has saved a thousand dollars."

"*Was!*" Grandma cried.

"How's that?" asked Hugo.

Elise said to Hugo, laughing, "Mama promised Charlotte they could get married as soon as Leon'd saved a thousand dollars, and now he's done it sooner than expected."

"How could he? A *thousand dollars!*" exclaimed Grandma.

"It looks bad." Elise sort of sang the words as though she was enjoying her mother's discomfiture. "Now Charlotte's sure to get married before Sophie."

"Good!" Sophie said, getting up and carrying the coffee cups to the sink.

Grandma was really taking the news hard. "I can't understand it. A thousand dollars. And he's such a *Schlemiel.*"

"Is that a way to talk about your future son-in-law?" Elise teased. "Your immediately-in-the-future son-in-law?"

"Let's get out of here, Hugo," Sophie said suddenly. "Let's go for a walk."

"Now? So late?" Grandma asked.

"I *like* walking in the dark," Sophie answered defiantly. "It makes it so much harder not to walk on the cracks in the sidewalk."

Hugo laughed. "Step on a crack, break your mother's back. You're like a kid, Sophie."

Grandma interjected quickly, "That's what I say! She's young—she should get married!"

Sophie raised her hands to her ears in exasperation, and her brother said sternly, "Now, Mama! Now, Mama—enough with Sophie!"

Meanwhile I heard Charlotte come in the front door and approach down the hall. I moved quickly into the shadows

so no light would fall upon me when she passed my stair-
well. I heard Elise ask her, "Leon go?"

"Yes."

"How many times did you kiss him good night?"

"Just once, if you really want to know."

"All right, Sophie," Hugo said, "let's go for a walk."
They left by the back door, and there was no talk for a
while, only the sounds of cups and saucers being washed
at the sink.

At last Grandma said, "I hear Leon's making lots of
money."

"Yes. Yes, he is, Mama."

Grandma sounded casual. "I hear he's got the thousand
dollars."

"Yes. That's what I wanted to talk to you about." Charlotte burst out with what was on her mind. "Mama, we
want to get married right away!"

"Right away? I never heard of such a thing! Crazy!"

"You said when he had a thousand dollars, and now he
has it."

"Ah," said Elise, "but Mama thought it would take him
ten years."

"Well, it didn't," said Charlotte. "Mama, we want to get
married *now*."

"You'd do a thing like that before your sister Sophie
with a child was married?" Grandma said.

"Ermanie's married, so why does it matter so much about
me?"

"One sister is bad enough; two, it looks terrible for
Sophie."

"She'll never get married, Mama." Charlotte moaned.

Grandma was indignant. "Is that so?"

"Well, there isn't a sign of anything. And meanwhile
you'll just keep Leon and me dangling and dangling." Charlotte's voice broke. "You'll never let us get married."

"Not so! I just want to give Sophie a little more chance. Just a little more."

"She's had a good thirty years," Elise put in.

Charlotte was really crying now. "Sophie hasn't got a beau in sight, and you're asking Leon and me to wait on the flimsy hope that somebody'll pop up and . . ." She was unable to go on.

"It so happens," Grandma said, "that I know Sophie's got a beau in New York."

"What!" Elise cried.

"From her buying trips," Grandma said.

"But she's never mentioned a word about anybody in New York," Charlotte said in disbelief.

"Because he's a traveling salesman!" Grandma cried triumphantly. "She got two letters from him from Denver."

One day a letter had come. We always read return addresses and looked at postmarks, so I examined the envelope when I brought it in from the mailbox. I had put it on the hall table, where it waited till Sophie came home in the evening. She had picked it up and given a little cry of astonishment when she'd pulled the letter out of the envelope and looked at the signature. She sat down on a hall chair to read it, then crammed it into her pocket and went immediately upstairs. Half an hour later when I went into her room she was still staring at it. She had not said anything to me about it, and I had thought no more of it until now.

"Did you read them, Mama?" Elise asked.

"Do I read other people's letters? Even my own children's?"

"I wouldn't put it past you. But all right. Did Sophie tell you what they said?"

"*Nein.*"

"Then how do you know they're from a fellow?"

"I know, I know."

"They could be from some woman friend, or maybe they're business letters."

"*Ich sage* she's got a beau!"

"I don't believe it," Charlotte said, her voice all choked up, "I don't believe it, and I'll give you one month. I'll give you one month—and then I'm going to marry Leon, come hell or high water!"

She came running out of the kitchen into the corridor, and for one terrible moment I thought she was going to dash up the back stairs and stumble over me. But she flew past to the main hall.

Grandma pounded her hand on the drainboard. "That settles it! Sophie gets married immediately!"

"Now that you've made up your mind, all our troubles are over," Elise said.

Grandma moved a chair and must have sat down at the kitchen table to study her notes because Elise said, "Aha! The list!"

"*Ja*, the list," Grandma said in a businesslike way. "This one looked like a bum. No good. This one no good—warts. This one too old."

"Better to be an old man's darling than a young man's slave," Elise said.

Grandma said sharply, "You want Sophie to be a widow so soon?"

"She isn't married yet, Mama."

"Still, you never know how it's going to turn out," Grandma said musingly. "Remember Essie Wasserman? She got married, and everybody said, 'Such an old man.' But in two years Essie was dead and her husband is still living. So what did she worry for, marrying an old man?" She was quiet for a minute, then said, "This one too poor. I cross him out entirely." I heard her pencil scratch, eliminating him forever. "This one looks like he drinks."

"Suppose he does. Can you afford to be choosy?"

"I will *not* let Sophie marry a man who drinks!"

"All right, go ahead and bust up another romance."

"This one's the best. Not perfect, but good. *Ja*, this one's the best."

"Why? What about him?"

"He makes a good living with Smith and McCabe Wholesale Jewelers, he's an orphan—so no in-laws—he's a *Landsmann*, he talks beautiful *Deutsch*, his shirt was good and clean, he went all through the *Gymnasium* in Frankfurt, he's thirty-three last February, doesn't drink and only smokes cigars, he knows Mrs. Biederkranz and Mrs. Biederkranz is the cream of the cream, he's in A-one condition except he gets rose fever—and how many roses do you see in a year?—he's got his own horse and buggy but he's not a wild spender, he went with a girl once but she moved away, he's a good eater and he's a member from the Allegheny *Liedertafel und Turnverein*."

"Say, what did you do? Hire Sherlock Holmes?"

"*Ja*, this one's the best."

"That's all you know about him?"

"How much can you find out in ten minutes?" Grandma asked. Then, rising from her chair, she decided. "Tomorrow I get in touch with him. I give him the room. Half past ten, Elise—bed!"

"I'm a big girl, Mama. I may stay up till a quarter of eleven.

"*Ach, Kinder!*" Grandma moved toward the pantry; her voice dwindled in volume as she continued. "I don't expect this late, but if any more boarders come, call me."

"No, I'm going to sit out on the porch and marry them myself."

"Then put the lights out downstairs," Grandma called back to Elise. "Gas costs money." She stayed in the dining room a minute and then I heard her going down the main hall on her way to the stairs.

Elise turned off the jet in the kitchen and left. I heard her humming "The Yama Yama Man" as she moved through the downstairs rooms dousing the lights. I waited until she went out to the front porch, letting the screen door slam behind her. Then, the house silent, I tiptoed through the kitchen to the pantry, where I put my hand into the bread box and pinched off a little piece of a loaf. Trying to return to the kitchen, I stubbed my big toe on the doorjamb in the darkness. The pain was so severe that I had to sit down on the pantry floor and, trying not to groan, waited till the ache subsided. It seemed to take ages. Then, just as I was standing up, I heard a noise in the dining room as if a window was being raised. Wondering who was there, I pushed the swinging door open just far enough to peep.

I saw on the opposite wall of the dining room the three windows illuminated faintly by moonlight. The middle window was open. Then through it, to my astonishment, a man's leg appeared. I remembered what Hugo had said about robberies in the vicinity, and the realization came to me that a burglar was breaking into the house. I wanted to scream, but held my breath. I wanted to drop my hand and run, but if I did the door might squeak, giving me away, and the intruder might get me. Not knowing what else to do, I stayed frozen where I was, staring at him as he came through the window.

He seemed enormously tall to me when, landed inside, he raised himself to his full height and looked about him. Then, moving gracefully, he slithered over to the sideboard, opened a drawer, and slowly began putting silver into the carpetbag he carried. I admired the precision and stillness with which he opened one drawer after another. A few times he carried objects to the window in order to see them better. Some of them he put in his bag, some he returned to their places.

Finished with the dining room, he was just about to tiptoe into the hall when Grandma, in a wrapper and carpet slippers, her braid down her back, silently crossed the threshold and nearly bumped into him.

What happened then became family history and was told and retold many times while I was living with the Webers, and probably a hundred times more afterward. Of course, I never could tell my part in it, how I had seen it all, and, as the story got more exaggerated in each recounting, I did not even dare to make corrections. It was the price I paid for doing something wrong in being downstairs at all that night, and I knew that everyone, if the truth were known, would be horribly cross with me. We were grown up before I even told Trixie, and then how we laughed!

"*Lieber Gott,* you poor man!" Grandma cried. "She let you wait here in the dark! That Elise!"

Run! Run! I wanted to yell to the burglar, but he was so startled he could only stand there grasping his carpetbag, gulping.

"No sense, that girl," Grandma went on. "Let me put on a light. It's a good thing I came downstairs." While she groped on the mantelpiece for matches, the man darted toward the dining-room table, put down his carpetbag, and tried to kick it under a chair but did not entirely succeed. "I wanted to read the *Volksblatt,* my son's paper, but I left my glasses down here," Grandma said, lighting the gas jet. Then, looking about the room: "Now, where are they? I could swear I left them in here."

"They're on your head," the burglar said helpfully.

Grandma felt in her hair and beamed when she found he was right. "What do you think of that!" She pulled the glasses down, settled them on her nose, and took a good look at the man. "My, you're handsome!"

He was, too. His hair was light and wavy, his eyes blue, his complexion clear, and, as I had already observed, he was tall and graceful. He was also, at this moment, completely flabbergasted by Grandma. Not knowing what to make of what was going on, he merely murmured, "Thank you."

I knew Grandma was a little flustered too because she used more German than usual, always an indication. "*Setzen Sie sich*," she invited, pointing to a chair. The man must have decided to go along with things, whatever they were, for he sat down. "Tell me first, are you a single man?" Grandma inquired.

I wanted to cry out, No, no, Grandma! He's not a boarder, he's a burglar!—but of course I could not.

"Not married, you mean?" he asked, dumfounded.

"*Ja.*"

"No, I'm not married."

Grandma nodded with satisfaction. "Fine. And now, *bitte*, your name."

"Smith."

Grandma seemed pleased. "Aaaah, Schmidt!" She seized his hand and shook it vigorously. "*Wie geht's?* I'm Mrs. Weber. You've got a good handshake. I like a good handshake. My daughter Charlotte's fiancé—like a fish. What do you do for a living, Mr. Schmidt?"

Our robber was startled. "Why, I—"

"Excuse me asking so much. But I'm so particular. You don't mind?"

"Oh, not at all."

"Then—your business?"

He was ready now. "Finance," he said firmly.

"Finance! Is that so? Like J. P. Morgan."

"Not exactly."

"Why not exactly?"

"Well, he operates on a larger scale."

"*Natürlich.* He's a big man. You like your work?"

"Yes. It has its hazards—but it's interesting."

"A man's work must be interesting, especially to the man."

"I've always thought so."

Our burglar was looking at Grandma as if she were a

conundrum impossible to figure out but still worth trying. However, when she leaned over, touched his shirt, and asked, "Who does your laundry?" he was even more perplexed.

"Why, a Chinese laundryman, I guess."

Grandma shook her head sorrowfully. "You need a wife." Then, going on more cheerfully: "Yes, a man must like his work, I have a friend, her husband never liked his work, and as soon as he had half a million dollars he retired."

"Really?"

"Forty-eight years old and he retired. Imagine!"

"Must have been just lazy," the burglar said.

"So true," said Grandma and shot another question. "How old are you?"

He gasped out an answer. "Thirty."

Grandma was pleased and immediately asked him if he would care to see the room.

Having no idea what she was talking about, but willing to go along with anything that would prolong his innocent role, he said that he would be glad to see it.

"*Kommen Sie mit mir,*" Grandma ordered, beckoning him to follow her. He did so as soon as he'd picked up the carpetbag. Before they went upstairs, though, Grandma persuaded him to leave it in the hall. I'm sure he didn't want to, but he was in the position of having to do anything she suggested. Up they went, their voices fading away.

While I wondered what I should do if Grandma really gave him the room, I heard Sophie and Hugo and Elise come in the front door, arguing. Most of their words were lost to me. The first sentence I was able to make out came from Elise. "Well, I'm sick of being her slavey."

"Oh, don't be silly. You're not her slavey," Sophie said.

"Listen, Elise," Hugo said, "Sophie and I were having a nice pleasant walk till you caught up with us."

"Well, I'm mad. If you lived with all that energy all day long like I do— Say, who put the light on in the dining room again? And what's this bag doing here?"

"I don't know," Sophie said.

"Maybe we've got another boarder," Hugo suggested.

"Let's take a peep inside," said Elise.

"You can't do that. It's not yours."

"If Mama can examine the underwear they have on," said Elise, "I can examine the underwear they have off."

I held my breath, sure she was going to look into the bag. I didn't know whether to be happy that our silver would be discovered and I would be relieved of any necessity of accusing the burglar, or to be sorry for him. I didn't have time to decide, because Grandma came downstairs with him, announcing, "Mr. Schmidt is going to take the room" —and I realized that Elise had not had a chance to open the bag.

"Is that so?"

"Yes, isn't that nice? Now I want you to meet my daughter Sophie, my son Hugo, my daughter Elise. Mr. Schmidt—of finance."

In contrast to his earlier attitude of caution, our burglar now sounded confident, even gay. "I'm delighted to know you." A moment's pause, during which he must have bowed. "Ladies! Mr. Weber!"

Grandma was gay too. "What do you think, he brought his baggage. He *felt* something."

"I feel something too," Sophie said dryly.

"Come in the dining room." Mesmerized, I kept my eye to the tiny chink between the edge of the swinging door and the wall. "And now we celebrate our boarder," Grandma said. "Would you care for a glass of kümmel, Mr. Schmidt? Or would you rather have port?"

"Kümmel, if you please," he answered confidently.

"Good taste," commented Grandma, beaming. "Elise, get the kümmel."

She went to the sideboard. I think if Grandma had gone, she would have noticed that silver was missing, but

Elise noticed nothing, just brought out the bottle and snatched up a few wineglasses.

"Before I do anything else," said the burglar, taking out his wallet and handing three dollars to Grandma, "I want to do this. A week's board in advance."

Grandma pushed the money away. "I wouldn't think of it! *Nein, nein,* put it away! I'm not a bit worried. You've got an honest face."

The man hesitated only a moment. "Well, if you insist . . ." And he put the money back in his wallet.

The kümmel was poured and passed. Our new boarder was the first to raise his glass to his lips.

I fled. The little wad of bread was still clutched moistly in my hand when I reached my room.

The rest of the story took quite a long time to unravel. "Mr. Schmidt" was with us for two weeks, and I must say I liked him and had a hard time remembering that at the nickelodeon he would be a villain. I had to ask myself on whose side I was, his or ours, for sometimes I worried when he went out at night. Having witnessed him at work, stumbled upon so easily by Grandma, I knew he was not too competent in his chosen profession and feared he would be arrested, maybe even shot.

Liking him as I did, I found it easy to keep silent about him, but at times when I lay in my bed I would have qualms of conscience and make up scenes in which I announced to the family that our boarder was a housebreaker and that we all must watch out. I had heard the phrase, "second-story man," but since he had come in the dining-room window I thought of him as a "first-story man." However, the scenes always ended with my getting punished for coming downstairs in my bare feet and spying on my elders, so I was never able to put anything into action.

He ate prodigiously and never paid his rent, in spite of his grand gesture in the beginning. But he made up for it in other ways, and no one would have dreamed of asking him for a cent. He was very kind to us children and gave lavish gifts to the ladies of the family, which they accepted only after strenuous insistence on his part and equally strenuous protests on theirs. Since the robberies in our neighborhood continued, I had a pretty good idea where those presents came from. I tried to salve my guilt by thinking of him as a Robin Hood, but, even though he may have stolen from the rich, we were not poor, so that little self-deception didn't work.

I was sorry when the end came and he was taken away. I believe he was sorry to leave us too, not only because he had to face a trial at which most of the family testified when it eventually came up, but because he had been happy with us.

His sentence was light, mostly because Grandma extolled his virtues so highly. I don't know what became of him after he left jail, but I hope he went straight. He was too handsome, too bright, and too gay to have stayed with burglary and surely must have made a success in some other field. But, whatever happened to him later, his memory lingered on with us, for we spoke of him again and again.

One day when Mrs. Zimit was visiting, the whole story was repeated. Mrs. Zimit was Grandma's friend from Cleveland. Whenever Grandma had out-of-town visitors she took them to the Heinz factory. She showed them through, getting a sample of baked beans, then a sample of pickle, than a sample of spaghetti, then other things, and before long the visitor was too full to go to a restaurant for lunch. Grandma saved lots of money that way. Though she must have cost Mr. Heinz a fortune, he could afford it.

That's where Grandma had taken Mrs. Zimit. Afterward they went to a nickelodeon, looked through some of the department stores, and finally returned to the house for a *Kaffeeklatsch*. I listened to the women chatting of this and that, and then Mrs. Zimit asked, "Well, what happened here lately?"

"Oh, plenty," said Elise, who was serving. "Mama nearly married Sophie off, you know."

Grandma glared at her daughter. "Now, Elise, don't start!"

But Elise was irrepressible, and Mrs. Zimit gazed at her encouragingly. "Mama put an ad in the paper for a boarder, and after looking all the applicants over with an eye toward a prospective husband for Sophie, she chose Mr. Right."

"Silence, Elise!"

"All right, all right."

But Grandma couldn't drop the subject herself and, shaking her head regretfully, said, "I don't understand it yet. He was so *gemütlich!*"

"Yes, he was a pet the whole time he lasted," Elise said. "He didn't pay his rent, of course, but he gave us the most beautiful presents! A jet necklace to me, a mother-of-pearl inlaid fan to Sophie, a cameo brooch to Charlotte, a harp to Mama—"

"A harp!" cried Mrs. Zimit.

Grandma smiled. "*Ja,* I always wanted a harp."

"Well, you got it," Elise said.

"It was beautiful. He was a nice man."

"Yes, sir! And we went right on thinking so till the police came."

"The police!" cried Mrs. Zimit.

"The police," Elise said firmly.

"He was a handsome man—and so neat," Grandma insisted in spite of everything.

"Yes, he was neat," Elise agreed. "You should have seen his room. He kept his loot so tidy."

"I don't care—he was nice."

"He certainly was," Elise told Mrs. Zimit. "There was only one little thing wrong with him—he was a burglar."

"A burglar!" the guest exclaimed.

"Mama hand-picked him," said Elise almost proudly.

"So! A burglar!"

"He even burgled *us* the night he came. He said so in court. But he put it back."

"For a burglar he was so honest," Grandma pleaded in his behalf.

"Well, I tell you," said Elise, "it was a sad day when the police came and took him and three trunkfuls of evidence from his room away. *And* all the presents he gave us."

"You had to give them back!" Mrs. Zimit cried in her staccato fashion.

"They were returned to their rightful owners."

Grandma sighed. "And I always wanted a harp." Then, probably feeling guilty to be thinking of herself instead of the poor felon, she said, "I don't care! He was a nice man."

"Yes, sir!" Elise admitted. "Sophie certainly lost something when she lost him."

4

The Fourth of July

BEFORE SCHOOL was over in June I had become notorious. No action of mine brought this about; it was because Trixie had been unable to keep her mouth shut.

I had not realized until then that Hugo's children listened to the adults as avidly as I did. That they had learned more about me than I had was beyond all credence. Had I known, I would have questioned them freely, for we did not sit in judgment of one another, and they would not have disdained me for asking. They did not mention to me what they knew, either because they had been warned by their father not to speak to me of such matters, or because of innate tact. Certainly Trixie had not meant to harm me. She had only found it irresistible to boast in school about my bloodstained past.

One warm Sunday, Trixie, Walter, and I were jumping rope on our tennis court with some boys we knew from school. Trixie and I were enjoying ourselves enormously because rope-jumping was a girls' game and our natural superiority to the boys was exhilarating. We smirked at their clumsiness and laughed when they tripped, and the more we did so, the more sweaty they became and earnestly determined to master the business.

Way down South on my grandfather's farm,
I sat on the fence, and the fence broke down,
An alligator bit me on the seater of my pants
And made me do the hootchy-kootchy
  gitchy-gootchy dance.

The boys *never* were able to jump the whole way
through without catching their feet on the rope. Trixie
and I flitted at will in and out of its ellipse, but the turning
had to be stopped and started all over again for the boys.

Around and around the heavy eight-foot rope went, held
in turn by two of us, plopping weightily and in rhythm
against the dirt court. The others jumped, trying not to
jostle each other, chanting:

Ice-cream soda, Delaware punch,
  Tell me the name of your honeybunch.

Trixie's favorite chant was:

All in together, girls,
This fine weather, girls,
January, February, March . . .

Each person was supposed to skip out of the rope's orbit
as the month of his birthday was called, and since Trixie's
was in December, she got to stay the longest.

Sophie came out of the house, wearing a blue linen dress,
plain but with a flounce at the bottom. The color set off
the red of her hair to perfection. In the brilliance of the
sunshine she seemed to me utterly beautiful. My heart
throbbed with love and admiration for her. She carried a
book with her, looking for a comfortable place to read.
She walked slowly toward us, smiling at the words of our
singsongs, but when she saw the rut the rope was digging
into the tennis court she asked us to move off into the grass,
where no harm could be done.

Seymour and Sylvester had made the court the year the
house was bought, leveled it and packed it, erected the high

wire barriers at each end. They still took care of it. In the
winter it was forgotten, but in the summer every rain was
regarded with apprehension lest the court be put out of
operation for too long. Generally, after two days of drying,
it could be rolled and re-marked and was ready for use again.

Walter, Trixie, and I, knowing what work the court
entailed, willingly left it, but the other boys were a little
sulky after that, and anyhow it wasn't much fun jumping
on grass because the rope turned harder and more slowly.
Sophie went off into a little grove of four or five trees at
the end of our property. She was hidden from us by elder-
berry bushes and syringa, but I knew she was lying in the
hammock that hung between two oaks, reading. I pictured
her there even while I was jumping to:

> *Mabel, Mabel, set the table,*
> *Don't forget the salt, vinegar, mustard, pepper.*

And then the fight broke out. I complained that the beat
was supposed to accelerate as the condiments were named,
and one of the rope-turners, a boy named Bert, said nobody
could speed it up in rotten old grass. I said I could if I
wanted to, and he said I couldn't, and one thing led to
another and then he was screaming at me, "You don't need
to think you're such a much! Your father murdered your
mother! Yah, yah, yah!"

I took the accusation at first just as one of the awful
but meaningless things one child yells at another in a rage,
but its sense became clear the moment I saw Sophie, white-
faced, coming out from behind the bushes. She walked
straight to Bert, took him by the shoulders, and shook him
until his head seemed to be coming loose. "Don't you ever
say that again! Not ever! Because it's just a plain lie! Do
you hear me?"

He was nodding so much from the shaking that I don't
know how he could have let her know he heard her, be-

cause he wasn't able to speak either. But she let him go with
a final little shove.

She turned to the rest of us and in no time at all "got to
the root of this," as she said she would. Trixie admitted
she had repeated at school things she had heard at home.

Of course! Had I not heard murder mentioned the very
first night I came to the Webers'? Since then had not a
hundred other things been said in my presence that should
have told me in what way it pertained to me? Why had I
been so dense?

"All right, Trixie," Sophie said, "thanks for owning up.
But I want you and everyone here to know something—
you heard wrong. Is that clear?"

Everyone agreed it was clear, and Sophie dismissed the
boys, who were glad to be off, told Trixie she'd deal with
her later, took me by the hand, and led me toward the
house.

Suddenly I was furious because Trixie knew more about
me than I did myself. Why had people hidden the truth
from me? Nobody had told me that my father had killed
my mother, an important thing like that!

I did not believe Sophie's denial. I believed Trixie had
been right and that I was branded forever. Everyone knew
now what sort my parents were. I burned with shame.

How innocent I had been, how trusting, never dreaming
of this! Trixie knew, but not I. I held Sophie responsible.
She should have warned me—if only so that I might have
had a clever answer ready when Bert had pointed his finger
at me, an answer that would have turned the tables on him.
But she had not thought of that.

I hated her so much I wanted to strike her. Not to have
told me my father murdered my mother was the worst
thing anyone could have done, ever! I was wild with rage.
I wished my father would come now and kill Sophie!

She took me to her room, sat down on the bed, and

pulled me to a place beside her. When she put her arm around me I wriggled away from her, and she did not try to touch me again. "I should have told you this sooner, Jane," she said, "but I thought I was saving you pain. I don't know what Trixie thought she heard, but it wasn't that way. You believe me, don't you?"

"No," I said, doubling over and hiding my face against the bedspread.

Sophie sighed and spoke to me gently. "Let me begin at the beginning so you'll understand. When I went to New York in February to buy, I used to see you in the hall on my floor of the hotel, or in the lobby. We spoke to each other the very first day. You were so sweet and smart, and we became friends. I would take you into my room sometimes, and you would play with my things, my brooches, my hatpins, or you would try on my veils. You lived in the room next to mine with your father and mother. I didn't know them, but I found out later your father was in vaudeville, a singer. You had checked into the hotel the same day I had. Your father had just closed in Baltimore but was not working in New York. Anyhow, you and I were friends, and one day I came back from the wholesale district about five-thirty in the afternoon. I was in my room taking off my hat when I heard a scream. It was coming from your room and it frightened me dreadfully. I ran out into the hall, and just as I got there I saw a man running away at the far end, ducking down the staircase. I didn't know who he was and I didn't even pay any attention. I was concentrated on the door of your room, which was open. Other people were coming into the hall now, but I only glanced at them and went in. You were standing on the bed in your little nightgown—you had a cold, and I suppose your mother had kept you in—and you were still screaming. You were looking down at the floor and—" She hesitated.

I asked, "And what?"

"Your poor mother was lying there, and she was dead. She'd been killed, I'm sorry to say. The police told me afterward she'd been stabbed, though they never did find the weapon. Anyhow, I took you in my arms and, though I don't know if you recognized me or not in that terrible moment, you clung to me as if you never wanted to let go. Well, then the room filled with lots of people, and I heard somebody say they were sending for the police, and I held you and tried to get you quieted down, and then I just told the people I was taking you out of there, away from that sight, into my room. So I picked you up and took you out and I've kept you with me ever since."

Dozens of questions popped into my mind, but I would not ask them. I would not help her. Having withheld this story from me so long, she must tell it as best she could.

"Naturally I was examined over and over again by the police," she said. "I was a witness—I'd seen the murderer running away. I want to emphasize this, though: I never knew your father, but I'm sure he wasn't the man running away. I don't know who the man was, but I know it wasn't your father."

Stubbornly I kept my silence, fought against a pain in my throat that was getting so bad I feared it would erupt in great sobs and tears.

"At the hearing," Sophie went on, "there were people who knew your parents, friends from the stage and so forth, and they testified how kind and good and in love with each other your mother and father were. They could think of no reason why he would have killed her, and I believe them."

I held the sobs at bay because, vow or no vow to keep silent, I had to ask, "Then where is he? Why did he go away? Why didn't he stay and say he didn't do it?" My voice sounded strange, not at all like mine.

"There's a reason, Jane."

I waited for her to tell me the reason. Though I still lay

huddled up on the bed, my back to her, I knew she was looking at me, trying to decide whether to go on or not.

"Some day, dear," she said at last, "some day everything will be clear to you. Meanwhile, it's best not to think of it. Or of what Trixie did, for she misunderstood whatever she heard."

That was all the explanation I was going to get. She wasn't going to tell me any more in case I would misunderstand like Trixie, a baby of six! I loathed Sophie. When she took me in her arms and smoothed my hair, I made myself stiff as a marble statue so she would be able to tell I didn't want her holding me. But I felt her warmth and softness, and inhaled the faint scent of lavender in her clothes from the sachet bags that were kept in her bureau drawers. I thought it would be bliss to let myself go and weep and clutch at her and be comforted. But I couldn't do that any more because she had deceived me.

Sick with frustration and grief, I wrenched myself away from her and went to the window. Though I looked out, I saw nothing, nothing!

Then Grandma called from downstairs. "Company, Sophie! Company!"

"I have to go," Sophie said. "Get cleaned up, dear, and come down. I'll make lemonade. And, Jane, you must believe what I say about your father. You have to trust me. You can look anybody in the eye, no matter what they say, because he didn't do it! He didn't do it, Jane!"

I waited until she left the room, and then I pushed the door shut and said, as loud as I dared without her hearing me, "He did, he did, he did!"

Then, blinded by tears I groped my way into my room, for I had to get out of Sophie's as quickly as possible. I threw myself on my bed and cried until the pain in my throat, which always came to me with tears or even the threat of them, was unbearable. Always? How did I know it was always? Had it happened before I had come to

Wilkins Avenue? If I remembered that, why couldn't I remember other things? My mother's murder? My father's flight? Why did I know certain things, that I *always* got a terrible ache in my throat when I cried, that I *always* liked strawberry jam, that I *always* played a game with myself of betting which raindrop, racing down a window pane, would reach the bottom first?

After a while I got up from the bed and looked at my cocoon on a twig. I had brought it into the house in April in hopes of seeing, one bright morning, a beautiful butterfly hatch out of its mummy case. I'd waited in vain, and now I forced nature by breaking open the cocoon with my fingernails. But all I found inside was an ugly chrysalis, very black and very dead.

I threw it away and tried to read a book. But Elsie Dinsmore's father, who had always seemed sound enough to me before, seemed now an utter idiot. If he forbade poor Elsie the playing of jacks lest her knuckles become enlarged from such exercise of her hands, why did he make her sit at the piano so long that she fainted?

I put the book aside and tried mumblety-peg on the floor. The game was forbidden in the house because the penknife made nicks on the floorboards, but I played it anyhow, out of a spirit of revolt. Even that could not divert me, for thoughts whirled in my mind. I could feel suspicion and anger and hate spinning around inside me

Then I had a new sensation—terror. Where was my father? Did Sophie know where he was? If so, why did she not produce him? Maybe together they had murdered my mother. Who knew what fearful deeds the two of them were capable of? Nothing seemed too outrageous now. I thought of the letters Sophie had received from Denver. Were they from my father? Was he there, and was she in correspondence with him? But only two letters had come. Besides, I had heard Grandma say they were from a beau, a traveling man Sophie had met in New York on a buying

trip. Perhaps Grandma was right. I hoped so desperately.
I made up my mind that in the future I would obey
Sophie and be courteous for the sake of the other Webers,
but I would always detest her. And I would never ask her
another question as long as I lived!

She came back, slipped quietly into my room, and took
the mumblety-peg knife out of my hand. She did not scold
me, only led me into the bathroom, where she washed my
face with cool water and dabbed it with eau de cologne.

Fifteen minutes later I was in the parlor, sipping lemonade. If my face was still red from crying, nobody mentioned it. The company was Tante Yohanna, old and wrinkled and frail. It was hard to believe she had ever been
young enough to have had a baby and been made to get
married. I answered politely her questions about my grades
at school and listened to the long story she told of how she
broke her hip and how it had mended.

For a few days after that I was self-conscious at school,
but nothing more happened. Perhaps the children had never
believed Trixie at all. Perhaps they liked the idea of a girl
whose father had murdered her mother, and had never met
anyone so interesting.

Though my first brief flight into infamy was at an end, it
had left its mark. Sophie had hurt me deeply. How angry
I was with myself when I thought of New York and wanting to buy her a house like Mr. Frick's! I no longer sought
her company; on the contrary, I avoided her because she
sometimes did or said things I admired, and I would not
give her the satisfaction of seeing me respond. How glad
I was now to have a room all of my own, where, when I
remembered to do so, I could be luxuriously sorry for myself.

June melted away, and everything pointed to the Fourth
of July. From the moment school let out for vacation, with
us swarming out of the building, screaming,

"No more pencils, no more books,
No more teachers' nasty looks,"

the talk veered more and more toward firecrackers and Roman candles. I could scarcely wait for the great day to
come, and when it did, it was even more wonderful than I
had anticipated. In the early morning, before the adults
were up, we started shooting lady fingers. We went steadily
through the day, pausing only for meals. We exploded so
many crackers, so many squibs and torpedoes and whiz-
bangs, that the grounds and the pavement and even the
street were littered with shreds of red paper and charred
bits of cardboard.

In the early evening Trixie and I went into the kitchen
for a drink of water. Grandma and Elise, with the help of
Max Hermansdorfer, who had been a dinner guest, were
finishing up the dishes and putting them away. Grandma
was so clean she even wiped the soap.

"Whew, it's hot!" she said, taking off her apron.

"Well," said Elise, "you insisted on doing the dishes now
in this heat, didn't you? You wouldn't stack them, would
you?"

"Stack the dishes! Do I look like a pig?"

"You could have let the colored girl do them when she
comes in the morning."

"If she washes dishes like she washes curtains," Grandma
said, "there'd still be enough pot roast sticking on the plates
for tomorrow's supper." She turned to Mr. Hermansdorfer.
"*Danke schön* for helping with the dishes, Max."

"His first day home from his tour, and she makes him
wash dishes!" Elise exclaimed.

"Who made him?" Grandma asked.

"You did."

"He offered."

"Because of the way you looked at him!"

"I looked at him?" Grandma asked in outraged innocence, while poor Mr. Hermansdorfer turned from mother to daughter in distress, feeling guilty because he was the cause of their disagreement.

"It was my pleasure anyhow, Mrs. Weber," he said.

But Elise paid no attention. "Sixteen people for supper, but can we stack? Oh, no!"

"What's that—sixteen people?" Grandma asked scornfully. "And five of them *Kinder!*"

"Children use dishes too."

"In Andernach there were twenty for supper every night —when the family was home alone, even."

"I can imagine it when there was company." Elise sighed.

"Mama, Papa, me, my sisters and brothers, *Grossvater, Grossmutter,*" Grandma recounted, "and the teacher. He lived with us."

"How many children did your parents have, Mrs. Weber?" Mr. Hermansdorfer inquired.

"Eighteen." And she added proudly, "Fifteen of us lived."

"Well, you certainly didn't take after your mother," Elise said, "you and your measly seven!"

Grandma heaved a long, heavy sigh. "*Ja.* I had a weakness. Well, Max, tell us about your tour. What happened?"

"A tour. The usual—music."

"Did you have a good time?"

"Of course he had a good time!" Elise put in. "You know what it's like, a musician on the road. Wine, women, and song. Wild revels every night, throwing money around like water, drinking champagne out of ladies' slippers."

Mr. Hermansdorfer looked so shocked that Elise twisted her head sideways and looked at him pertly. "Well, didn't you?"

"Nothing of the kind!"

Trixie and I had finished our glasses of water, but we stayed about, fascinated, listening to Elise tease him.

"Oh, I bet you carry on to beat the band when you get the chance," she said.

"No, Elise."

"You're sure? You didn't seduce any opera divas while you were away, or jump naked into a harem pool full of claret cup?"

"My God, no!"

"Enough, Elise!" Grandma cried. "Enough! *Vorsicht vor den Kindern!*"

"Oh, all right."

"It must have been a nice tour, though," Grandma said as she left the kitchen. "Very exciting. Imagine—a harem pool full of claret cup!"

Mr. Hermansdorfer must have known that he would never be able to erase that picture from her mind, no matter what he said, for he said nothing at all.

When the others went out to the porch, Trixie and I decided to go with them, partly because we didn't want to miss anything, partly because we were tired and needed to rest a few minutes from firecrackers.

I loved the porch in summer. It was shaded by red and white striped awnings; fresh-smelling rush carpets covered the floorboards; there were so many plants standing about that I thought of them as a flowerpot forest. Max and Elise sat down on the swing.

"What happened here during my absence?" he asked.

"Oh, plenty," Elise said. "Sophie nearly married a burglar."

"Silence, Elise!" cried Grandma so loudly Mr. Hermansdorfer looked as if he felt bad all over again. Was he always to start trouble?

From the side of the porch where the boardwalk led to the back of the house came Grandma's three sons and her son-in-law Theodore, all wearing white shirts and duck pants.

"My, I'm tired," Hugo said as they crossed the lawn.

"Too much tennis today," Seymour remarked.

"Sophie's still playing?" Grandma asked.

"Yes. Singles now with Charlotte's Leon."

The men joined us on the porch. Trixie and I sat still in our wicker chairs, so quiet we never even squeaked them. Everyone was gazing into the dying sunlight, waiting for the dark to come.

"Ermanie's still upstairs with the baby?" Theodore asked, taking off his pince-nez and wiping the glass with his handkerchief.

Elise told him yes, and there was complete silence, and then a particularly loud explosion shattered the air.

"Cannon cracker," Seymour said casually.

"Shot off under a tin can," Sylvester murmured.

"Those children!"

"When are their firecrackers going to run out?" Hugo asked. "I don't see how they manage to make them last all day."

Grandma shot a reproachful look at Seymour and Sylvester. "Five dollars' worth of firecrackers. No wonder! They should last a week."

"Now, Mama, we always buy five dollars' worth of firecrackers," Seymour said.

"Last year three dollars," Grandma argued. "It was always three dollars."

"There's Jane to think of now."

"Two dollars extra for Jane? Next it will be two dollars extra for the baby."

"Oh, I'll buy the baby's firecrackers," Theodore said.

"No, you won't," said Seymour. "Firecrackers are always on Sylvester and me." He poked Theodore with his forefinger. "The way you rush that baby into doing everything, it's a wonder you haven't got her shooting off a skyrocket right now."

"I wonder if she'd like one," Theodore said dreamily.

"Go on upstairs and get her," Elise said. "Find out. Try it. You tried everything else."

"You really ought to give that baby some peace, Theodore."

"I give her peace."

"Three months old and she's already been in an automobile."

"She loved it!"

"Oh, go on! She slept the whole time."

"She was wide awake! She took everything in. Didn't miss anything."

"Next he'll take her up in a flying machine."

"Anyhow, Theodore, you could stop picking her up at night every time there's company."

"Then how could he show her off to everybody?"

Walter and Ernest came racing around the side of the house and across the lawn.

"Sparkler time yet?" Walter asked.

"Sparkler time yet?" Ernest asked.

"Not yet," said Seymour.

"How soon?"

"Pretty soon."

The little boys vanished as quickly as they had appeared. Grandma said, "That reminds me, what time is it?"

"Why?"

"Sophie should stop playing tennis. She should get dressed. Mr. Auerbach's coming."

"Mr. Auerbach?"

"Mr. Auerbach of the Auerbach Theatre."

"From where do you know him?"

"From where do you think? From his theater. How many stock company matinees do I have to go to to meet Mr. Auerbach of the Auerbach Theatre?"

"Leave it to Mama."

"And you invited him here tonight to meet Sophie?"

"Why not? Don't I owe him something? He lets me sit in a box for the balcony price. Such a nice man!"

"It starts again!" Elise cried. "Run for Sophie!"

"*Ja*, Trixie," Grandma said sweetly, looking at her.

"*Ja*, Trixie," Elise aped. "Hurry!"

We knew how Grandma picked the child who was to be sent on an errand. She always looked around and chose the youngest one in sight. Trixie stood up.

I went with her out of sympathy. For some reason Sylvester came along too, perhaps because in his generation he'd often been his mother's choice. Our feet resounded on the boardwalk that ran along the side of the house to the back lawn. Before we had gone far, we saw Sophie, with Charlotte and her fiancé, coming toward us from the court. We stopped and waited, listening to what they were saying. Sophie had a tennis racket slung over her shoulder. Her red hair, damp from the heat, curled around her cheeks. Her face was flushed, and she was so pretty she reminded me of a girl I had seen pictured on a candy box. Exercise must be good for her, I thought; she looked and sounded so gay tonight.

"If I could only correct my backhand," Leon Bauer said.

"And your forehand," Sophie added, laughing.

"I think you play beautifully, Leon," Charlotte said loyally as they came up beside us and we turned around to walk along with them, "even though Sophie won."

"She plays the best game of any of us," Sylvester said.

"Well, it's a lady's game, but it's accurate," Leon admitted.

Sylvester sounded indignant. "It is not a lady's game!"

"Oh, that's all right, Sylvester," Sophie said cheerfully. "I don't mind playing a lady's game. I am a lady, you know. I consider it rather a compliment, as a matter of fact. Thanks, Leon."

"I think it was getting dark," he said, still trying to explain losing. "I was having trouble seeing the ball."

"Some excuse!" Sylvester mumbled.

We had all returned to the porch before Trixie remembered to say to Sophie, "Your mother wants you."

Sophie looked inquiringly at her mother, but before Grandma could give her any orders Walter and Ernest were back, saying it was surely sparkler time by now.

"Wait till it gets a little darker," their father told them.

"It's pretty dark," Walter insisted.

"Well, I still wouldn't construe it as dark enough."

"It's twilight."

"Well, partial twilight, maybe."

"Oh, let them start," Sophie said. "What difference does it make?"

The boys shrieked with pleasure, and so did Trixie. All three began tugging at Seymour, coaxing him to the cellar to get the sparklers and pass them out. Though, to my knowledge, I had never had an experience with a sparkler and was as anxious to try one as anybody, I did not go with them. I stayed on the porch with the adults because I had to find out about Sophie's immediate future. I wanted her to meet Mr. Auerbach, fall in love with him, and marry him. No, I did not care whether she fell in love with him or not. It would be better if she were made to marry him, even though she loathed him. Then she would suffer, and I wanted her to suffer. But the important thing was that she get married as quickly as possible.

I wished it because I was terrified of my theory that Sophie and my father had connived together to murder my mother. I could not bear it if that had been the case. If Sophie got married to someone else, I reasoned, the odds were less that she and my father had collaborated in the fatal stabbing. Then they could have had no plans for the future and so no reason to have killed my mother. Perhaps if I could believe she and my father were not guilty together, I could believe they were not guilty separately.

"Somebody make the children bring the sparklers here to the porch," Hugo said. "I like to watch."

"Me too," Sylvester said, swiping at a fly buzzing over his head. "I've got to watch everything—get my money's worth."

"I like sparkler time better than any other time there is," Sophie said.

"It's after that I like," Charlotte said. "I like the things that shoot up and light up the sky."

"Which reminds me," said Sylvester, rising, "I'd better start getting them laid out." He and Mr. Hermansdorfer went down to the cellar to get the night pyrotechnics ready. There was to be a great and ordered spectacle; even during the heaven of the day's activities I had been told by the Fourth-of-July-experienced others to look forward to the night.

"Well, Mama, what do you want?" Sophie asked.

"A Mr. Auerbach is coming," Grandma said, moving forward in her chair, her wiry little body braced at the edge.

"Who's Mr. Auerbach?" Sophie wanted to know.

"Never mind."

"He's a man," Elise said. "What else do you have to know?"

"Oh, not again, Mama!" Sophie cried.

"I want you to get dressed nice," her mother told her. "I want you to look like a million dollars."

"Oh, naturally! And what would you suggest I wear to look like that? My diamond tiara and my emerald stomacher? Or *ein goldenes Nichtschen oder ein silbernes Bischen?*"

Grandma accepted this sarcasm, which translated into "a golden nothing or a silver little bit," with calm. "Don't make fun, Sophie," she said.

"No, I certainly won't. Because it isn't funny. It's very sad. All right, Mama, I'll take the path of least resistance. I'll go get dressed and spend a delightful evening boring a man crazy, as usual. It's the easiest way out."

Sophie turned to go into the house. Grandma raised her hand and said with great dignity, "One minute. I want to make a hint."

Sophie closed her eyes and stood stock still, waiting in dread for the rest of it, but when Grandma continued, it was in as kindly a voice as she was capable of. "With Mr. Auerbach you should be fascinating—not like you are with everybody else."

"Some hint!" Elise declared.

"I should be fascinating!" Sophie exclaimed. "What do you think of that!"

"Do what your mother tells you," Elise said.

Sophie turned around to look her mother in the eye. "Mama, if I knew how to be fascinating, I would have been fascinating years ago."

Grandma looked back at her and asked innocently, "What's so hard about it?"

"Well, I know it's easy for you, but for me it's hard. However, you're such a good hinter, maybe you can hint to me how it's done."

Grandma was happy to oblige. She wriggled backward into her chair. "Well, the charm must fit the man. Take Mr. Auerbach—a bachelor, in show business, mixes with actresses, he's a little fast maybe. So you shouldn't be slow."

"What should I do? Race around the room?"

"You know what I mean. You shouldn't be so serious. You shouldn't talk about business. You should be—more of a temptress."

"A temptress!" Sophie gasped.

Elise laughed heartily, but Grandma ignored her. "You know what I mean."

"No, I don't," Sophie said.

"Well, take the nickelodeon I saw yesterday. There was a temptress in it."

"There was?"

"Yes. It said right on the screen. The men were wild for her."

"What did she do to get them that way?"

"Well, she wore a dress, very low cut." Grandma indicated the bosom line with her hand. "And her hair was like this." She made imaginary spitcurls on her forehead. "And when there was a man in the room she wiggled up to him." Grandma stood up and wiggled over to Hugo. "And she made goo-goo eyes like this." Grandma rolled her eyes at Hugo. "And then she lay down on a tiger skin."

"A tiger skin!"

"You know, like the one upstairs in the sitting room, only ours is a bearskin.'

"Well, I have to admit she does sound facsinating," Elise said.

"*Ja*, she knew how to make up with a man!" Grandma said in fond reminiscence, then added, a slight frown crossing her face, "Of course, she wasn't a nice girl."

There was a bitter edge to Sophie's voice. "Oh, she wasn't?"

"How did you know?" Elise asked.

"She smoked," Grandma answered.

"Oh, well, of course," said Elise. "That explains it."

Grandma looked squarely at Sophie. "So go upstairs and get dressed pretty."

Sophie, her face flushed, her eyes glaring, cried in outrage, "A temptress!" I had never seen her so angry. I could tell Hugo was worried about her, for he put his arm across her shoulders, but she shoved him away, spun suddenly on her heel, and stalked into the house, slamming the screen door behind her.

A bit later, when I was sitting on the porch steps with the four cousins, my first sparkler in one hand, a piece of burning punk in the other, I was glad she had gone. I did not have to think of her now, so nothing could spoil the dusk's contentment. It was complete. A sparkler, I learned from Sylvester, was a long wire which had been dipped halfway into a combustible solution, which then solidified, and when it was fired by the application of a stick of aromatic punk, it burned more slowly than a fuse, giving off thousands of tiny sparks. Holding one was like holding in one's hand, at the end of a baton, a twinkling star.

Sometimes Pauline twirled her sparkler; Walter and Ernest, one in each hand, made boat signals; but Trixie and I just sat silently, absorbed, watching the sparks fly against the curtain of coming night. I could hear crickets close at hand in the grass, and somewhere, farther off, locusts singing in the trees. The talk of the Webers was part of the dusk sound, just like the locusts. I hoped sparkler time would never end and, seeing how many boxes of sparklers Seymour and Sylvester had bought, I thought it seemed as though I would get my wish.

Ermanie came outside with her baby. "I thought we'd sit out on the porch a while," she said. "I thought a little cool air would be good for her."

"Well, it's not very cool out here either," Theodore said, making room for her beside him on the swing, "but I guess it's even hotter upstairs."

"That's what I thought," said Ermanie.

"Did she take all her bottle?" Theodore asked.

"She left about an ounce."

Theodore's voice was suddenly shrill with alarm. "An ounce! Did you give her time? Was the milk warm enough? Maybe the nipple clogged up!"

Grandma said to him, "Don't worry. She won't drop dead because she didn't finish her bottle."

"But I do worry," Theodore said. "I wonder why she won't eat. Do you think she's sick?"

"Everything's perfectly all right," Ermanie said. "She just wouldn't take it."

"Maybe it's the heat," Charlotte said. "I know I didn't eat very much today. Too hot."

"Go make some lemonade, Elise," Grandma said.

"I've hardly got through drying dishes!" Elise cried. "Now I've got to go make lemonade! Don't tell me I'm not her slavey!"

The screen door scraped as she went inside. And then Grandma got up and pulled it open so she could holler inside after her, "And don't make your regular dishwater. Put some lemons in it," before going to sit down again.

Hugo came and sat on the steps with us. Behind me, the conversation had turned to cod-liver oil. "Well, I didn't mean to forget!" I heard Ermanie exclaim, a bit miffed.

"You didn't mean!" Her husband groaned. "You want the baby to get rickets?"

"With all the noise today, I just forgot it, that's all."

"I don't know how you could forget an important thing like that."

"I don't know either, but I just forgot to give it to her."

"Thirty-six hours already," Theodore cried unbelievingly, "and no cod-liver oil!"

Grandma said, "*Ach!* You know how many children I had personally?"

"Seven," Trixie said.

"Thank you for telling me," Grandma said to Trixie before turning to Theodore. "None of them ever had any cod-liver oil and they all lived."

"Oh," said Theodore, "you Webers always stick together."

Hugo said, "No. Mama isn't against cod-liver oil. She's against nothing except Sophie. What she's for is picking on her."

There was the thought of Sophie again. I lit a new sparkler as a drunkard pours a new drink, trying to forget what bothered me.

Theodore looked at the baby. "You think she's warm enough with nothing on but diapers?"

"On a hot night like this? Anyhow, I've got this blanket around her, haven't I?"

"It's mighty lightweight."

"Oh, it's plenty heavy, Theodore!"

There was a pause and then he asked, "You think it's maybe too heavy? She might get prickly heat."

"No. It's a very loose weave. The air goes right through it. Besides, her diapers are wet, and that's nice and cooling."

Elise came outside with a large tray bearing a pitcher of lemonade and glasses. Then the sound of tinkling ice was added to the other music of the evening.

"I just saw a shooting star," Pauline said.

"If you did, it's dark enough for the fireworks," her father told her. "Come on, let's see if Seymour and Sylvester are ready. Come on, everybody."

It was impossible to believe all the sparklers could be used up, but when I looked around, the boxes were strewn helter-skelter, all empty. I got to my feet, eager for what came next.

"To the back yard!" roared Walter.

Trixie wanted to come with us, but was held back by the last sparkler, clutched in her hand. "Come on, Trixie," her father said. "Finish that up."

She looked at him wistfully. "I can't make it sparkle any faster."

"Why can't we shoot off skyrockets right here in front?" I asked.

"Because the back yard is the place for skyrockets," Hugo said.

"We always shoot off skyrockets in the back yard," Ernest said.

It was impossible to break with tradition at the Webers', I knew, so I trotted around the side of the house with the others. "I can't wait!" I cried.

"You never saw any fireworks before? Wait till you see!"

"Our skyrockets are better than any others in the world. Our Roman candles too."

"And listen to me for a moment, everybody," Hugo said sternly. "Only the men set the fireworks off. The children watch. Understood? I don't want any little kids yelling with burned fingers."

"Why?" I asked Trixie, who caught up with us, her sparkler nearly burned out. "Why can we do crackers ourselves, but not Roman candles and everything?"

She looked at me solemnly. "The night things are very dangerous."

Seymour and Sylvester were ready. An arsenal of rockets was stabbed into the grass; dozens of pinwheels pierced the bark of trees. Everything was waiting for the scrape of a match. Hugo herded us back and lit the first, a girandole. A chorus of "ah"s went up with the rocket, almost drowning out Hugo's cry of pain. It was not until the last cascade of light had died away from the sky that I realized he had burned himself like any little kid and had to go in the house for ointment and bandage.

We were able to do without his services. Seymour and Sylvester, assisted by Mr. Hermansdorfer, set off pyrotechnics, one after the other, like madmen. I was in ecstasy as Catherine wheel followed Roman candle and flowerpot followed Catherine wheel. Elise, Charlotte, and Theodore, even Ermanie after she'd put the baby down to sleep, came to watch. They pulled the wooden benches out of the grape arbor and sat on them. Not far off, other people were shooting off their fireworks, and there was a great public display in Schenley Park. But all that existed for me was the sky over our own back yard.

I had put it off as long as I could, but now I really had to go inside to the bathroom. I hurried into the house, through the kitchen, and up the back stairs.

When I came out of the bathroom I saw Sophie going down the main staircase. She looked so odd that, instead of returning the way I had come, I followed her. At the foot of the steps she crossed the hall and went into the parlor. I could not see into that room until I reached the landing, and then I stopped in amazement, watching Sophie.

She was dressed fantastically. Her hair was done in an elaborate fashion with immense spitcurls on forehead and cheeks. She wore dangling earrings so long they looked like clock pendulums. Her dress was a ball gown I had never seen, and she must have robbed every bureau in the house of jewelry. Over her shoulder she carried the enormous white bearskin rug complete with head. Unaware of me, she stalked around the parlor like a bird looking for a place to nest, finally chose the very center of the room, and slapped the bear rug determinedly to the floor. At once she lay down on it in what I supposed was prescribed temptress conduct, pulled the neckline of her dress over her shoulders, took a man's pipe and matches out of a reticule she carried, and proceeded to light up.

So rapt had I been that I scarcely noticed Hugo come into the hall from the front porch. He had a patch on his hand where it had been burned and he gaped at Sophie in astonishment. "What the devil are you doing?"

She looked up at him, a bit startled, but spoke calmly enough. "I'm waiting for my gentleman caller."

"Huh?"

"I'm showing Mama a thing or two, that's what," Sophie explained.

"Come again."

"She wants me to be a temptress. So I'm a temptress."

"Oh, Sophie!" Hugo said, starting to laugh.

"I'll teach her a lesson once and for all! We'll see if she ever invites a man here to meet me again. This is the last time I'm going to be embarrassed. I'll cure her." All this time she had been trying to light the pipe, and at last she got it going. "All right, I'm ready," she said. "Let Mr. Auerbach come."

Hugo wasn't smiling any more. "But that's just what I came inside to tell you. He isn't coming."

"What!"

"I was just sitting on the porch with Mama, having my bandage put on, when a messenger came. Mr. Auerbach can't get here tonight."

"Oh, no! You mean I went to all this trouble for nothing?" She looked down at herself, the beads, the low-cut dress, the pipe held in her hand. "This is all going to be wasted?"

Hugo grinned. "I guess."

"Oh, damn," Sophie said, "all this trouble and now no man."

But just then Mr. Hermansdorfer came into the hall from the kitchen on his way to the porch and was going past the parlor when Sophie saw him. Her face lit up, and she pointed at him with the stem of her pipe. "Aha!" she cried softly, triumphantly, to Hugo.

Mr. Hermansdorfer noticed Hugo and said, "Elise told me to fetch—" but he never finished his sentence. He just stood in the hall, staring at Sophie through the doorway.

She got right to work and wriggled sirenishly on the rug. "Max, *mon amour*," she said in a throaty voice that didn't belong to her at all. "You're so handsome. I was intrigued by you the first moment I saw you. Come here, *chéri*, I want to look into your eyes."

And Mr. Hermansdorfer went toward her like a man mesmerized! Hugo made some sort of little stifled sound and ran. As I heard the screen door slam on him it crossed my mind that he was being cowardly. But I was going to keep on watching, no matter what the consequences, no matter if I missed a hundred skyrockets. Because I had to know what Sophie was going to do next.

She took Mr. Hermansdorfer's hand and pulled him down

on the rug too. Then she ran her fingers slowly through his hair and down the back of his neck and then up again. "Ah, Max," she said in that strange, whispery voice, "you are so manly, so strong, so brave. I have been thinking all this time what it would be like to touch you, to caress you." He stared at her, scarcely breathing. She went on, "I have contained myself for so long, but I cannot any longer. I must make my feelings known. At last."

She pulled his head down onto her shoulder and breathed so heavily into his hair it parted in little rivulets. Grandma came in from the porch, letting the screen door slam. Neither Sophie nor Mr. Hermansdorfer stirred, but I noticed a little smile cross Sophie's lips when she saw her mother appear in the hall. "Kiss me, Max, my sweet," she said. "Kiss me!"

Grandma heard her and turned.

Sophie drew Mr. Hermansdorfer even closer, put a hand under his chin and raised his head, and pressed her lips against his. She kissed him lengthily, holding the back of his head with one hand and her smoldering pipe up in the air with the other.

From where I stood on the landing I looked down on Grandma studying the scene on the rug. She shook her head. "*Nein! Nein*, Sophie!" she cried. "Not a pipe—a cigarette."

After that we did not see Mr. Hermansdorfer again until after Christmas. He jumped up the moment Sophie released him and ran. Her laughter followed him out of the house. She said, "The pipe is wrong? Mama, you certainly are the limit!"

He did not even come back to see Elise. In late fall we heard he had gone on another concert tour, but he sent us not a postcard. Sophie did not mention him except to say she hoped she had not offended him as she had not meant anything by her actions, and though Elise spoke of him sometimes she was too busy with other young gentlemen to miss him very much. I think Grandma regretted his absence the most. When he was present she had taken his virtues in stride, but now that he was no longer in our midst she magnified them a thousand times. He was the nicest, the best-bred, the most polite, the finest piano-player, the smartest, the neatest of all the callers we had ever had.

"All right, Mama, enough, enough!" I heard Sophie, exasperated, exclaim several times.

Though Grandma never came right out and said it, I think she felt that, although the trap had been set for Mr. Auerbach, if Sophie had followed directions more carefully Mr. Hermansdorfer might now be a member of the family. But, since Sophie refused to discuss it, Grandma never got to express herself fully on the matter.

5

Labor Day

THE SUMMER drifted away slowly like clouds on a still
day. How much a summer encompassed then! There
were band concerts at Exposition Park, a balloon ascension
in Schenley Park, buggy rides, a riverboat excursion. Mary
Garden was singing, Billy Sunday was preaching, Honus
Wagner was batting. To me the summer was one great
name after another, either spoken of or seen in person. And
there was the store picnic.

It was held every year on a Sunday in July at Kenny-
wood Park, which could be reached by trolley from almost
any direction, and everyone who worked in the store was
invited and so was her husband or sweetheart or other
chosen companion. For weeks beforehand the salesgirls
chattered about it. The ones who were married had no
problems about whom to bring, but the others were in a
dither of indecision almost up to the day of the picnic. We
brought baskets of food so loaded they creaked with every
lurch of the streetcar. And no wonder! Grandma and
Elise had been baking and boiling and beating for days.
When everyone met at the agreed-upon spot by the
wishing-well, Seymour and Sylvester passed out long strips
of tickets for rides on the chute-the-chutes or the tunnel of
love or for other delights. The girls blushed when they in-

troduced new beaux to the Webers, and tried to act casual about old ones. The Webers made a great point of remembering names from last year. "Well, Mike, how are you? Put on a little weight since last year, I see. You look fine. . . ." "For heaven's sake, Mrs. Cvesko! I'm so glad you came! I told Anna, you bring your mother, rheumatism or no rheumatism, I would be heartbroken if she didn't come. . . ." "Well, well, well, look who's here—Mr. Humphrey! Still going steady, eh, Ruth? When is he going to pop the question? When are you going to be Mrs. Ruth Humphrey?"

The glorious day stretched on into evening with supper on the wooden tables under the trees, and continued afterwards with all of us surging to the roller-skating rink.

Sophie turned out to be a marvelous skater, so skilled that perfectly strange men she'd never seen before came over to her and asked her to skate with them. She took their arms graciously and went off with them, arm crossing arm, her skirt flying, her hair coming loose and falling attractively down her back, her face animated and happy. She had learned to skate when a child in Germany, Grandma told me. Every winter portions of the Rhine froze over. Sometimes she had had to walk miles to a place where the ice was right, but it had been worth it to her.

From the rink we went to the steeplechase, where some of us lay down on a smooth wooden disk twenty feet in diameter, and when it began to spin, faster and faster, we clung as long as we could to its slippery surface, but all of us were finally flung off, dizzy, laughing helplessly. At the steeplechase our skirts were blown up unexpectedly. We slid down tunnels, tried to remain erect in great turning barrels, had our fortunes told. Then it was time to go to the dance pavilion.

This was what the girls in the store had been looking forward to all day. Not so Sophie. As a dancer she looked awkward and ill at ease. Because she was a hostess, she was

asked to dance frequently by the men in our party, but before making half a turn of the pavilion and long before the
music was over she felt sorry for her partners and asked to
sit down. So it was not the men's fault. They were not quit-
ters.

"If dance halls were skating rinks," I heard her say to
Hugo, sighing, "I would be the belle of the ball."

We children did not take part in the dancing, and by
this hour were too tired to care. We sat on the benches or
leaned on the railing, watching the adults hazily. When at
last we left the pavilion the good-bys seemed to go on
endlessly, people parting as though they would not see each
other again in fifty years, though most of them would
be together the next morning at eight-thirty at the store. At
last the Webers and I were on the trolley, limp with fatigue
but deeply satisfied, our baskets empty, our money spent. I
was sitting between Hugo and Sophie. When I started to
doze off I felt her arm go around me and I let my head fall
against her breast. It was not in me, after so wonderful a
day, to feel anything but peace, even with her, so I went
to sleep contentedly, leaning against her.

When I became conscious again I was being talked about.
I listened, without moving, to Hugo's voice. "Are you going to be able to keep her or aren't you? Your suspense
must be terrible. What if her father turns up?"

"I'm certainly hoping he will."

"What makes you think he'd let you keep her?"

"I just do."

"If he's guilty, yes, for he'll go to jail or worse. But if he's
innocent, why would he?"

"Oh, because."

"Sophie—"

"Maybe out of gratitude. Did that ever occur to you?"

"No. You don't know anything about him. What makes
you think he's capable of gratitude or any other decent
emotion? Sophie, I think you're making a mistake with the

child. The longer you keep her, the harder it's going to be
to part with her. And you count on it so, keeping her. You
won't face the probabilities. You love her too much,
Sophie."

"I can't help it."

"It's wrong. I admit she's a nice child, I'm very fond of
her myself, but she doesn't care for you, Sophie."

I felt Sophie's body give a sudden start, and it was not
from the movement of the streetcar. "What do you mean!"

"Just that. The way she acts toward you."

"How? She's as good as can be, polite and obedient.
She—"

"Good, yes. Polite and obedient, yes. But that's all."

Though Sophie sometimes flew out at other members of
the family or ordered them about, she never spoke to Hugo
with anything but respect and affection. But now she
sounded furious with him. "Are you such a great authority
on children, because you have four of them, that you know
everything?"

"I just don't want you to get hurt, Sophie. You're putting all your eggs in one basket, and the basket doesn't
care about you one way or the other."

I think she realized that Hugo meant what he said for
her own good, for she spoke now without resentment. "Do
you really believe that?"

"Yes, *Liebchen*," Hugo said. "I believe she loves the rest
of us better than she loves you."

Sophie's heart beat four times against my ear before she
spoke again. "Then I'll just make her love me," she said at
last, quietly and gently.

Sudden tears stung my eyes, and I had to squeeze up my
face to keep them from spilling. Could I be wrong about
her? She must be telling Hugo the truth. He was her favorite brother, the only person in the family with whom she
shared all her interests—books, the stage, heavyweight
prize fights, politics, art galleries, the desire to travel. They

understood each other so well and talked so freely that if there was something she wouldn't tell even Hugo, she must have a reason.

And I had made another mistake. Hugo had noticed my coldness to Sophie, and now she too was aware of it. What if she became discouraged with me and made my grandmother take me or gave me to an orphanage? I would rather die than leave the Webers. I must be nice again. And I wanted to be. Oh, I wanted to be!

On hot afternoons Pauline and I made hollyhock dolls, using the blooms for skirts and buds for heads. We cut out paper dolls too, and filled cigar box after cigar box with their clothes, so many that we smelled of paste all summer. Walter and Ernest got caught smoking Sweet Caporals in a neighboring carriage house, and also got caught with pictures they'd sent away for of ladies with nothing on but shoes and stockings. Boys were very silly.

On hot evenings just when everyone was dying of thirst, the honkytonk man came. He was welcome from the moment we heard the tinkle of the Japanese prisms that hung from his pushcart. We would plead with the adults on the porch to give us pennies, and, if they did not, we would run inside and get our own savings. Then we stood in line while he slowly filled the order of the first-comer, our eyes big, our mouths watering, as he filled a paper cup with shaved ice, built it into a high round mound, and then sprinkled it with red or green or yellow flavor from an array of bottles that had once held hair tonic. Was there anything the honkytonk man could buy as delicious as the wares he sold?

Inexplicably Trixie fell in love with Nancy Myrtle May and wanted me to give her to her, saying that I had had her so long without her wig coming off that it probably never would. I clutched my doll to my breast and refused, but later when I caught Trixie in my room playing with her

I pretended not to notice. I loved Nancy Myrtle May, but I loved Trixie too.

Once when I went with the cousins to visit their mother where she lived with her parents, we played Indians and Settlers after supper in the dusk. Trixie was a Settler. We captured her and tied her up against the foot of an old rusty fire escape in the back yard of a vacant house. We left her there, saying we would come back and burn her as soon as we captured some other Settlers. But back on the street we ran into a crowd of hide-and-seek players and joined them.

When it started to grow really dark we had to go home, and I was undressed and in bed before I heard Hugo bawling, "Where's Trixie? She's not here! Where is she?" We remembered where we'd left her, a little shocked that we had forgotten her so completely, and Hugo made us all get dressed and go with him to retrieve her.

We found her still tied up, slumped against the fire escape, her eyes closed, asleep. Hugo untied her gently, but she woke up and smiled at us and asked, "Are you going to burn me now?" When we told her that we had already been in bed and it was too late, she seemed disappointed.

It was a wonderful summer of petunia beds and rows of sunflowers by day, and fireflies and hoot owls by night. It lasted almost until school started again, until the night the store caught fire.

It was not a serious fire, the building itself had hardly burned at all, but there was a great deal of damage to the merchandise from smoke and water. Sophie spoke of the overzealousness of the Braddock fire department, including its horses, for one of them, inexplicably, had put its hoof through a plate-glass window. But she did not make any formal accusations. She was too busy getting ready for the great fire sale.

And so were we all. As in any crisis, the whole family pitched in. The store was closed for three days while, sun or moon, some of us, or all of us, worked at cleaning up, drying out, repairing holes in the floor, repainting walls, washing windows, wiping out display cases, and all the other things that today would involve a dozen unions and thousands of dollars but then was accomplished by a large family. We children were put to work sorting out goods— the wet, the singed, the hopeless, the undamaged. Sylvester painted gigantic signs announcing the sale, and Seymour plastered them all over the outside of the building. Ads were taken in all the local papers. And Sophie bought a ton of extra merchandise because as long as we were having a big sale we might as well have plenty to sell. She bought it from the Pittsburgh wholesalers; there was no time to go to New York, for every day the store was closed was a day of irretrievable loss.

Late one afternoon I got a splinter in my finger and went up to Sophie's little office on the landing to look for a needle to get it out. Sophie was not there—she was downtown at the time—and her office was chaos. Ledgers, bankbooks, bills, and receipts were spread over the floor, drying out. I stepped around them and sat down at her desk. On it were some keys and two strongboxes. I was tired, and I felt that my splinter entitled me to a short respite, so I lolled at the desk, fighting off the temptation to open the strongboxes. I lost. In one of them I found more bankbooks, a roll of cash girded by a rubber band, a lease, some bonds, insurance policies. The insurance policies were on top. Sophie had probably been looking at them to determine what fire coverage she had, just before she went downtown. She must have forgotten to put the keys away.

In the other box I found letters. I expected them to be business letters and nearly closed the lid on them when a Denver postmark caught my eye. These were letters from Sophie's New York beau, I thought. But they were not. They were from my father.

The only one I read (for I did not have the stomach for

more) was signed E. C. in a bold, beautifully formed script. Edwin Carlyle, I thought, my heart pounding. I stared at the initials, hoping they would change into others, H. M. or G. B., anything but what they were. However, they held steady, and I began to read.

"Dear Lady Bountiful," my father had written, "Thank you with all my heart for the packet of treasures. Such wonders straight from the hands of my dearest one cannot help but lighten these dark and frustrating days. Sometimes I despair of ever emerging from my hiding hole, but each letter from you brings me so much encouragement that I determine anew to fight the enemy with all my power for my girl's sake. Ever yours."

Suddenly I felt ill. I could no longer doubt that a conspiracy between Sophie and my father existed. What was she to him? She was "my girl" and "my dearest one." I fingered the other letters in the box. There were dozens of them, all but the first two addressed to the store—to put off our suspicions at home, I guessed. Then, as quickly as I had opened the box, I locked it and pushed it away. But, try as I might to forget the letter, phrases from it sang in my ears long after I had fled the office and returned to my work, and for days afterward. And, for the first time, I began to wonder what my mother had been like. How did she look? I made up a mother so lovely and gentle that tears of pity for her formed in my eyes as I visualized my father running away along a hall corridor and Sophie coming from the hotel room next door pretending to be my friend.

Naturally I told no one of the letters. It did not occur to me to confide in Hugo, who understood me very well, or in his children, my contemporaries, who understood me not at all but who would be ever so sympathetic. I, like all other youngsters, was a reservoir of secrets, not because I meant to be, but because I was unable to reveal anything that put me in a "bad" light. Once during the spring, after a severe head cold, I had been nearly deaf for a week, but

I never mentioned the fact and had pretended to be thinking of something else when I had not known I was being addressed. During the summer I had concealed the loss of a library book for agonizing days, only to learn, at the end of all that suffering, that Pauline had returned it. And now I could not mention the letters.

The next time "my policeman," as Trixie called him, came for his monthly visit and asked the question he always asked, "Has Jane heard from her father?" Sophie shook her head as usual.

"No communication at all?"

"No."

I wanted to scream, "But *you've* heard from him, Sophie! Why don't you say it? Why don't you tell him?" It was all I could do to keep silent.

"It's amazing to everyone," Mr. Flynn said, "that, in spite of all the efforts made, no trace of him has been found."

"But you're still working on it, of course," Sophie said.

"Of course."

After that she went away on another buying trip, and I was relieved to have her out of the house.

When she came back I avoided her more than ever. I kept myself especially neat so she would not have to touch me to wipe a smudge from my face or rearrange my hair or straighten my dress. In the beginning she was so busy catching up at the store that she did not notice my evasiveness. But when things returned to normal she came into my bedroom one night and said, "Jane, dear, why is it, when I want to talk to you lately, you are never around?"

"I'm around," I murmured, not looking her in the eye.

"No, you're not. And why, when I wanted to help you with your shoelace this evening, did you jerk away from me?"

"Oh, did I?" I asked innocently.

Her attempts achieved nothing. I slipped from her conversationally as well as physically but, as Hugo had said, I was always polite, and now I was even apologetic. "I'm sorry, Sophie. I didn't mean to leave the room." "I'm sorry. I didn't realize you were talking to *me*." "I just thought I'd let Grandma wash my back, that's all. I'm sorry."

I conversed with her only inside my head. "I'll never let you adopt me," I said, but never to her, "because my mother is dead and my father is hiding, and it's your fault." Then: "Oh, yes, adopt me! Adopt me, please. Because I never want to go away from here as long as I live."

Evening after evening, through the long summer, before I fell asleep I lay in my bed listening to the night sounds. If the Webers were sitting on the front porch the voices were far-off and indistinguishable, but if the weather was rainy or cool they stayed in the upstairs sitting room and I could hear almost everything said. What great questions of the day there were! Would Admiral Peary reach the North Pole or would he not? Were the Chicago Cubs unbeatable in this year's pennant race or did the Pirates still stand a chance? Could the English Channel really be crossed by an aeroplane? Now that Oklahoma had been admitted as a state, would that be the end, or were there going to be more stars to come in our flag? Wasn't the price Mr. Mellon had paid for a Velázquez staggering—twenty thousand dollars? Was Sarah Bernhardt the greatest actress in the world, or had there been better in another era, Sarah Siddons, or Fanny Kemble? Would Jack Johnson win his fight in Australia?

Among the names I heard so often during those conversations, there crept in, more and more frequently, that of Hilda Klopstock, who was not famous at all except in Allegheny because her father was so rich. It was in Allegheny, Pittsburgh's north side, that the Germans, arriving in the great waves of immigration from Europe in the eighties and nineties, settled, living at first in modest frame houses, then, as they prospered, building Victorian mansions of red brick or brown stone, with wide lawns and picket fences and sometimes an iron stag for ornamentation.

There was a marble statue of a nymph on Hilda Klopstock's lawn in Allegheny, with one arm raised and the other holding up her draperies at her middle. Though none of the Webers had ever counted Hilda's money, the nymph was an assurance that there was plenty of it. Indeed they spoke of her as "an heiress." And who was keeping company with her? Sylvester!

He had met her early in the summer and spoke seriously about her from the very beginning. He said that several times in the past he had had his heart set on certain young ladies, but that the family had talked him out of taking steps. Though he had not appreciated it at the time, now he was glad because he was free to marry Hilda. And if anyone thought this time they could talk him out of Hilda, they—

Grandma said, "Not so fast! Not so fast, Sylvester! Maybe she's a nice girl, she comes from a good German family, but don't jump so fast."

"Now, Mama, you're going to do just like you did with the others. But this time I'm not going to let you."

"I did something?" Grandma asked, fiercely indignant.

"You and the rest of the family. But you're the worst. So critical. There was something wrong with one girl, she never got up till ten o'clock in the morning. There was something wrong with another girl, her mother cooked with lard. Always something. But not even you can find anything wrong with Hilda."

It was true. She arose at a decent hour in the morning, her mother cooked with the best of unsalted country butter, her father was an honest harness manufacturer, Hilda was in good health, pretty, and there was no scandal attached to her. There was only one question—was she *too* rich? Would Sylvester be looked down upon by the Klopstocks and their well-to-do friends? Would there develop a problem like Hugo's—whether to keep on doing what he was doing or go into business with his wife's father? Could a girl as rich as Hilda refrain from bullying her husband? Would Sylvester be happy living partly on his wife's money, for she'd surely want a big house right away and a maid or two, and what he made at the store might pay for a little flat some place and that's all. Would it not be better, Grandma asked, to wait till Sophie was married and then decide?

But Sylvester wanted a decision now, and all summer the family went over the pros and cons until a phalanx, led by Sophie, won out, and it was decided that yes, Sylvester could marry Hilda.

After that there was a day-after-day discussion about the proposal. It was finally decided he would do it on Labor Day because he would not be working and could give enough time to the rendezvous to make it outstanding. In some states the holiday was not even recognized then, and in some towns it went uncelebrated. But it was not ignored in Braddock, perhaps because the memory of the Homestead Steel strike was unfaded in the minds of its inhabitants, and our store was closed.

So Sylvester made an appointment to meet Hilda downtown at six o'clock in the evening in the lobby of the Fort Pitt Hotel, following an afternoon tea she was going to attend. She and Sylvester would have dinner in the grand dining room, then go to the theater, then to Hummel's Rathskeller, where Victor Herbert, when he was in town, could be seen drinking beer with his good friend Hummel. Somewhere, dining amid the romantic marble pillars and palms of the hotel, or perhaps on the drive back to Allegheny in the hansom cab, he would ask her to become engaged to him.

And so, with the Webers' complete approval, Sylvester dressed and went out our front door but met more fuss before he got off the porch. He looked very nice, but was his handkerchief clean? Did he have his wallet? He hadn't forgotten the theater tickets, had he? And then Sophie put in his lapel a carnation she had bought at the florist's. He was astounded. "What? A bought flower? For me?"

She smiled at him. "There was nothing blooming in the back yard but asters and marigolds, and I couldn't let you go to your doom with an aster in your lapel."

He thanked her but still hesitated, his round face bland but his eyes glazed. "I wonder, should I spring it on her while we're dancing, or do you think the hansom?"

"Feel it out. When the moment seems right."

"I hope I have everything."

"Take your time, be careful. It would be terrible if you got excited and had an accident on your way to such an important event."

"I'll be careful."

"Put on your hat. My, that looks nice. Button your jacket."

"Yes."

"Well, good-by, Sylvester. Good luck."

He went down the front steps, and we watched him till he was out of sight. After so much controversy as to whether or not Hilda was the wife for him, and when and where he should propose, it never occurred to any of us that she might refuse him.

The evening progressed as usual, with the children running in and out of the house and being told a dozen times not to let the screen door slam, and Elise making lemonade, and Grandma telling the plot of the latest picture she'd seen at the nickelodeon, but all of us seemed a little nervous, as though waiting for something. We knew Sylvester would not be home until after midnight and we could expect no news from him until then, but still we waited.

At eight o'clock Leon Bauer, Charlotte's fiancé, arrived and sat down beside her in the swing, apologizing for being so late, but he had had supper with his sister who lived in Allegheny, had missed a streetcar, then had lost his transfer, so had walked from Forbes and Murray. Nobody listened to him but Charlotte until he said, "Say, did you hear about Hilda Klopstock?"—and then everyone's ears pricked up.

"What about her?"

"She eloped."

"Eloped! What on earth could have come over Sylvester?"

"*Lieber Gott!*" Grandma cried. "He didn't even have a clean nightshirt with him!"

"My," said Elise, "and he didn't even ask our permission."

"A sudden impulse, I suppose," Seymour said.

"Oh, what a shame," Charlotte said. "I was looking forward to the wedding. The Klopstocks would have had such a big one, and so many parties and everything for the bride beforehand. What a shame. Still, I'm happy for Sylvester if this is the way he wanted it."

"So Sylvester's the lucky man!" Leon exclaimed. "I never dreamed."

"Well, I think this calls for a celebration," Sophie said.

"I should say so," Hugo agreed. "What do you say to breaking out a bottle of champagne?"

"All right," said Grandma. "All right! We drink a toast to Sylvester and Hilda. She comes from a good German family, even if she does put too many ruffles in her bosom so she sticks out."

So champagne was brought from the cellar, the bottles dusted, the corks popped, the contents poured into hock glasses and passed about to the adults full to the brim, and half full to the children.

"To the heiress!" cried Hugo, laughing.

"To the newlyweds!" Seymour exclaimed more gravely.

"To a groom who deserves the best in life," Sophie said, "and to a bride I know will give it to him."

There was a great clinking of glasses. Hugo announced

that all the children could stay up half an hour later than usual, and we all sat around, grown-ups and children, not talking too much but feeling happy and pleased, as though at the end of a job well done. How fascinating, I thought as I sipped my wine, that one minute you can be somebody you've been all your life, and the next you're Mrs. Somebody Else.

Leon had his arm around Charlotte. He had never gone that far in front of the family, but now, proud of himself because he had brought the news, he took the liberty. "Yes, sir," he said, hoping to spin out the glory a little further, "there I was at my sister's when a neighbor dropped in, and she told us. 'Guess what, Hilda Klopstock ran off and got married this morning.' My sister asked who to, but this woman didn't—"

He had to stop because Sophie screamed, "This *morning!*" and Seymour dropped his hock glass on the porch floor, where it shattered into a thousand bits.

"Why, yes, she—"

"But Sylvester didn't even leave the house till five-thirty this afternoon!" Charlotte exclaimed.

"He couldn't have eloped this morning," Trixie said. "He would have said something about it."

"Be quiet, Trixie!" her father said.

"All right," said Sophie. "Let's face it. She ran off with some other man."

"Leon, are you sure you have your information straight? Are you sure this woman said . . . ?"

"Oh, positively."

"Well," said Hugo, rising, "I'm going to go some place where there's a phone and try to get the truth. All the children, go to bed!"

"But Papa, you said a half hour. You—"

"I don't care what I said. Now I say 'Go to bed!' "

And we had to. We stalled as long as we could, kissing everyone good night. Hugo marched off the porch and up the street. Charlotte said, "But I wonder where Sylvester is? Why hasn't he come back? He must have known hours ago that things weren't going to come off as planned."

Elise laughed. "As planned? That's a scream."

"What do you suppose he's doing?"

"He's still standing in the lobby of the Fort Pitt, waiting," Elise said, "but he's beginning to wonder if she's going to leave him in the lurch."

"He would have gone out to her house hours ago to see what happened to her."

"He would not have. He'd be too embarrassed."

"Why doesn't he come home?"

"Heavens, eight-thirty already!"

At the mention of time, we were really forced to go. "That Trixie's such a kissing bug," Grandma said sadly as we went inside. "She'll elope before she's sixteen."

I slept lightly, waking up now and then and listening for developments in Sylvester's case. Hours seemed to go by and nothing changed, and then I heard the family move from the porch to the upstairs sitting room. Hugo was with them but what he had ascertained from his phone call I did not hear. Nobody was talking much. Once Grandma said, *"Ach, du Lieber!"* and once Sophie said, "I don't care how long it takes, I'm not budging." The only thing I knew was that none of the family had gone to bed, all were staying together, keeping the vigil till Sylvester got home.

I don't know how many more times I dozed off, but at last I was brought back to consciousness by the sound of a horse's hoofs clop-clopping to a halt in front of our house. I went to the window and looked out, forgetting that the roof over the front porch obstructed my view of the street. Still, I was sure Sylvester had come home in a hansom. He was very quiet unlocking the door and coming upstairs. He must have been terribly surprised to see the sitting-room door open and, inside, the gas lights blazing and the whole family there.

"Well, for heaven's sakes," he said, "why are you up so late?"

"Why were you out so late?" Grandma shot back at him.

"Well, for heaven's sake," Sylvester said, and I realized not only that he stuttered a little but that there was a note of false joviality in his voice, "can't a fellow have a big night without everybody sitting up for him?"

"Big night? What did you do?"

"You knew what I did. Dinner and theater and everything."

"Oh, you went to dinner and theater and everything?"

"Well, of course!" He sounded quite jolly. "Isn't that what I said I was going to do?"

"And did Hilda like the play?" Elise asked.

"She thought it was pretty good."

"She enjoy the dinner too?"

"Said it was delicious."

"What did she think about Hummel's?"

Sylvester started to answer, but Sophie said, "That's enough, Elise! Leave him alone!"

Sylvester wasn't to be stopped, even though Elise was. He insisted on answering. He said they'd had a fine time at Hummel's, but a strange thing had occurred there. He'd had occasion to take a good look at Hilda and decided he wasn't really in love with her and he was darned if he was going to be blinded by her money, so he had simply taken her home without proposing to her. He had been as cordial and friendly as usual to her, but—

Sophie cried out, "I can't stand it! I don't know how the rest of you can just sit here and listen to this! Sylvester, no more of this masquerade. Hilda eloped with Kurt Epps this morning."

Even though I got out of bed and strained to hear, Sylvester spoke so low that I missed what he said next. I got only the tone and realized he was taken completely by surprise. And then so many people talked at once I couldn't make out anything, but when there was quiet again Sylvester kept saying over and over again, "So that's why she didn't show up, so that's why she didn't show up."

"What did you do all this time?" Charlotte asked.

He said he'd waited an hour and a half, then had gone to four nickelodeons, had a beer in a saloon, and had come home in a hansom. He'd had nothing to eat. Grandma had a fit when she heard that and said she was going right downstairs to fix him something. I ducked into my bed, and as the family came out of the sitting room I heard Hugo say, "We wouldn't have thought any less of you, you know, if you'd come right back here and admitted you'd been left standing."

"After all that talk about should I or should I not marry an heiress? After Sophie gave me a bought flower?" Sylvester asked.

He recovered quickly from the fiasco with Hilda Klopstock. As Hugo said, it was probably his pride that had been hurt the most. Indeed, the tension he had been showing most of the summer was missing after Labor Day. Maybe Elise was right, that Sylvester had nearly bitten off more than he could chew and was relieved that he didn't have to be an heiress's husband. Elise said it was not in his character, that he would be better off with some little wife he could lord it over, and the family had been insane to think he really wanted Hilda. For the moment he had wanted limelight, she said, and in the end he had got it, though not in the way he'd intended.

Grandma recovered too. In time she began to believe Sylvester's invention when he came home the night of the debacle, and I heard her tell Mrs. Zimit that he kept company with Hilda for a while and then decided he wasn't serious and she had married Mr. Epps on the rebound.

Grandma carried on as she always had, scrubbing floors and washing windows when nobody was around to catch

her at it, and doing lighter work when we were present. I
see her still, walking about the kitchen, beating with a
wooden spoon the contents of an enormous bowl she held
under her arm, and at the same time giving orders or calling one of us in from play. It was "Yoohoo, Walter! Yoohoo!" through the window, but never a break in the beat.
When she made yeast cake she could be seen time and time
again impatiently peeping under the towel to see if the
dough had risen yet. We children were there whenever
there was an opportunity to lick bowls, see dough painted
with egg yolk, smell the wonderful odors of baking, and
taste a sample fresh from the oven. What fun it was to
watch her cutting up apples for strudel, shelling the nuts,
stretching an elastic dough to paper thinness over the whole
of the kitchen table, cutting and tucking it over the fruit,
popping in raisins she'd forgotten, and sprinkling on the
sugar. And when there was nothing more to do at home,
she would be off to the nickelodeon.

One day she took Trixie and me to a new one in East
Liberty, the three of us riding there in the iceman's wagon.
And who was the owner of the new place, only yesterday
converted from a jewelry store? Mr. Auerbach! He shook
hands with Grandma vigorously and told us that in addition
to his stock company he now had four nickelodeons and
intended to acquire more. He was going into the picture-
show business in a big way. I could see why Grandma
wanted him for Sophie. He was a man of bountiful energy,
with flashing dark eyes and rather nice features. His smile
bespoke warmth and generosity and an easy camaraderie
with people of all sorts and ages. He showed Trixie and me
the same deference and respect he showed Grandma.

Suddenly I remembered this was the man I had hoped
would marry Sophie on the night he had been expected at
our house. Oh, but Sophie wouldn't have married him anyhow, because of my father. Why was she involved with murder? Why was she my father's "dearest one," why couldn't

she be plain Sophie Weber, whom I could love as I did the rest of the family?

I was wrenched away from my miserable brooding by Mr. Auerbach's pleasant laughter and Grandma's appreciative utterance. "Mr. Auerbach, you tell a funny joke better than Harry Lauder or Weber and Fields even."

Then he invited us to be his guests at the show and escorted us right down the aisle and to our seats. Grandma whispered her thanks and told him he must come to our house to supper and meet Sophie. A man in back of us said, "Shut up!" but Mr. Auerbach paid no attention to him and whispered he would be very happy to have supper with us any time he was invited. Then he tiptoed away and we turned our attention to the screen.

Film was sometimes interrupted by signs flashed on the screen by the projectionist, "Please Don't Stamp, the Floor May Cave In," or "One Minute Please While the Operator Repairs the Broken Film," or "Keep Your Child from Crying." The one I liked best was, "A Woman Who Left a Baby Carriage Outside Is Wanted Immediately." The audience responded with obedience, or groans and boos. When the woman who left a baby carriage outside rose to find out why she was wanted, there was general laughter.

Nickelodeons held from fifty to a hundred people, and Mr. Auerbach's was one of the larger. We knew he was a good theater man and would get ahead, because his audience sat on chairs instead of on the uncomfortable wooden benches still used at the Pictorium, Dreamland, Jewel, and Theatorium. His piano player, we thought, was good but not nearly as good as Mr. Hermansdorfer. The show lasted about an hour, and the four or five one-reelers we saw were all new. Even Grandma hadn't seen any of them before, and to her, a nickelodeon-goer of such magnitude, that hardly ever happened.

We went home in a happy mood, taking the streetcar to Shady Avenue and Wilkins, and getting a ride the rest of the way on the fire engine, which was out for practice. Grandma knew one of the firemen, of course.

Before September was over, Sylvester took the Weber children and me to the Phipps Conservatory for the yearly chrysanthemum show, and he was in marvelous spirits. Trixie said she saw him flirting with a young lady who was going through at the same time we were, but I missed that because I was too excited by the spicy-scented flowers, great masses of them, all white or yellow, with blooms as round and big as a child's head. How wealthy Mr. Phipps must be, I thought, to afford all the gardeners necessary, all the glass in the ceilings in room after room, all the palms and tropicals to give background to the flowers, all the imaginative vistas of stone and moss and wrought iron planned to delight and surprise.

No matter what terrible things were said about Pittsburgh's great multimillionaires—that they robbed the poor, forced the weak out of business, carried Senators and cabinet members in their pockets, made secret agreements with foreign powers—at least two of them gave me much pleasure that year of 1908, Mr. Phipps and Mr. Carnegie. It was true, I mused, that Mr. Mellon hadn't done anything for me so far. I resolved that the next time I saw him taking a walk I would suggest he give Pittsburgh something. However, I never did, and I almost blamed myself when, many years later, the magnificent Mellon art collection went to Washington.

I had lingered behind the others to study the sun filtering through immense fronds of tree ferns under a glass roof when I heard a hoarse voice call to me, "Jane, Jane." I turned my head, but all I could see was a man's hat on the other side of a clump of tall flowers.

"Jane," the voice came again, "do you remember the stabbing? Do you remember how it happened?"

The answer was on my lips, but before I could utter it Pauline appeared in the doorway at my left, returned from the room beyond to look for me.

"We wondered where you got to. You—" And then, shrilly: "That's him! That's the reporter!"

The hat moved swiftly along the tops of the chrysanthemums. Feet pattered on the marble floor, and the man emerged and ran so quickly out the door at my right that my impression of him was a blur and all I could be sure of was that he had a black patch over one eye.

Pauline came toward me, frowning in perplexity. "I wonder why he ran away. Did you say anything to him?"

"No, but I was just going to."

"What do you suppose he wanted?"

"To talk to me."

"How did he know you were here?"

"Maybe he followed us from home," I said.

"Then why didn't he stay and talk?"

"I don't know."

She looked off. "We've got to tell Sylvester."

"No!" I cried so sharply that she turned back to me and stared.

"Why not?"

"Because I don't want you to. I don't want you to tell anybody."

"That's silly. It might be very important. The folks will want to know."

"Pauline, please."

"But why?"

I looked at my shoes and said softly, "I think he's my father."

"Oh, he is not. He's a reporter."

"He just said that to you. It's not true." I gave a great sigh and groped for clarity. My father had been writing to Sophie from Denver, but he could have come to Pittsburgh, twice now, in order to—what? Find out how much I knew? "Pauline, they think my father did it—the murder."

"Who does?"

"Oh, you *know*, Pauline—the police, everybody. If we tell them he's here they'll capture him." Then everything about the crime would come to a head. Sophie's part in it, the letters she received, her failure to report them, all would be out in the open. I could not let it happen to the Webers—not to the Webers. "Please, Pauline."

She looked doubtful. I could tell she hated to give up the telling, the excitement of being questioned by the family, becoming the cause of authorities' being called in, but when I tugged at her sleeve and looked into her eyes appealingly she said, "All right."

"Cross your heart?"

She crossed it, and I breathed with relief.

She stuck to her word too. The only time she mentioned the incident was when she whispered to me that night on our way up to bed, "I don't think your father did it, do you?"

"No," I fibbed.

"Well, as long as they suspect him . . ." And she crossed her heart again.

"I love you, Pauline," I said.

In bed that night I lay awake, thinking. Pauline had said she did not believe my father to be guilty, but if he was not why did he hide from the police and why was Sophie concealing his whereabouts? She had had her chance to say to Mr. Flynn, "I know where he is. I write letters to him and he writes letters to me." But she had let the opportunity slip by. Surely this was wickedness.

But still, how could she, a Weber, be a murderess? Was a Weber capable of so terrible a deed? The inconsistency made my head reel. There must be some other explanation for her silence, something I did not understand but which would be revealed to me some day, some day. . . .

Suddenly I sat up in bed. What if my father had come to Pittsburgh to see me because he *wanted* me to remember the stabbing? What had he asked me? "Do you remember how it happened?" If he wanted me to, then it was because he was innocent and I could prove it!

I put my head back on my pillow to rearrange my thinking, to exonerate my father. It was not difficult. Because I desired him to be guiltless, he was. Being a child, I was omnipotent. I could easily reason that he was only hiding until the day I could recall the past and clear him of suspicion. If he wrote affectionate letters to Sophie it was because he did not know she was the criminal. And maybe she wasn't. Maybe someone else entirely had murdered my mother. No, that was too good to be true; Sophie had done too many strange things for me to believe it.

For my father's sake I tried once more to recall the murder as I had witnessed it, but no matter how I strained and squeezed and pushed inside my head, nothing came to me. I turned to Nancy Myrtle May beside me in bed and spoke to her in a whisper. "I can't remember the murder. But you were there. Do you remember it?" There was no reply. Her china face felt cold to the touch, and her eyes were shut. Whenever she was sat up her eyes sprang open with a loud metallic click, and Trixie said if you saw them from the inside of her head they looked terribly nasty, all balls and wire. I had never seen the inside of Nancy Myrtle May's head, but I knew one thing—her eyes had been closed during the murder.

Oh, it was useless to churn everything over. I would stop thinking about Sophie's guilt or non-guilt. I, who had forgotten so much, would forget everything except that she was a member of the Weber family.

Having made that resolution, I went to sleep.

6

Christmas

———◄•••►———

THE WARM DAYS were gone. There was an end to watching tadpoles in a pond, to finding toadstools on the
lawn sprung up overnight, to making halos from sprigs of
the bridal-wreath bush, to picking elderberries. Autumn
had come.

There was a sunny day in September when, without
warning, rain began to plop surprisingly upon the leaves of
the asters and blue gentians in the garden, first a few drops
nearby, then others spreading to the ivy and the hedge and
the trees across the street, plop plop, harder and harder, a
symphony played on greenery.

There was an October electric storm when the iron
lamppost in front of our house was struck by lightning
twice in ten minutes, disproving all theories to the contrary and filling us with such delight at making the discov-
ery that we recovered quickly from our fright at the noise.

Though children have a strong tendency to look ahead,
to anticipate, I treasured each day of the autumn and relin-
quished it unwillingly. It was a time of peace for me, when
nothing new occurred to heighten my suspicions and my
truce with Sophie could be maintained. While nature was
ranging from violent storms to gentle days of Indian Summer, displaying riots of color on maple and oak, blowing

the loudest or whispering the softest, carrying on like a banshee or tiptoeing across the lawn—while all this was going on, for me there was a lull.

The summer clothes were washed and hung in the great wardrobes on the third floor. The wools and furs and overshoes were taken out in expectation of the cold. The tennis net was folded and put away. The wicker furniture was brought in from the front porch and the swing taken down.

I was told to untie the hammock and store it in the cellar, but I wanted to hold on to the autumn a little longer, so I left it up, and since nobody but children went near once the tennis court was out of use, it stayed up even when cold weather came. Leaves drifted into it, and ice froze its strings, but still it remained—a monument to golden days.

Why was time so precious to me, a little girl who should be looking forward to the holidays? Why did I relish each day, when other children were in the habit of wishing time away, hardly able to wait for Christmas? I think I knew that I would never have another year at Wilkins Avenue.

In spite of holiday business, the children did not help out at the store. We had had an epidemic of head colds after Thanksgiving, and it was thought best to keep us at home. Mine had been so severe that Sophie had sent for the doctor. Grandma was aghast. She had heard of sending for the doctor for strokes, smallpox, and babies but never for colds. However, Sophie was adamant and Dr. Reichart came, though not without having to be coaxed because of the way Grandma had acted the day Ermanie's baby was born. He was still muttering when he came into my room, and Sophie tried to put an end to it by offering to pay him before he examined me, but this insulted him in another way and he had to be appeased all over again.

While they talked I fell asleep and had to be awakened to stick out my tongue and say ahhhhh. My temperature was taken while Sophie looked on worriedly. Then he put his ear to my chest and back and admitted he had found some congestion. Sophie cried anxiously, "It's not consumption, is it?"

"That's rich! Consumption! No, blast it, woman! It's a common cold!"

Sophie smiled. "Good. Well, what should she do for it?"

The doctor rose angrily from the bed, where he had been sitting beside me. "She should blow her nose!"

He refused to take any money for the visit because I wasn't sick. When he left, Sophie said he took that position only to make us feel even guiltier for having sent him away when the baby came. Grandma said she didn't care, it served him right because he could have been reached in time if he hadn't been playing pinochle.

Denied his ministrations, I became the object of Grandma's care. This meant mustard plasters fore and aft, my feet put into a dishpan of steaming hot water, my neck wrapped in a cold wet rag. Now thoroughly miserable, I had no place to go but up and recovered quickly.

Now and then during the year I had received letters from the Merriweathers and from other people of the stage, people who knew me, but whom I did not know. "Dearest Jane," they would write, "we miss you very much and hope you're getting along well. Have two new bicycles in the act now. You'd love it." Or: "Jane, darling: Thought of you today when I gave Fifi a fish and she clapped her flippers. Remember what you said once when that happened?" I didn't.

Now Christmas cards began to come for me from all over the country. Sophie answered them for me, as she had the letters, with thanks and assurances of my well-being.

At last it was Christmas Eve. We children were sent to bed at our usual time but got up one by one until we all met in the hall. We began to play hunt the slipper, the boys in their nightshirts, we girls in long flannel nightgowns. Aside from Ermanie's baby, asleep in the guest room because Ermanie and Theodore were at the store, nobody was home but Grandma, and we were able to hide from her nearly half an hour, up steps and down, till Walter forgot he was hiding and began to pump out "The Blue Danube" on the player piano. The sound brought Grandma swiftly to his side.

"What a terrible boy you are, Walter!" she cried in her sternest tone. "Get back to bed!"

He stood up from the piano, but he said defiantly, "I don't have to go to bed yet. I'm eight years old."

"I'm sixty years old and I say—go to bed!"

He started out of the room reluctantly. "Will you wake me up when the folks come home?"

"No, I won't! On Christmas Eve they don't get through at the store till nearly midnight. Then it takes an hour nearly on the streetcar. Do you want me to wake you up at one in the morning? Do you think I'm crazy?"

He went upstairs then and there. A rapping was heard at the front door. Grandma went to see who had come, and we children appeared from wherever we were, too curious to fear banishment. Grandma opened the door, and the hall light flooded outside, revealing Elise and a snowy night landscape behind her. Immediately Grandma was filled with alarm. "Elise! Home from the store so early? What happened?"

"Wait a minute, Mama. Don't close the door. Hugo is coming."

"Hugo! *Himmel! Was ist los?*"

The tragic pitch of her voice so frightened us that we drew back a little, but Grandma ran outside on the porch in her bedroom slippers and with her apron still on. Hugo, his arm in a sling, and supported by Leon Bauer, was just turning in at the walk. Grandma ran right down into the snow, pushed Leon aside, and held Hugo herself. Though he remonstrated with her, begged her to go back on the porch and not to make a fuss, she never let go of him.

"It's nothing, Mama! Don't get excited. I broke my arm, that's all."

"Then why are you limping?"

"Because I sprained my ankle a little, too. But it's nothing. Mama, for heaven's sake, let Leon help me."

But she wouldn't, and got him into the house personally, crying, "What happened? What happened?"

"He fell off a ladder, that's all, Mrs. Weber," Leon said.

"That's all! He's crippled for life and you say, 'That's all.'"

"He was trying to reach some high boxes and he fell off."

"Hugo, quick. Sit down."

She got him onto a hall chair, removed his hat, and felt his forehead. "Stop worrying, Mama," Hugo said, while she struggled to get him out of his overcoat. "It's just a simple fracture. Elise and Leon went with me to a doctor, and he set my arm. The ankle he bound, and it'll be all right in a few days."

"Everybody thought Leon and I better go with him," Elise said, "in case he got faint."

"Everybody thought Elise and I could best be spared from the store," Leon said.

For once Grandma agreed with him. She admitted that, of all people, he and Elise could best be spared.

"It's a shame," Hugo said, "a freak accident like this just when Sophie needs me on Christmas Eve."

"Oh, the store is so jammed with relatives, nobody'll miss you," Elise said.

"Do relatives know the stock?" Hugo asked.

"Who needs to know the stock on Christmas Eve? The customers'll buy anything."

"Elise, please," her brother begged. "I'm not in the mood for arguing."

"I'm not arguing. I'm just saying you don't need to feel bad about leaving the store."

Grandma put an end to any more of that discussion. "Go make some coffee, Elise!" she ordered.

"Yes, a cup of coffee would taste fine," Hugo said.

Elise went out to the kitchen. Leon stood by, still in his overcoat and not knowing what to do with himself. Grandma felt Hugo's forehead and tested the pulse of his good wrist. She was worried, so he tried to cheer her up.

"Business was really big at the store," he said.

"That's nice."

"I see the children are fine." He nodded to us. "Only where's Walter?"

"Asleep," Grandma said. "Asleep like a little angel."

Pauline nudged me, and for a minute we had to fight off a sudden attack of the giggles. Grandma noticed our glee and yelled to us to go upstairs at once. We started off rapidly, but slowed at the top of the steps. Looking down, I saw Hugo bow his head into the crook of his good arm and blurt, "I can't do without Daisy any longer! I just can't!"

We children stared at one another in amazement. We had never heard of a grown man's showing so much emotion. We didn't know what to make of it. We leaned over the balcony rail and watched.

"He's been talking about his wife ever since he fell off the ladder," Leon Bauer said.

"The longer we're apart," Hugo went on, "the harder it is to get back together again. I don't think we'll ever get back together again now."

"Shush, shush," said Grandma, patting his head.

"I shouldn't have left her. Whatever she said, whatever she did, I shouldn't have closed up the house and left."

"This is the way he's been for an hour," Leon said.

After a long pause, Grandma said, "I'm thinking. I'm thinking. Hugo, *Lieber,* go to bed."

He raised his head and brushed his eyes with his free hand. "No, I'd like a cup of coffee first."

"I'll bring it to you in bed," Grandma coaxed.

He rose, and we children scattered, I to my room next to Sophie's, and the Webers to theirs on the third floor.

Ten minutes later I got up to go to the bathroom, but found it already occupied by Grandma and Elise. The door was open and I saw them standing there, Elise with a glass of wine in her hand. "But he just had a cup of coffee," Elise said. "What does he need wine now for?"

"Because he does."

There was silence except for the creak of a cabinet door and some faint clinking, and then Elise cried out, "Mama, what are you doing?"

"Never mind."

"What are you putting in the wine?"

"Nothing."

"Mama, do you know what's in that bottle?"

"What's in it?"

"It's chloral hydrate!"

"Is that so?"

"You used a couple of drops of it for a sedative when you had your dyspepsia, remember?"

"Yes, yes."

"But all that you're putting in the wine will knock Hugo out."

"Is that so?" Grandma sounded extraordinarily calm.

"Seymour said once it's what they use in a saloon when a customer gets disorderly. Eight drops."

"I heard him say."

"It's a Mickey Finn, Mama."

"That's nice, a Mickey Finn."

"It'll make him unconscious."

"Good, it'll make him unconscious."

"But, Mama!"

"Elise, go for Daisy."

"What?"

"Go for Daisy. Right away." Elise evidently was rendered speechless, for Grandma continued, "Don't say anything about Hugo. Just say, 'Come—an emergency.' "

There was a long pause, and then Elise said, "Mama, you fascinate me." There was in her voice honest admiration for her mother.

As they came out of the bathroom, Grandma to take the wine up to the third floor, and Elise to put on her coat and hat, I bobbed back to my room. The events of the evening were as good as a play at the Alvin Theatre. I could scarcely wait for the next act.

Before it began, there was a little curtain-raiser between Trixie and Leon Bauer. After Grandma gave Hugo the wine she went down to the kitchen by the back stairs as Leon came up the front ones. He went into the sitting room and was just taking off his overcoat when Trixie appeared, out of her bed again and down from the third floor. He must have been startled by the little apparition in a nightgown, because he gave a very loud gasp.

"Hello, Mr. Bauer," Trixie said.

"Hello, Trixie."

"Why don't you go back to the store?"

"I don't know if I ought to so late," he said peevishly. "I wish somebody'd tell me what they want me to do."

"I think you ought to go back. How was business so far?"

"They were very busy."

"That's good." Then she added, pride in her tone, "The store did RTE yesterday."

"What's RTE?"

"Don't you know?"

"No."

"RTE is nine hundred and seventy dollars."

"Why?"

"Because—the code. Don't you know the code?"

"No."

"The key to it is LUCKY STORE. L stands for one, U stands for two, C stands for three, K stands for four, Y stands for five—"

"And so on."

"You have to keep in mind that E is zero," Trixie warned.

"I see."

"Didn't you know about the code?"

"No."

"It's a wonderful one. We all can talk about money and nobody but us knows how much money we're talking about. You see the secret?"

"Yes, but it's not going to be a secret very long if you go around telling everybody the key."

"Oh, I wouldn't tell just anybody. I'm telling you because you're going to marry Aunt Charlotte and then it won't matter if you know the secret because you'll be in the family."

Grandma materialized in the doorway suddenly, having come up the back stairs silently in her slippers, frightening both the performers in the entr'acte.

"Not again!" she cried. "Not again, Trixie! This is the third time you got up since you went to bed."

"Second," Trixie said.

"What's the excuse—what is it this time?"

"It's Walter, Grandma. What he does."

"What does he do?"

"He jumps up and down on his bed and makes faces, and acts all kinds of horrible things to annoy me."

"The boys go into the girls' room?" Grandma inquired sharply.

"No."

"The girls go into the boys' room?"

"No."

"How do you know what Walter does in his room, then?"

"Well, you know the picture on the wall in my room, 'The Horse Fair' by Rosa Bonheur?" Grandma nodded, and Trixie went on. "Well, right behind the horses there's a hole in the wall, and if you stand on a chair and push the picture sideways, you can see right into the boys' room."

"*Ach Gott!*" Grandma cried.

"You better make him stop doing things, Grandma," Trixie said.

"I'll make him stop doing things! I'll make him lie down and go to sleep and I'll make you stop looking through the wall! With a whip!"

"But, Grandma—"

"Go to bed now! Go to bed and don't let me hear of you again till tomorrow morning."

Trixie scooted off, and Grandma turned her attention to her son-in-law-to-be. "Well, Leon, what are you going to do? Stand around here all night?"

"Oh. Do you think I ought to go back to the store?"

"Well, Leon, you know how it is. You're so anxious to marry my Charlotte, but everybody who marries somebody in this family works in the store before Easter and Christmas."

"Oh, I intended to go back," Leon said.

"You don't have to. Nobody's making you marry Charlotte."

"I'll go right back. I'll just put on my coat and—I guess I can get in an hour or two of work still tonight, even after the streetcar—"

Grandma interrupted him, but she sounded far away, as if she had sat down at the far end of the sitting room, or as if she were talking from another county. "Leon, do you ever hear from Max?"

"Max Hermansdorfer?" Leon asked. "No, I hardly ever see him."

Grandma sighed. "I wonder why he never comes here any more. Such a nice man."

"Oh, Elise isn't missing anything," Leon said.

"Not since the Fourth of July," Grandma murmured mournfully. "He hasn't been here since the Fourth of July. And it's Christmas already."

"Well, I haven't wanted to say anything, but, since you bring it up—Max doesn't belong in this house. You wouldn't want him here if you knew."

"What's to know?"

"He's getting a very bad reputation. Very wild."

"Max?" Grandma cried.

"You have no idea how he's been carrying on, Mrs. Weber. He's got a new horse and buggy, and you should hear what goes on in it. And the crowd he runs with— actresses, even."

When Grandma spoke again she sounded pleasantly bewitched. "Is that so?"

"I was never going to open my mouth as long as he had the decency to stay away from here, but you asked."

"What else do you know?" she demanded avidly.

"Well, I don't like to tell tales out of school, but I ran into him one night and—well, I don't like to say he was drunk, but he was drinking!"

"*Ja, ja,*" she said after digesting this information. "He always did drink claret cup from swimming pools."

Leon sighed. "Tsk, tsk. I'm not surprised."

Then Grandma said, "Leon, on your way back to the store, go by where he lives. Say he should come and see us."

Leon was shocked. "Mrs. Weber! After what I told you!"

"It was exciting."

"You certainly don't want Elise to keep company again with a man like that?"

"No, not Elise!"

"Then . . . ?"

"Me," Grandma said tartly. "I'd like to keep company with a man like that."

"But Mrs. Weber!" From the way he said it I could picture him goggle-eyed and his mouth slack.

"You heard me, Leon. Go!"

"You shouldn't talk that way to me, Mrs. Weber," he protested mildly, his feelings hurt.

"I have a bad temper," Grandma said. "If you don't want me for a mother-in-law, you know how to get out of it."

Through my open door I saw him emerge from the sitting room, jamming on his hat. Grandma called him, "And when you get back to the store after you see Max, work!"

"I will," Leon muttered, going down the stairs.

"Work hard!" Grandma yelled. She must have heard the front door open and close on him, as I had, but she still spoke to him. "You and your thousand dollars!"

Then there was nothing else for me to do but lie in bed until the next thing happened. I wondered how much I'd missed by the sheer necessity of having to sleep sometimes. I decided to train myself to get along with less sleep in the future.

But staying awake had its hazards, because I was soon thinking of the strongbox with my father's letters in it, of Sophie's unaccountable falsehoods, of the man at the chrysanthemum show. And then a new thought struck me. What if he was not my father, but an unknown murderer at large who was going to kill me as he had killed my mother? But why would he? What had I done to deserve such a fate? For that matter, what had my poor mother done?

I might have worked myself into a froth of anxiety and sorrow had not Trixie come down from the third floor again. Walter was with her. She marched right into the sitting room and said, "Grandma, Walter pulled up his nightshirt."

"I did not," Walter claimed.

"He did too."

"I did not. I was only scratching a mosquito bite."

Trixie said, "There aren't any mosquitoes in December, ya, ya, ya."

"There are too. Look!" Walter cried.

He must have pulled up his nightshirt to prove his contention, because Grandma screamed, "Shame on you, Walter! In front of a girl! Shame on you!"

"Well, it itches."

"Go to bed! Go upstairs! Both of you!"

But Trixie wasn't quite ready. "Grandma," she said imploringly, "has Santa Claus come yet?"

"No!" Grandma shouted. "He never comes till the store is closed!"

"Oh."

"Back to your rooms! You hear me?" Grandma screamed. "In a minute I'm going to be furious!"

After that there was silence until Elise came back with Daisy. I sat up in bed in sheer excitement, because it was the first time she had been in the house for so many years. She reached the top of the stairs, her coat askew and her hair tumbled, loosened by fallen hairpins in her race from home. Grandma bustled out of the sitting room and clasped her long-lost daughter-in-law in her arms. "Daisy, *Liebchen!* You're still in time!"

"For what?" Daisy demanded frantically. "What's wrong? Elise wouldn't tell me anything. Is it one of the children?"

"It's Hugo."

"What's the matter with Hugo?"

"Go up to him, Daisy. He's in the third floor front. Go up while there's still time."

"Still time?" Then Daisy gave a little shriek and flew to the steps like an insane woman.

Elise was very angry. "What are you doing to that poor woman, Mama? What are you doing to her? I think you're terrible! Oh, I'm all out of breath. Daisy can certainly run if she wants to."

"Quiet, Elise."

"Why?"

"I'm thinking."

"It seems to me," Elise said, "you've already thought quite a bit tonight. And I must say, Mama, you really are the limit. Honestly! Poor Daisy. And now what next?"

"How was business at the store?" Grandma asked.

"All right, but—"

"You were in blouses?"

"No, Charlotte was in blouses. Sophie had me in handkerchiefs all day."

"Good," Grandma said. "You're fine for handkerchiefs. Blouses I wouldn't trust you with."

"Mama, for heaven's sake, how can you talk about the store? Aren't you afraid you may have poisoned Hugo?"

"Pooh! A Mickey Finn."

"And what about Daisy? Aren't you afraid—"

She didn't finish her sentence because Daisy came down from the third floor, wailing. "He's unconscious! Oh, Mama, he's unconscious!"

"He's unconscious," Grandma admitted when Daisy fell weeping into her arms. "Elise, go downstairs and make some coffee."

"I already made some!"

"Then bake a cake!" Grandma ordered.

"Bah!" Elise said, going.

Grandma patted Daisy's back. "Don't cry. It'll be all right."

"What happened to him?" Daisy asked piteously.

"He had an accident at the store."

"Then why isn't the doctor here? He can't just lie there suffering."

"The doctor has seen him already," Grandma said, truthfully enough. "There's nothing that can be done right now. We must wait."

"Is he going to die?"

Grandma answered in funereal tones, "When a man has no will to live, anything can happen."

Daisy sounded hysterical. "Hugo has no will to live?"

"He's an unhappy man."

"Oh, I know. It's all my fault! It's all my fault!"

"Daisy, a man must do what he has to do. Hugo is a man who must feel what he's working at."

"I know, I know. The *Volksblatt* is everything to him."

"Yes, it is."

"Oh, Mama!"

"Some men say what is in their hearts when they make money," Grandma said. "But Hugo is not like that. He says what is in his heart when he writes words. It's a beautiful thing."

"I know that now."

Grandma sighed. "And poor Hugo got unconscious before he found out you knew." She sighed again. "Well, it wasn't your fault. You couldn't help it. You were the way you were."

"He was right. He was always right. I was selfish and ambitious. Oh, Mama, I'd do anything if he'd only live!"

"Maybe," Grandma said hopefully, "if you went upstairs and sat with him—who knows? Maybe he'll pull through."

"Do you think he might?"

"He has a good chance."

"All right. Maybe, even though he's unconscious, he'll feel I'm there. And if he comes to, I'll tell him how I . . ."

"He might be unconscious for a long time," Grandma called after her.

"I don't care if it takes all night."

She went upstairs, and there was silence for at least two whole minutes after that. Then somebody was at the player piano, pumping out the clear and mechanical notes of "The Blue Danube." It had an amazingly triumphant sound. Grandma must have slipped downstairs, I thought. Only she could be playing, because Elise was hollering, "What's that for? A funeral or a fancy-dress ball?"

When I woke up it was one-thirty in the morning, and the folks were coming back from the store. Ordinarily, when they came home late, I slept on undisturbed, but the excitement of Christmas was upon me and I heard everything, the rapping on the front door, and then Seymour crying, "Merry Christmas, Mama!"

"My, look at all the packages!"

"Merry Christmas, Mama," Sylvester said. "Got a kiss for a fellow?"

"How's Hugo?" Seymour asked.

"Fine." She didn't say a word about Daisy. "The others are with you?"

"Yes, but we walked the fastest."

"Walked? We *ran* all the way from the streetcar," Sylvester said.

"Good exercise," Grandma said approvingly.

While the first contingent of the family was taking off its wraps there were knuckles against the stained glass in the door again, and the next came in. Charlotte cried, "Merry Christmas!" and was echoed, less heartily, by her fiancé.

And Sophie asked, "How's Hugo?"

"Fine."

"Jane?"

"Asleep like an angel."

"I was thinking. Tomorrow I want to sleep till noon for

a change. I really do, Mama. I'm going to stay in bed till noon if it kills me. And that means the children will be in a dither all morning waiting for me to get up so they can open their presents. Why don't we wake them up tonight and get it over with?"

"At this hour?"

"They can sleep late tomorrow."

But I was out of bed already and calling over the balcony to them in the hall below, "I'm awake! I'm awake!" And, without waiting for Sophie to change her mind, I scurried up the steps to the third floor and shook the girls and then the boys. "Sophie says we can open our presents tonight! Sophie says we can come down now!"

I didn't think of Hugo until I was back in my room, putting on my kimono and slippers at the suggestion of Pauline, who thought we all ought to repay Sophie's kindness by being as nice as possible. Then I remembered seeing the light streaming from under his closed door. If Daisy, sitting at his bedside, heard our commotion, she gave no sign of it.

We were very well behaved downstairs, first kissing everybody, then listening quietly and waiting for Christmas to start, happily eying the presents in the hall.

"How did you do in blouses?" Grandma asked Charlotte.

"I sold LKE personally."

"Pretty good—for blouses," Sylvester said.

Grandma asked, "Who took handkerchiefs after Elise left?"

"One of the girls on the floor," Sophie answered. "And then when Leon came back I put him there."

Grandma raised her eyes heavenward. "So now you're stuck with a lot of left-over handkerchiefs!"

"He sold very good, Mama," Charlotte cried defensively. "Very."

For a person who never went out to the store, Grandma kept up with its operations remarkably well.

Theodore and Ermanie were the next ones to shake the snow from their shoes on the doormat and rap on the pane. "Merry Christmas!" he cried, entering. "My, what are the children doing up?"

"Christmas is starting early this year," Sylvester said.

"How's Hugo?" asked Ermanie.

"Fine," Grandma told her.

"Where is he?"

"In bed."

"Why's Papa in bed?" Walter, who had been sent to his room before Hugo came home, asked the question.

"He broke his arm a little," Grandma told him. "Don't worry."

Ermanie asked, "How's the baby?"

"Asleep since six o'clock like an angel."

"I'm exhausted," Ermanie said, being helped out of her coat by her husband. "Just exhausted."

"You're not used to being on your feet so long," he said. "Sit down."

"Are we going to trim the tree before or after we eat?" Seymour asked.

"Let's trim it first," Sophie said. "All right, Mama?"

"Elise!" Grandma called in the general direction of the kitchen. "Put the soup back in the pot!"

Theodore and Leon brought the fir in from the back porch. It was a lovely one, with heavy tufts of long needles. I'd gone out to smell it a dozen times since the wagon had brought it. When set up in the parlor, it was so tall it nearly touched the ceiling. It was marvelous, everyone said, one of the nicest we'd ever had.

Seymour and Sylvester brought out boxes of ornaments that had been stored away since last year, and while the tree was being dressed conversation wafted around it.

Sylvester said, "Mama, you'll die laughing. I had one

customer, a Polack, he wanted to buy a doll for his baby, it was the funniest thing."

"I had a customer," Charlotte interrupted, "just before Hugo fell off the ladder. She was a scream."

"Such customers tonight!" Seymour exclaimed. "Crazy!"

"Mama, this Polack," Sylvester continued, "he said to me, 'Have you got a doll opens and shuts her eyes?' I said yes, and he said, 'She walks?' and I said yes, she walks. He said, 'She says Mama?' I said yes she says 'Mama.' And he said, 'She eats?' I said no, she doesn't *eat*. And you know what he said? He said, 'No eat, no buy.' " I didn't think the story was very funny, but Sylvester roared with laughter.

"Honestly," Charlotte said, "I had more insane customers tonight than I ever had in my life."

"Imagine—'No eat, no buy'!" Sylvester gasped, wiping his eyes.

"What will they want next?" Seymour asked.

"I had one lady I nearly slapped," Ermanie said.

"You know what Sophie did, Mama?" Seymour asked. "What?"

"She got rid of the PMs in coats."

Grandma looked impressed. "In coats! What do you think of that!"

Leon seemed puzzled. "What's a PM?" he asked.

I knew he must be thinking of LUCKY STORE and realizing it didn't have a P or an M in it.

Theodore was amazed at the question. "You worked in the store before Easter and every night this week and all day today, and you don't know what a PM is?"

"No."

"Means 'premium,' " Theodore explained. "Anybody sells a piece of merchandise marked PM—old stuff we can't get rid of—gets ten cents bonus."

Sophie laughed. "Listen to the big store executive talking!"

"For a man who makes his living selling insurance," Seymour said, "Theodore sure knows all about the mercantile business."

"Well, my lord, how many years is it that I've helped out in the store? I ought to know something."

"PMs." Leon mused. "I did sell things marked PM. Ten cents, eh? I bet I sold five PMs, at least."

"So add the fifty cents to your thousand dollars!" Grandma said.

"Too late, Leon," said Seymour. "No proof. You should have saved the tickets."

Ermanie said, "I know I ought to go upstairs and look at the baby. And I will as soon as I get my strength back."

"I'll look," her husband told her.

After he went out, Sophie asked, "What's the matter, Mama? You look sad."

"I was just thinking of Papa. He died three years ago tonight—at a quarter after eleven."

Charlotte explained to Leon, who might not have heard the story, "He wouldn't die till the store was closed."

Grandma nodded thoughtfully. "I'd do the same myself."

"Oh, Mama!"

Sylvester tried to make a joke out of it. "Well, don't you flatter yourself! What makes you think we'd ever close the store in *your* memory?"

"We would too," Seymour said loyally. "We'd close it for a week."

"A day is enough!" Grandma exclaimed tartly.

"Well, let's not sit around here talking about dying. It's Christmas."

"Yes, we could start with the presents."

But we didn't get to them yet. Somebody was at the door.

"My goodness, who can that be?"

"At nearly two in the morning!"

"We're all here, aren't we?"

"Of course."

Charlotte opened the door, and there stood Max Hermansdorfer. I hardly recognized him. He was not the same shy Mr. Hermansdorfer we used to know. This was a different Mr. Hermansdorfer, a suave, sophisticated one, wearing a high hat and an opera cloak. The sideburns were gone. He looked taller and smelled excitingly of pomade.

"Max!" Charlotte cried, gaping at him, at the wing collar and the white tie, the gold-knob cane, the revised and improved mustache.

"Yes, where on earth did you drop from?" Seymour asked.

Grandma shot Leon Bauer the first look of approval I had ever seen her give him and turned to the guest. "Imagine! You, Max! Such a surprise!"

"I got your message, Mrs. Weber."

"What message?" Charlotte asked.

"Never mind," Grandma said. "My, don't you look handsome, Max!"

"I'll go get Elise. She's in the kitchen," said Sophie.

"I'll do it," Walter said and scooted away.

Mr. Hermansdorfer looked coldly at Sophie, then winked at Grandma and said, "I happened to be passing the house after a small supper party in the neighborhood. I saw the lights and I thought I'd stop in a moment and wish you all a Merry Christmas."

"Wonderful! Make yourself at home!"

Hands stretched out to take his cane and hat and cloak, but he shook his head. "No, I'm sorry, but I can only stay a few minutes. As a matter of fact, I'm on my way to another party."

Elise came down the hall and when she saw our guest she gazed at him, all smiles, and said, "Max! I don't believe it! Well, if you don't look like a million dollars!"

"Thank you so much, Elise," Max said with complete composure.

"You just look *dashing!* You really do. Why don't you take your cloak off?"

"He has to go," Seymour said. "He's going to another party."

"Another?" Elise asked. "Tonight?"

"Yes. So far it's been a very gay season, and I see no signs of its letting up."

Suddenly Daisy called from the top of the steps, "He's conscious! He's conscious!" We all turned and looked up, but she had disappeared.

"What was that?" Mr. Hermansdorfer asked.

"I don't know," said Sophie, looking perplexed.

"It was nothing," Grandma said. "Well, Max, tell me—"

"Was that Daisy?" Sophie asked. "What's she doing here?"

"Don't ask me," Elise said. "Don't ask me what's going on tonight. Ask your mother if you want to know. I'm not being told anything. But queerer things I've never seen."

"Why is Daisy here?" Sophie persisted.

"You'll have to get it directly from the Sphinx," Elise said.

"Well, Mama?"

"Daisy?" Grandma asked.

"Yes, Daisy!"

"You remember her," Elise said to Grandma. "The woman Hugo married. The mother of the four children we've had around here all year."

"You called Daisy on account of Hugo's broken arm," Seymour suggested.

"*Ja,* on account of his arm."

"And a certain other condition he may have developed since he got home," Elise added.

"He's got something else?" Sophie cried, alarmed.

"*Nein, nein!* He'll feel fine soon. He just needs a little rest."

"He's getting it, all right," Elise said.

"Don't forget Max is here," Grandma reminded her. "Max, *wie geht's?*"

"Yes, what have you been doing?" asked Seymour.

"Oh, you know how it is with an orchestra. In and out of town. Have you heard any of the concerts?"

"I have," said Sophie. "Several."

"You should have let me know you were in the audience."

"I never thought of it," Sophie said.

"Miss Weber," Mr. Hermansdorfer said, "could I speak to you a moment alone?"

Sophie looked confused. "Who—me?"

"Yes."

"Well, I suppose so, but . . ." She looked around, wondering where they could be alone in this house.

"The music room will be fine," he said, taking her arm and steering her straight through the parlor past everyone. The members of the family looked at one another, puzzled. Not one of them thought of following the couple to the music room to find out what was going to happen, but I did. I wanted to know, and so I went.

"The last time I was here," Mr. Hermansdorfer was saying, "you succeeded in making quite a fool of me, Sophie Weber. I was rather unworldly then, but I've been around a bit since, and I would hardly describe myself as unworldly now. As I recall, you kissed me that time. This time I'm going to kiss you."

And with my own eyes I saw him lean his cane against the piano, take Sophie gracefully into his arms, one hand at her waist bending her body into a gentle arch, the other at the back of her head. Then he pressed his lips against hers, his eyes closed, and remained in that position so long it was like a show at the Alvin.

When he let her go, she was out of breath. She stared at him solemnly, gasping, but he turned away, picked up his cane, nodded to me as he stalked past through the parlor and into the hall. He was smiling. "Good night, everyone!" he called gaily, turning the handle of the front door. "A very Merry Christmas!"

And he was gone.

The family surged toward the music room. "What did he want, Sophie? What did he say?"

"Nothing."

And she would not say another word about him. Indeed, she scarcely spoke again, except to ask questions about Hugo. Grandma assured her the best thing for him was to let him rest undisturbed. Besides, Daisy was with him if he needed anything.

Sophie kept quiet but looked preoccupied the rest of the night. The men finished trimming the tree, Seymour holding Theodore on his shoulders so he could reach to the top to put on the star. "My," Grandma said, "that's as good a stunt as the acrobats at the vaudeville show."

The presents were brought into the parlor from the hall and we all began to look for our names on the tags. "T-R-I-X-I-E," said Sylvester. "That spells Walter."

"It does not!" Trixie cried, outraged. "It spells me."

"Oh, I beg your pardon," Sylvester said.

Seymour was the first to unwrap a package. "I bet this is a necktie," he heard him say. "Yes, it's a necktie—from Charlotte." He held it up. "This is the prettiest one I ever had."

Charlotte asked anxiously if he was sure he liked the pattern.

"Do I like it? I like it so much, the first time I saw it I ordered two dozen from the wholesaler myself!"

"I'm glad," Charlotte said.

It was a wonderful sight, all of us so busy, some kneeling on the floor, some sitting, all studying packages, sometimes shaking them to guess what was inside, or ripping off the paper. I was so pleased to be a part of that scene that I couldn't open anything right away; I had to watch other people first.

Ermanie begged, "Open my present first, Mama. Open mine first."

"In a minute!"

Charlotte pulled the tissue paper off something blue and woolly in one of her boxes and exclaimed, "For heaven's sake, a coat! Oh, what do you think of that! Oh, thanks."

"Do you like it?" Sophie asked. "It was the last PM in stock and I thought the color would be very good for you."

Seymour laughed. "So that's how you got rid of the PMs?"

Charlotte stood up and tried on the coat. It fitted her nicely. "It's just beautiful," she said, smoothing it over her hips and trying to catch a reflection of herself in the window pane.

"Anybody who gives me a PM," Elise said, "can put it right back in stock."

"Some day," Sophie said wistfully, "maybe we'll be rich enough so we can give each other things from other stores. Just walk in any place and buy what we like—at retail prices.

"I bought my present to Mama at retail price," Ermanie said proudly. "At Kaufmann's. Hurry up and get it open, Mama."

Grandma asked, horrified, "You went in somebody else's store and spent your money?"

"Yes, you traitor!" Seymour exclaimed.

Elise murmured, "Well, you know how it is. Come easy, go easy."

Ermanie was very hurt. "But I thought—"

"Oh, never mind, Ermanie," Sophie said. "It's all right."

"I didn't think everybody was going to—"

"Nobody's offended. They were just teasing you."

Grandma was holding up the present, something made of velvet and lace, by the sleeves. "What is it?"

"It's a bed jacket," Ermanie told her.

"A bed jacket? What for? I'm never sick."

"You don't have to be sick to wear it," Ermanie said. "You can wear it for breakfast in bed, for instance."

Grandma broke into helpless laughter. I never saw her, before or after, lose such control of herself. She laughed until her face was crimson and tears rolled down from her eyes. Seymour and Sylvester got worried and patted her on the back as though she had hiccups. But nothing helped. Her laugh just had to run its full course.

Finally it was over, and Ermanie said, very disappointed, "You don't like it."

Grandma stood up, came over to Ermanie, and gave her a big hug. "I'm crazy about it. It's just what I always wanted."

"Oh, I'm so glad," Ermanie said.

"Kaufmann's!" Grandma muttered. "They haven't got bed jackets at Weber's?"

As more boxes were unwrapped, paper began to cover the floor and some of the chairs too.

"Look—suspenders!" Walter said, feigning joy, and not succeeding very well. "I wonder what else I got."

"Look and see," Sylvester told him.

Once I started to open my presents, I forgot all about the other people. I tore away the paper from a very large box and found inside an enormous doll, the most beautiful I had ever seen. She was dressed like a bride with a veil on her head, and she held a bouquet of the tiniest white flowers one could imagine. Her hair was in long, dark corkscrew curls down to her waist. I lifted her gingerly out of her box and gazed at her raptly.

Trixie, who was sitting beside me on the floor, glanced at my doll and shuddered. "Wait till her wig comes off," she said. "There'll be a great big hole in the top of her head."

"Her wig will never come off!" I cried. "Never as long as she and I live!" Nothing could spoil my happiness, not even when I found out the doll was from Sophie. I wished the gift had been from anyone in the world but her, but I was not going to let that bother me. I would pretend somebody else had given her to me, Mr. Auerbach of the Auerbach Theatre, or maybe Mr. Hermansdorfer of the opera cloak.

Theodore complimented me on my doll and asked me what I would name her.

I said I would have to give that matter a great deal of thought.

Suddenly he got to his feet, crying, "My baby is not going to miss this!" as he raced out of the parlor. He charged up the stairs, but nobody seemed to think his reactions unusual.

"In the worst of the rush tonight," Charlotte said, "a lady wanted to try on a corset."

"Try on a corset? Well, that's being mighty particular. Whoever heard of such a thing?" Seymour asked.

"And who buys corsets, anyhow, on Christmas Eve?" Ermanie wanted to know.

"Maybe she wanted to give herself a present," Elise suggested.

Seymour couldn't get over it. "Try on a corset! That's understandable downtown, but in Braddock who tries on a corset?"

"Well, she tried it on," Charlotte said. "Right in the aisle. I was too busy to stop her."

Theodore came back with his baby wrapped in a blanket and held against his shoulder. "Well, here she is, here she is!"

"Oh, Theodore, it's just criminal to wake her up.'

"Who says she's awake?" he asked, grinning

"Well, how is she going to enjoy all this if she's asleep?"

"She'll enjoy it," Theodore said, sitting down on a love seat and patting the sleeping baby gently on the behind.

"She can always say she was here," Elise said.

"A toy set of dishes! A toy set of dishes!" Trixie cried.

"So far all I've opened," complained Walter, "is darn old clothes."

"Don't worry," Seymour said, "there are toys for you too."

"What have you got there?" Charlotte asked, watching her mother open a tiny package. "Why, it's a thimble. Is it sterling silver? It is? How beautiful."

"Now wouldn't it be nice," Grandma asked, "if I had a trousseau to sew on?"

"You have," Leon Bauer said boldly. "Charlotte's."

"Charlotte's is finished," Grandma snapped at him.

"Oh, good," he said. "Then I think we can tell you. We're going to be married on New Year's Eve."

"What!"

"The store'll be closed the next day. It's a good time," Charlotte pleaded.

There might have been more opposition had not Daisy appeared on the stairs just then with another bulletin from the third floor. "He's going to be all right!" she cried. "He's going to live!" And then she disappeared again.

"Who's going to live?" Seymour asked.

"Hugo," Elise told him.

"Hugo's that sick?" Sophie turned furiously on her mother. "He's that sick, and you didn't tell me?" She ran out of the parlor, heading for the stairs, but Grandma ran after her and stopped her.

"*Nein*, Sophie! Stay here. He's not sick."

"Just a little unconscious, that's all," Elise said.

"What happened?"

"Mama gave him knock-out drops," Elise told Sophie.

"Knock-out drops!"

"I was trying to fix it so he and Daisy would make up and go back together again."

There was a pause, and then Sophie started to say, "Mama, you . . ." but she didn't finish. I don't know if she was going to say something complimentary or damning. I don't think she knew herself.

Anyhow, Daisy was back, this time helping Hugo down the stairs. He wore a bathrobe and seemed very groggy. "I begged him not to come down," Daisy said, "but he insisted."

Sylvester helped her get him into the parlor.

"You're all right, Hugo?" Grandma asked.

"Fine," he answered, sounding as if his tongue were as thick as a cow's. He sank onto the nearest chair. "I don't know what hit me."

"You'd be surprised," Elise said.

"He's going to be all right," Daisy told us all, as friendly as if she'd been speaking to the family every day all those years. "As soon as I told him that I— Well, he made the most remarkable recovery."

Hugo reached for her hand and held it tight. "We're going back together again."

"We're going home, children," Daisy announced. "We'll open up the house and we'll all be together again. Won't that be wonderful?"

"Aw, heck," Walter said, "I liked it here at Grandma's."

Several people laughed, but I didn't. Things were changing, and I was helpless to stop them. Charlotte was going to get married and go away, and the children and Hugo were leaving. What else would happen? Whatever it was, life on Wilkins Avenue could not be the same. I wanted the rooms to keep their present occupants; I wanted there to be twelve of us for breakfast every morning. I wanted everything to stay as it had been in 1908. I looked around the parlor, at all the people together whom I loved, and at Sophie, whom I hated, and I pleaded with them all silently: Stay here with me. Stay here with me always.

The children were playing with their toys. Ermanie took the baby from Theodore because she thought he'd held her long enough and it was her turn. Daisy and Hugo whispered while Grandma watched, pleased that her plot had hatched so well. The others were talking and laughing, except Sophie, who was picking up scraps of paper and ribbon from the floor, a faraway look in her eyes. No one knew what I was thinking.

"Well, this is a merry Christmas, all right!" Charlotte said.

"Oh, my Lord, I've been carrying around a present for Mama for three days and I forgot all about it!" Seymour exclaimed. He took a letter out of his pocket and read from the envelope, "For 'Mrs. Karoline Weber.' Is that you, madam?"

"That's me," Grandma said, and Seymour gave her the envelope. "I wonder what it is," she said as she tore it open. "Well, what do you think—it's from Mr. Auerbach. But what is it?"

"It's an all-year-around pass for the nickelodeon," Seymour told her.

"No!" Ermanie exclaimed.

"Yes, siree," said Seymour. "He gave it to me a few days ago when I ran into him downtown. Said it would save him the trouble of sending it. Said it was my mother's Christmas present."

"Oh, if that isn't sweet of Mr. Auerbach!" Charlotte cried.

Grandma could scarcely believe it. "I can go to the nickelodeon—for nothing?"

Seymour nodded. "All year. And you have the choice of any of his four nickelodeons."

"*Lieber Gott im Himmel!*"

"Just think of all the nickels you'll save, Mama."

"Nickels? I hear they're going to raise the price of picture shows to ten cents soon," Sylvester said.

"Ten cents! For a picture show?"

"Nobody'll go if they have to pay ten cents!"

"Well, I don't have to worry," Grandma said with satisfaction. "I've got my pass. I'll go every day."

"Oh, my! Is Mr. Auerbach going to lose money on this!"

"Now that's settled, could we eat?" Sylvester asked.

"Oh, yes!"

"To the dining room!" Theodore cried.

"May I escort you, mademoiselle?" Seymour asked, holding his arm out to Sophie.

"You may," she said, taking it.

Everybody fell into the spirit of gaiety and went in line, in pairs, out of the parlor and into the hall. Trixie and I came last.

"There should be music for the grand march," Daisy said.

"I wish Max had stayed," Grandma said. "He could have played us nickelodeon music. True Blue Harold to the rescue! Fire, fire! *Ach,* isn't he handsome?"

"Well, Mama," Elise said, "it's been a busy year for you, hasn't it?"

"Busy? Why? What have I done?"

"What have you done!" Elise gasped.

"*Ja,* what? Oh, yes, I was so nice to Mr. Auerbach he gave me a pass."

"You don't count the chloral hydrate and burglars and heiresses and—"

"Elise, get the soup tureen!"

We reached the dining room. I looked around at the familiar faces, at the fireplace aglow, the sconces on the wall giving off their jets of light, the holly on the mantelpiece, the *Kuchen* on the table, the windows covered with frost, and beyond them the dark. I said to Trixie, who was still holding my arm, "Don't you love nighttime?"

"Yes," she said, "especially middle-of-the-night time."

New Year's Eve

⟶ ❖ ⟵

O N THE EVENING of the twenty-sixth of December, Hugo
and the children left Wilkins Avenue and went home.
Daisy and a cleaning woman had worked all day putting
her house back in order after its long abandonment, and by
night it was ready. Daisy accomplished it without help from
Hugo because the after-Christmas sale was on at the store
and he was helping out. The *Volksblatt* always did without him this time of year, and, for once, Daisy made no
murmur. She even apologized for not coming to Braddock
herself.

Though I knew I would see the children at school, and
though they promised to come and play with me, there
was a great big lump in my throat as I waved good-by to
them. I remembered secret meetings in the dark, pillow
fights, whispered conspiracies against the adults, games at
odd moments while waiting for meals or to get into the
bathroom or for the grown-ups to get ready to take us some
place. It was good to have friends, but to have them under
the same roof, I thought, was the most satisfactory of all
companionships. Oh, good-by, Pauline. Good-by, Trixie.
Good-by, boys. Without you I will be a kite in the cupboard, a top nobody spins.

The day after they left, my lonely wandering from room

to room reminded Grandma of all the extra space we now had on the third floor, and that, in addition, Charlotte would soon be gone. Her marriage to Leon, so long a threat and now definite, goaded Grandma into putting another ad in the paper: "Room to Let With Board."

"After the burglar," Elise said, amused, "I don't know how you had the nerve."

Seymour added, "And it isn't as if we need the money."

Elise heard me sigh and said, "Jane hopes you rent to a man with four children."

Sylvester winked at me. "Cheer up. Maybe Hugo will have another fight with Daisy and come back."

Sophie was furious when she heard what Grandma had done. "Just you bring a man into this house," she said to her mother with such bitterness and vehemence the rest of us were astonished, "and you'll be very sorry you did!"

"Why would I be sorry?"

"Because I'm going to make him miserable! I'll be rude to him, and shrewish, and patronizing!"

"Is that a nice thing to do to a poor boarder?" Grandma asked indignantly.

"No, it's not, but I don't intend to be nice. I intend to be obnoxious and insulting."

"Tell me why! Give me one reason we can't have a simple little thing like a boarder."

"Because you're looking for a husband for me again! And I'm ever so disappointed in you, because I'd expect you to have a new idea and not do the same old thing all over again. Believe me, you're wasting your time, because I'm not going to marry a boarder or anyone else."

"*Ach*, Sophie! How can you be so stubborn?"

"Stubborn about what?"

"About not marrying anybody."

"Oh, Mama, you know nobody's ever asked me."

"The trouble is you don't let anybody ask you!" Grandma shouted.

Sophie laughed, but not because she thought anything was funny. "I'll let anybody ask who wants to. Tell them all, my suitors, to get in line! I'm right here. Let them ask." She paused a moment. "Well, where are they? I don't hear a thing."

"Sophie, *du bist ein Teufel.*"

"True. I'm a devil. And you'll be sure of it if you rent some man a room. So, if that's clearly understood, I will return to the reading of my book, *Jane Eyre*, in which there is a man a lot more exciting than anyone you could possibly introduce me to, with all your machinations!"

She stalked out haughtily, and Grandma asked, "What's machinations?"

"It means ads in the paper," Elise told her solemnly.

The next morning the notice appeared and, because Sophie had put her foot down, Grandma turned away the gentlemen who answered it. She was a marvelous linguist; otherwise she never could have picked up such good English in her middle years. She loved new words and used them at the first chance. "Oh, you saw my machinations," she said to the potential boarders. "Come right in."

She could have got rid of them at once by saying that the room was already let, or that she'd changed her mind, but that was not her way. She invited them in for coffee and a bite of cake, and after a pleasant session of conversation she explained that her children didn't want the room rented. She told me she gave them the time and the food because they'd come such a long way and she wanted to be kind to them. But it was not a real kindness to turn them away once they'd tasted her *Kuchen.*

In spite of everything, Grandma rented a room.

I must say here that when I write of Mrs. Grenoble, I write as I thought of this person then, not in the light of what I came to know. For it was to Mrs. Grenoble that Grandma gave the room, setting off, most unexpectedly, a whole chain of events.

Late in the afternoon, after Trixie and I had gone ice skating at a pond in the neighborhood, we returned to Wilkins Avenue for the cup of hot chocolate Grandma had promised us and saw an old lady standing in front of the house. As we passed her on the sidewalk she called to us, "Oh, little girls, little girls."

"Yes, ma'am?" I asked.

"Do you live here?"

"*She* does," Trixie said, pointing to me, "and I did, but now I've gone home because my mother and father have made up."

"Is that so? Well, that's very nice. I see you've been ice skating."

"Yes," I said, and shifted my skates from one hand to the other.

"Do you enjoy it?"

"I do," I told her, "but Trixie doesn't because her skates won't stay on."

"Maybe the straps need fixing," the old lady suggested.

"No," I said, "it's just that her skates are too big for her."

"Well, she'll grow into them."

"Not this year, I don't think," Trixie said, sighing.

"Perhaps next." She turned her gaze on me. "My, that's a pretty sweater you're wearing."

"Yes," I said, "it was a Christmas present."

"Oh," the woman said. "Did you get many Christmas presents?"

"Lots," I said. I was describing them when Grandma came out onto the porch.

"Trixie, Jane, what are you doing?" she called to us.

"We're talking to this old lady," Trixie said.

"Is that a nice thing to say? Shame on you!" She addressed our new-made friend. "Excuse her, please. To a child everybody's an old lady over forty."

"I quite understand." The woman smiled and moved timidly down the walk toward Grandma, trailed by Trixie and me. She was beautifully dressed, with a little wool cape over a dress of dark green broadcloth. Her hat, of the same material as the cape, perched on an elegantly waved head of gray hair scalloped becomingly around her face. She had scarcely a wrinkle, and I thought her quite pretty for a person of her age. Her clothes, her speech, the way she bore herself made her seem every inch a lady, except that her lips were rouged, so lightly that one could hardly tell, but still there flashed through my mind what Elise had said once about Mrs. Zimit: "The poor old thing paints because she's trying to look younger and because she lived in Paris once, where, I understand, cosmetics and even smoking by ladies are the custom."

"Your house is very charming from the outside," Mrs. Grenoble said to Grandma.

"Did you come about the ad in the paper?"

"The ad? Oh, yes."

"You didn't notice it said 'gentlemen only'?"

"No, I didn't."

"Oh, that's too bad. Now you've come all this way for nothing."

"What a shame."

"Well, come in. Come in, anyhow. Don't stand in the cold. Let me warm you up with some cocoa. I have plenty."

"Oh, I really shouldn't."

"Come in, come in! Don't be shy." Grandma started inside, and the old lady, after a glance at Trixie and me, got up the courage to follow.

"I really am cold," she admitted. "I don't think I'm dressed warmly enough for a day like today."

"You're shivering," Grandma said as she closed the door. "Your lips are blue."

Oh, they are not, I thought, they're red. But then I saw that Grandma didn't have her glasses on.

"How lovely it is in here," our guest said, looking about

the hall. "And how do you keep that rubber plant looking so healthy?"

Grandma told her the secret was in washing the leaves with milk, and then asked suddenly, "What's your name?"

"Why, Mrs. Grenoble."

"I'm Mrs. Weber."

While the two of them shook hands I asked, "Have you ever been in Paris?"

"Yes, I have. And in London too."

"My, my, such a traveler!" Grandma exclaimed. "Come in the parlor and take off your cape or you'll freeze when you go out again. Trixie and Jane, go upstairs and wash your hands. And when you come down you can serve the cocoa. Mrs. Grenoble and I will both be company, won't we, Mrs. Grenoble?"

The old lady nodded and complimented Grandma on her knack of bringing up children. "It's good to teach them to be resourceful. You never know in life when it will come in handy. Are they your grandchildren?"

"One is and one isn't," we heard Grandma say as we went up the stairs. "But I like them both the same."

Trixie and I chose the best doilies and the prettiest china. Trixie got out sterling spoons and filled the Meissen chocolate pot. I carried the tray into the parlor proudly, and got a nod of approval from Grandma. I gathered that while we'd been busy she'd told the story of her life, because Mrs. Grenoble was saying, "How lucky you are, Mrs. Weber, to have all your dear ones around you still, with the exception of your husband. I, personally, have no one left."

While Trixie and I handed out the cups and poured, she went on to say that once she'd had two little boys, but they'd died of diphtheria when very young, and now her husband was gone—epilepsy—and she was alone.

Grandma clucked her tongue in sympathy and sent

Trixie and me back to the kitchen for cake. When we returned, the ladies were speaking of the nickelodeon. They had a great deal in common, for Mrs. Grenoble was an admirer of motion pictures too. She had actually seen them being made! She knew a man who manufactured them in the loft of a building in New York. She'd stood beside him while he told the cameraman where to put his camera and the actors what to do. She said it was most interesting.

"I bet," Grandma said, impressed.

"How nicely the girls serve," Mrs. Grenoble said, sipping her cocoa. "Now, Trixie, tell me about you."

"What about me?"

"What you do."

"I go to school. I'm in the first grade."

"Isn't that lovely? Delicious cake, Mrs. Weber. Now you, Jane. Tell me about you."

"I'm in the fifth grade."

"Oh, you must be very bright."

"No," I said, "it's just that I'm ten years old."

"Are you? Then you must have started in the first grade when you were six, like Trixie. And did you go to kindergarten at your school too?"

"No," I said, "our school doesn't have kindergarten."

Trixie said, "Even if it did, she wouldn't have gone. Because she wasn't here."

"Oh, where was she?"

"In New York and every place."

Mrs. Grenoble turned back to me. "How exciting! New York and *every place!* And which city did you like best, Jane?"

"I like Pittsburgh best," I said, "and Braddock."

"Better than New York?"

"Yes," I said.

A new question was forming on Mrs. Grenoble's lips, but Grandma spoke up suddenly. "I've been thinking. Never mind about the 'gentlemen only,'" she said. "It's all right, because my daughter doesn't want a gentleman in the house, anyhow."

"I beg your pardon?" Mrs. Grenoble murmured.

"I decided I'm going to let you have a room," Grandma announced, giving the statement the importance of a manifesto. "You can take your choice of the whole third floor."

I was not too surprised. Our guest's interest in the nickelodeon probably had persuaded Grandma. How could she pass up having in her own home a woman who would go to the show with her, who would discuss so intelligently, from such intimate knowledge, the merits or demerits of the picture?

The ladies went upstairs, and Trixie and I washed the chocolate cups and put everything away. When we came back into the hall Mrs. Grenoble was getting ready to leave, smoothing her cape over her shoulders, touching chignon and hat with an expert hand, declaring that the rate Grandma asked was very satisfactory to her. "I'll be back this evening, bag and baggage, and take possession." She shook Grandma's hand and smiled. "Now, don't forget to hold it till then."

"I could hold it till forever if I listened to my children," Grandma said, smiling back.

"I'm anxious to meet them. Are they half as dear and warm as you are?"

"*Ach,* yes!" Grandma admitted.

"Oh, dear Mrs. Weber, it will be so nice to be here."

Grandma went out onto the porch with Mrs. Grenoble and waved good-by to her as if they were lifetime friends about to be separated by a voyage to Japan. When at last she came back into the house and closed the door, she sighed reflectively. "A lovely woman!"

When Sophie heard the story at the supper table, she was furious. With the wedding the day after tomorrow, with so much to do, we needed a boarder like we needed a typhoon. It just made no sense having a strange old woman in the house talking of death and diseases, especially when we didn't need the money. "Mama, how could you have done such a thing?"

"*Ach*, I hated to see the ad go to waste."

"Here we go," Seymour said. "Hide the silverware!"

Grandma ignored him. "I told her as soon as Charlotte gets married on New Year's Eve I'll move her down from the third floor. Why should she have two flights of stairs to climb?"

"You're going to give her Charlotte's room? Right in our midst? Oh, Mama!"

"You'll be crazy about her."

"Crazy or not, the deal is all off!"

"The deal is off?"

"I mean it, Mama. I'll go over to the Walkers' and telephone her not to come."

"I don't know where she lives."

"You didn't get an address?"

"No, why should I?"

"You're usually so thorough in these matters, or do you only ask questions when you're interviewing gentlemen? Oh, Mama, why do you do the things you do?"

"It sounds to me," Sylvester said, "like she was overanxious to meet this friend of Mrs. Grenoble's, the one who directs moving pictures."

Grandma shook her head. "*Nein, nein*, he lives in New York."

"Well, I want to go on record as being against the whole thing," Sophie said.

"Give her a chance," Grandma suggested, "and if you don't like her, we can say Charlotte doesn't like her husband and is going to come home again."

"Mama, you're terrible!" Charlotte cried. "I'm going to be very happy with Leon!"

Grandma shrugged her shoulders. "You can't wait a little with the wedding till your sister Sophie gets married?"

"No, she can't!" Sophie shouted.

"All right," Grandma conceded. "Don't yell."

True to her word, Mrs. Grenoble arrived that evening. Unexpectedly, the family found nothing objectionable about her. "But then," as Elise said, "we adored the burglar."

Grandma would have liked to spend the next day with the new boarder, but she had too much to do for the wedding. Mrs. Grenoble stayed in her room most of the time until she found out what was occupying Grandma, and then she helped her. It was she who packed the trousseau and rearranged furniture and made breathtakingly beautiful arrangements of the flowers that came from the florist's the day before the wedding. She was very good with a needle too, and took up the hems, not only of the wedding gown Charlotte bought at Kaufmann's but of her other new dresses (from our store).

But Mrs. Grenoble kept away from the family conference that took place that night in the sitting room. As Sophie remarked, the woman did make an effort not to be intrusive. She did urge *me* to visit her whenever I liked. Though she promised me candy from a box of bonbons she had if I'd help her get settled in her room, I shook my head and ran to my own.

Suddenly I put on my hat and coat, picked up Nancy Myrtle May, and went over to Hugo's house. There I held out my doll to Trixie. "Here, you can have her."

Trixie looked stunned. "But you like her so much."

"I don't like her any more," I said. I crammed Nancy Myrtle May into Trixie's arms and went home.

I never got to Mrs. Grenoble's room. I spent the daytime playing with other children, school being out for Christmas vacation, and in the evening I lingered with the family as long as I was permitted, absorbed with the problems of the wedding, where the minister was to stand, if the menu the caterer had presented for the dinner following the seven-o'clock ceremony was exactly right, whether or not everyone who should be was invited. It had been agreed that guests were to be limited to our family and Leon's and, of course, our Mrs. Grenoble; and then, in spite of all, Grandma asked Mr. Auerbach. She said it was the least she could do in view of the pass he had given her for Christmas.

How unimportant all those discussions, the pros and cons, heated as they were, seem in retrospect. We did not know that, before the wedding day was over, serious trouble was to strike. How innocent were our concerns, dealing as they did with wedding cake and new clothes and flowerpots.

I mention the flowerpots because the day before the wedding Tante Yohanna decided she was dying and, wishing to dispose of her possessions before she went to her grave, sent us a cartload of house plants, ones she had nursed for years, begonias and ferns and geraniums and cacti and agaves and two scraggly palms, all wrapped in newspaper against the cold. She gave them to us, she wrote in a note, because we had a conservatory and she considered us best able to care for them. When they were brought into the house and unwrapped, instead of carrying them through the dining room to the conservatory beyond, Seymour and Slyvester decided to make a background of foliage with them against the fireplace in the parlor, in front of which the wedding ceremony would take place. Then, to everyone's surprise, Tante Yohanna recovered sufficiently to come to the wedding and was quite angry with us for keeping her darlings in the parlor. We explained that they were only there temporarily until the wedding was over. But she was not too happy and, even while the guests were assembling, went about feeling at the roots to see if there was enough moisture and wiping imaginary dust from the leaves with her handkerchief. She kept her eye on her plants all during the ceremony, as though they were the principals in the marriage and not mere decor.

The store closed early that last day of December, and by five-thirty Sophie, Seymour, Sylvester, and the bride were home. They hurried into the house, through the confusion made by the caterers, up to their rooms to dress. They rushed to get ready, calling to one another, "Where did Mama put my studs?" "Do I have to wear a stiff shirt?" "I can't find my camisole. Oh, never mind, here it is!"

Mr. Auerbach came a full hour before the appointed time because he misunderstood Grandma's instructions, and since Sophie was the fastest one to get dressed, she had the job of entertaining him. She protested fiercely, but the man couldn't be left standing in the hall, so she went down to him. Her unwillingness sparked her eyes and complexion. Her blue-green dress of watered silk set off the red of her hair, and the low neckline, with ruching all around it and tiny sprigs of velvet forget-me-nots in the folds, revealed her lovely white shoulders.

Because I regarded the owner of the Auerbach Theatre and four nickelodeons as quite a celebrity, I was torn between listening to what he was saying to Sophie below and watching the bride get dressed. I tried to do both. First I went into Charlotte's room for a little while, and then I raced down to the parlor. Mr. Auerbach and Sophie were deep in a discussion of the difficulties besetting a film exhibitor, and she found the subject so much to her liking that she forgot to be self-conscious. And for a little while I too was intrigued.

He was a dynamic man and he spoke volubly and easily, his lips always on the verge of a smile, his dark eyes flashing. He was saying, "With so many new nickelodeons springing up—there must be nine or ten thousand across the country by now—it gets harder and harder to find enough product. It used to be that the pictures didn't have to be changed more than two or three times a week, but now there's so much competition that the bill has to be different each day. The average nickelodeon seats only about a hundred people, so you have to get people to come back again and again to make any real profit.

"You must love my mother," Sophie said.

"I do, I do!" he exclaimed with a radiant smile.

"You made a terrible mistake to give her a pass."

"I wouldn't want to get rich on Mrs. Weber. There are lots of other people I can rob."

"You need a constant turnover of customers?" Sophie mused. "Is that why the bills are so short, from half an hour to an hour?"

"Yes, and why we keep open from morning until midnight. And it gets harder and harder to get pictures."

"If there's such a demand for the product, why don't the manufacturers make more?"

"My dear girl, they're turning out pictures like sausages. Vitagraph, Biograph, Edison have enlarged their plants, and new companies are jumping up like mad."

"Then your problem will soon be solved."

"Oh, no. The pictures are just getting terrible, because all the companies think about is speed of output. They can sell whatever they make, so why should they worry about better pictures? They only worry about better prices. As time goes on I pay more and more for worse product."

"There must be something you can do."

"Well, *some* exhibitors are doing a little cheating. They pay the exchange a rental with the understanding it's for one theater only, but then they arrange their schedules of screenings so that a boy on a bicycle can race the same print under his arm from one theater to another."

"Honestly, Mr. Auerbach?"

"Dishonestly, Miss Weber."

Sophie laughed, and then he went on to say that the prices the exchanges were asking for first runs were enough to drive the exhibitors to any sort of ruse. However, not wanting to stoop to dishonesty himself, he had decided on another solution: he was going into production himself.

Sophie was impressed. "That's very smart. Then you can supply your own theaters with first runs and make a lot of other sales besides! But wouldn't it take a lot of capital?"

"Well, Miss Weber, I can cite you an actual case. Kalem —you've heard of that company, I'm sure—started three years ago with a cash investment of six hundred dollars. Now they clear five thousand a week."

"It sounds impossible."

"It isn't, I assure you."

"How many pictures do they make?"

"Two a week."

"There's that much profit to be had from only a hundred and four pictures a year?"

"Yes, and not very good ones at that. I, personally, have a whole new idea."

"What's that?"

He gave her one of his most dazzling smiles. "I'm going to make good pictures."

"Oh, Mr. Auerbach, in a minute you'll have me begging to put some money into your company."

"Think twice. I could fail, you know."

"I don't believe you will."

"At the risk of sounding swell-headed, I must tell you I feel rather confident myself. My plan is to spend five hundred dollars or more on each picture, manufacture them right in the heart of the theatrical district in New York, where good actors are available except on matinee days. And I intend to hire only the most experienced and imaginative of directors and cameramen."

"Mr. Auerbach," Sophie said earnestly, "I have two hundred dollars I would like to invest in your company."

He laughed. "Thank you for your confidence, but I warn you it's a risky business."

"I want to take a flier," she said firmly.

What strength there was in her, and what decisiveness! Oh, I thought, how tossed I am between my admiration for Sophie and my hatred! How much I might have loved her if only her path had never crossed my father's. Yet, if it had not, would I be here in this house, which gave me so much happiness in spite of my suspicions of her?

It was too much to make head or tail of, and I was too excited by what was happening to try. The caterers rushed about in the kitchen and set up extra tables in the dining room and hall. The groom arrived, wearing everything new and stiff from his collar to his shoes, and looking scared to death. Seymour lost the roll of the wedding march he was going to play on the player piano and found it again. Ernest got what was nearly a nonstop spell of hiccups and had to be pounded and frightened and made to drink water and have his upper lip pressed against his nose. The minister appeared. Grandma greeted guests, and carnations were passed by Ernest for the gentlemen's lapels. Trixie got her head stuck between the rails of the banister and was extricated by the minister after a terrible fuss.

I was in Charlotte's room when the last touches were put upon her bridal apparel by those experienced matrons Daisy and Ermanie. "Something old, something new, something borrowed, something blue," all had been accounted for, and now only the veil remained to be placed upon her head. It looked terrible at first, too skimpy and too short. Mrs. Grenoble had to be called, and after that resourceful person made her appearance in a wonderful dark blue gown that Ermanie said looked ever so expensive, the veil was taken apart, redraped, and sewn onto a little halo of silk blossoms. And when it was replaced on the bride-to-be she looked not the Charlotte I had known but a mysterious and beautiful stranger.

Grandma came up for an inspection and a kiss, and she too gazed with approval. But when she turned to leave she shook her head and said in wonderment, "I can't get over it! A thousand dollars!"

"A thousand two hundred now, Mama," Charlotte called out. I was glad she got in the last word, especially on her wedding day.

I went downstairs again. Seymour and Sylvester were already at the whisky. Walter was caught sampling the icing on the cake and had to be severely reprimanded. Then, when I was sure all the guests had come, Max Hermansdorfer arrived.

From the flush that appeared on Sophie's face I deduced that she had not known he was invited. Indeed, no one knew he was coming but Grandma, who had asked him without a word to the rest of us. He was made as welcome as though he had been expected, Elise telling him how handsome he looked, and Seymour and Sylvester shaking his hand two or three times over. Grandma took him about, introducing him to Leon's family and to Mrs. Grenoble. He was a great success with them all, especially with the minister, who was a frequent patron of the symphony. In scarcely any time at all he had snatched away from Mr. Auerbach the position of most honored guest.

As if it were not enough that he was so handsome and talked and laughed like an elegant gentleman, he had come in a motor car. Walter saw it from the window, standing there against the curb among the buggies and carriages and the horses stomping in the cold, round iron weights on the ground anchoring them in their places. He inquired of the guests whose machine it was, and, when Max admitted to its ownership, plied him with questions. Then all of us, family and guests alike, had to go outside and look at it. Without putting on coats, though some of the ladies were *décolleté*, we poured onto the porch and out to the sidewalk to see it at close range. It was a Reo, painted bright red, a four-seat runabout. Prompted by questions, Max informed us it had cost six hundred and seventy-five dollars and could move at a speed of twenty-six miles per hour.

It was only the cold and dampness that drove us back into the house; I think some of us would have liked to accept Max's invitation to a spin around the block, wedding or no wedding.

As we were returning I heard Grandma say, "My, my, I didn't know musicians made so much money!"

"Oh, Max has private means," Elise said airily.

"I didn't know."

"He's inherited, I've heard."

"*Ach du Lieber!* And such a good nickelodeon player, too."

Right after Christmas Sophie had ordered electricity put into the house. The gas jets had been closed off and the new wiring put in. Now bulbs hung from the ceiling in every room and gave off such brilliance that one could see into every corner. I gazed about at the guests, hoping to see admiration for the Webers reflected in every eye, but they took the electricity casually. Perhaps, after the Reo, it was an anticlimax—or perhaps other people were used to it and it was only I who thought it such a novelty.

When seven o'clock approached, Seymour went to the player piano. Voices died away the moment the Wedding March began resounding. Leon's family moved to one side of the parlor, and ours to the other. Trixie counted and whispered to me proudly that we outnumbered them. The minister and the groom took their places before the bank of foliage; heads turned expectantly toward the hall for the first view of the bride as she descended the staircase. Hugo waited at the foot of it to present his good arm to her (the other was still in a sling), for it was he who would lead her into the parlor and give her away in marriage.

My heart thumped in excitement and I squeezed Pauline's hand. Then Charlotte was there, her face invisible behind her veil but her hands plainly trembling, and the ritual began.

At first I listened to the words, solemn and beautiful, but my attention waned as I looked into the faces of those gathered here. Would they ever come together again, for a party maybe, or another wedding, Elise's or Sophie's? . . . No, never again. Next time there will be other faces, and some of those here tonight will never come again. Tante Yohanna may die, or Mrs. Grenoble, or even Grandma, who is old too. Mr. Auerbach will be in New York. And who knows where fortune will take the dazzling Max—to San Francisco or Chicago or the capitals of Europe? Oh, let the wedding last a long time, before death and change alter everything!

I suppose it was only natural that a little girl who had lost her memory should have had such thoughts. I had no past, only a present, and I feared the future—with what precise instinct!

For a little while time seemed suspended, and I looked at all the dresses and the faces. Everyone was intent upon the ceremony, all but Mr. Auerbach, who was looking at Sophie. Did he like her, and did I dare hope again that she would marry him and that I'd only imagined there was something between her and my father, that the letters I'd found in the strongbox in Braddock would turn out to be only a bad dream? Had she finally found a man to whom she could talk, one who was as interested as she was in business, one who would not think of her as a cash register?

Was Sophie thinking of Mr. Auerbach? No, she was gazing steadily at the back of Max Hermansdorfer's head. Once, when he turned and caught her, she averted her eyes quickly. Did she prefer Max to Mr. Auerbach? I recalled the kiss he had given her, and though I had seen no significance in it at the time, was it possible it had meant something to her? Had she been hurt when he'd walked out and stayed away so long? Oh, Sophie, what goes on in your head? Why can I never understand you? Is it because everything you do is a mystery and an enigma to me that I am so furious with you?

Unexpectedly the light went out and the room was plunged into darkness. The minister stopped in the middle of a sentence, and for a few moments there was silence as well as blackness. Then a babble of voices filled the room. The whole house was dark, whether from a city power failure or a fault in our own electric system we did not know at first. Seymour and Sylvester went to look for candles, feeling their way about, groping blindly, because the old gas jets were now useless.

Later we learned that the electric lights, left on in nearly every room in the house, had put too much strain upon our power allotment.

It was eerie standing there in the darkness, the ceremony interrupted, and Tante Yohanna said, "I'm afraid this is a bad omen, a curse on the marriage."

At this Grandma, who had fought the union from the beginning, did an about-face and became so angry at Tante Yohanna that she made the poor woman cower. "What nerve to say such a thing! *You* had a curse on your marriage, and it wasn't just the lights going out! I won't say what it was in front of the company, but don't you open your mouth again. My Charlotte will have a lovely marriage! Blessed, not cursed! Do you understand, Yohanna? Blessed!" Grandma had no tolerance for superstition, but neither did she put her faith in electricity. "With gas a thing like this would never have happened, but you had no right to say anything anyhow!"

Sophie had to interfere and calm her down before she could follow through her threat to eject Tante Yohanna's plants from the house on the instant.

With peace restored, Seymour and Sylvester returned, and the rest of the ceremony was conducted by candlelight. The "I do"s were said at last, then the final pronouncement, then everyone seemed to be kissing everyone else, and the champagne was poured. Max kissed the bride, then Elise and Grandma, but he did not go near Sophie.

I thought the wedding wonderful and that the lights' going out had given it an added sensation. By the time we went in to dinner Seymour had fumbled with fuses in the cellar until the electric bulbs illuminated suddenly, making everyone blink from the glare. There were "Ah"s and cheers, and a few of the men applauded gaily. The food provided by the caterers seemed deliciously different and exciting. There was squab and, for dessert, baked Alaska. I wondered if any other wedding was ever so luxurious. I was seated with the other children at a table in the hall but had only to turn my body slightly to see into the dining room. What chatter and laughter issued from it, and how sentimental or funny or verbose were the toasts to the bride and groom!

I hoped for more and more toasts, for the company to stay seated, for the departure of the married couple to be postponed indefinitely. We're still here, I thought, all of us, including Charlotte. While we remain the family is still a unit and no harm can come to any of us.

I did not know that, because of a hand which at that very moment was touching the front door, everything was going to change.

Walter heard the knock and rose. I saw him stand talking to someone through the half-opened door. It seemed a long time before he let a stranger into the hall and went to whisper something in Sophie's ear. Looking puzzled, she stood up and followed him out of the dining room.

The man at the door was young—perhaps twenty-five —with sandy hair and a clean-shaven but extremely freckled face. I couldn't imagine what he wanted with Sophie at such an hour. His manner was informal but polite, and I liked the sound of his soft, faintly burred voice.

"Miss Weber?" he asked.

"Yes."

"I'm Mr. Marcy of the New York police." I thought that odd because he wore no uniform. However, he took from his pocket some credentials which he showed to Sophie, who nodded after she had examined them and handed them back to him.

"Forgive me for coming at this time. I see you're having a party."

"A wedding."

"I'm in town because I brought in a prisoner for extradition this morning. I intended to see you this afternoon, but I got involved with some red tape on his case. You know how it is."

"Yes?"

"Well, this is nothing official. But before leaving New York I was asked to drop in on you while I was here."

"Oh?"

"Just to see how everything was going, especially with the little girl." He looked at the children. "Which is the one?"

"I am," I said.

"How do you feel?" he asked me.

"Fine," I said.

He turned to Sophie. "Miss Weber, I realize I've come at a very inconvenient time, but I would like to talk to you a little while and I'm catching a train out early in the morning. How long is all this"—he waved his hand toward the dining room—"going to go on?"

"I don't know exactly."

"Well, would it be possible for you to give me a little time later on? I'll wait if you want me to, because I hate taking you away from the middle of things."

"I understand. Have there been any new developments in the case?"

"Not much, but I have a few questions I'd like to ask."

"Would you like to wait here in the hall?"

"Is there some other place? This is rather central."

"There's an upstairs sitting room."

"Good."

Sophie asked me to take him upstairs. I saw him up and showed him a pile of magazines with which to amuse himself while he waited. He rejected the *Collier's* on top and chose a copy of *St. Nicholas Magazine* which Sylvester had bought for me. We talked a few minutes of *St. Nicholas's* wonderful illustrations and stories and poems. He told me it had been his favorite periodical when he was a boy, and I left him sitting on the sofa and chuckling over a page of Brownies. I thought he was a very nice man.

When I came back to the wedding Charlotte was just leaving the dining room to go upstairs to change into her traveling suit. She was not going to travel until the next day, because she was going to spend the night at a downtown hotel, but of course it was unthinkable to leave the house in her wedding gown.

While she changed, the people swarmed back to the parlor and music room, but eventually there came word that she was going to throw her bouquet, and everyone went into the hall. Charlotte stood at the top of the stairs, a traveling case in one hand, her bouquet in the other. Some of the women began to yell, and one of the groom's sisters kept screaming, "Me, me!" I wondered why, so Pauline told me that the maiden who caught the bouquet was the next to be married, and I held out my hands at once.

"Me, me!" I yelled too. Charlotte raised her arm and tossed, and the flowers flew as though they were on a wire straight to Sophie. She had not even tried to catch them, so they struck her on the shoulder and fell at her feet. She had to lean over to pick them up.

I heard Trixie say above the noise, "It's Sophie. Oh, goody!" and Pauline pinched Grandma's arm and asked, "Isn't that nice, Grandma?"

But my heart thumped. Whom was Sophie going to marry? My father? I looked at Mr. Auerbach, and he was smiling so broadly that I was able to hope it would be he. Oh, let her put money into his motion-picture company, I wished, and let it bring them together so that he will ask her to marry him!

There was more kissing, then a hundred adieux before Charlotte and Leon were gone. Hugo gathered his children to take them home, but told Daisy to stay on a while, as she was having such a good time, and he would come back for her. A few of the guests left, but most of Leon's family remained to drink the last drops of the wine of festivity.

"Who was that man in the hall before?" I heard Grandma ask Sophie.

"Just someone from New York."

Grandma gasped. "From New York! And I never believed in bouquets before!"

"Bouquets?"

"It's your beau from New York—so fast!"

Sophie glared at her mother. "Mama, he's a policeman."

"I thought a traveling man. Still—a policeman—he could be Commissioner some day."

"Mama, he's here on business, about the case!"

Grandma sighed, and I said, "Maybe the bouquet meant Mr. Auerbach. Or Mr. Hermansdorfer."

Sophie kissed me on the top of the head and said, "That's enough out of you too! Go to bed!"

Grandma was right about one thing, as I was to learn much later. Mr. Marcy, an asset to the force, and a graduate of New York University, did become Commissioner.

Sophie went upstairs with me, and I saw her slip into the sitting room to talk to him. I went into my room, but left the door open and undressed in the cupboard so no one could see me.

Pretty soon Grandma and some other people came upstairs and went into the sitting room, and just as I got into bed I heard Sophie enter her bedroom with Mr. Marcy. "I don't know where else we can be alone," she was saying, "with the house so full of people still."

"That's all right, Miss Weber. Let's get to the questions and I'll be on my way."

"Wait a minute," she said and closed the door between her room and mine.

I was angry, not only because I would have liked to hear what they were saying to each other, but because Sophie had deliberately shut me out. For ten minutes or so their voices rose and fell, but not a word was intelligible to me. I lay in my bed, not consciously apprehensive, but nervous enough to itch until I had to scratch my arms and my legs too. I tried to concentrate only on the wedding, on the funny things that had happened—the lights going out, Walter gouging a piece of icing out of the cake, Grandma's threat to put Tante Yohanna's plants out of the house though not Tante Yohanna herself, my own desire to catch the bouquet, all of us going outside to look at the red Reo.

I succeeded so well that I was startled when Sophie opened my door suddenly. "See for yourself," she said to Mr. Marcy, and then she told me to get up, put on my kimono, and come into her room.

I did so as quickly as possible. Mr. Marcy smiled at me and to put me at my ease told me how much he had enjoyed the *St. Nicholas.* Then he said to me gently, "Jane, has anything come back to you, anything at all, about your father or your mother or anything that happened?"

"No, sir."

"You can't remember any more than you did in New York at the hearings?"

"I don't even remember the hearings," I said.

"All's blank," Sophie said, "until she came here. How many times must we go over the same thing, Mr. Marcy? Don't they tell you what I say to them when I'm in New York? Don't you get the report of the policeman here?"

"Yes. I'm sorry. And do you like it here, Jane?"

"Oh, I do!"

"It's nice that you're so happy. Miss Weber here must be an excellent foster mother."

"Yes, sir," I said.

"You must love her very much."

I said, looking away, "Yes."

The policeman turned to Sophie. "Well, Miss Weber, I guess that's all there is to it. Though we were certainly hoping that after this passage of time the little girl would begin recalling. The doctor said she would, sooner or later."

"That was his opinion," Sophie said. "Though he also said there were instances where the memory never came back."

They went on talking. I turned my back on them and idly began to play with the familiar objects on Sophie's bureau, the shoe-horn, the shoe-buttoner, the hair receiver, the pincushion, the pomade jar, the hairpin tray. I laid out a little design on the marble top with her curlicue bone hairpins.

Mr. Marcy, emboldened by my apparent inattention, permitted himself to say in my presence, "What I'll never understand is how the paterfamilias could have disappeared so completely—vanished from the face of the earth, it seems as though. If we could only catch him."

"You're so sure he's the culprit?"

"You saw him running down the hall yourself."

"Mr. Marcy," Sophie said testily, "I never said it was Mr. Carlyle! And if it was, I couldn't have identified him because I never met the man!"

"Who else could it have been?"

"It could have been anyone, a lunatic, a drunk, a thief who broke into the room, anyone!"

"We get right back to the main issue: if it was somebody else, why would Mr. Carlyle have run off?"

"He might have reasons and be perfectly innocent."

"Then you'd think he'd communicate with somebody if he had any regard at all for . . ." In the mirror I saw the gesture with which he finished his sentence. He nodded toward me. "You'd think he'd wonder where she was."

"I believe the newspapers mentioned I was taking her. He could have seen them."

"Wouldn't he worry about what kind of a person you were?"

"Why should he?"

"You've never heard from him, Miss Weber?"

"Of course not," Sophie said.

She's lying again, I told myself, numb with misery. She's lying, and I'm not going to think about it. I'm not going to think about it at all, but instead I'm going to play with her hatpins. If I take them out of the holder, one by one, I can arrange them in my hand to look like flowers in a bouquet, a bridal bouquet.

"Well," Mr. Marcy said, "I'm sorry I had to disturb you on an occasion like this, and thank you very much for your courtesy."

"That's perfectly all right."

"Sophie," I said, "didn't there used to be a butterfly hatpin?"

Mr. Marcy, who had started toward the door, turned around quickly.

"What, Jane?" Sophie asked, trying to concentrate on me. "Why, yes. I did have a butterfly hatpin once, but I lost it."

"Where did you lose it, Miss Weber?" the policeman asked casually.

"I don't know. Oh, yes, I do. In New York."

"Before or after the murder?" Mr. Marcy asked.

"I really can't remember, but what difference does it make?"

"Oh, it just might be interesting to know when."

"Well, it was on that trip I lost it."

"Then how would Jane remember it? Didn't you say everything was a blank till she came here?"

"That's true." Sophie bent toward me and took my hand. "Why, Jane, dear, your memory's coming back."

I shook my head.

"It must be. You could only have seen the butterfly hatpin in New York that time, because I never brought it back with me."

"What was it like, Miss Weber?" the policeman asked.

"Just a long hatpin, eight inches or so, with a head shaped like a butterfly—of colored enamel."

"Blue and purple?"

"Yes." Sophie's eyes were lowered, but now the lashes suddenly flew up as she stared straight at Mr. Marcy. "How would you know?"

He sighed deeply, as if he regretted the revelation he was about to make. Or perhaps I misread his thought because I liked him, and the sigh was of relief, a policeman's satisfaction in a glimmer of light shining into a dark cave of mystification.

"Miss Weber, that hatpin was found a few weeks ago, when the hotel decided to repaint, in the room occupied by the Carlyles."

"Where Jane . . . ?"

"Shall we call it 'the scene of the crime'? It had been thrown into the grille of a hot-air register and naturally wasn't found until the grilles were removed. It was several days before we realized its significance."

"And what is its significance?"

"A very serious one. Since the hatpin is yours, I fear you're our prime suspect as of this minute."

"I'm what!"

"Do I have to say it in front of the little girl? Should she—"

"No, let her stay. She's heard this much, and she'll only

worry." Her voice rose. "Speak out, Mr. Marcy, for heaven's sake! Why am I the prime suspect?"

"Because the hatpin was the murder weapon, Miss Weber."

In spite of my previous suspicions, the accusation against Sophie was no sooner voiced than I rejected it. She stood at my side, too astonished to speak, staring at the policeman while laughter came to us from the upstairs sitting room, while music drifted up to us from below, where Max was playing the piano.

Suddenly she seemed almost unbearably beautiful to me. Her red hair, always so striking, looked brighter than ever above the blue-green of her gown. A little tendril had escaped from her coiffure and curled disarmingly at the nape of her neck. On her shoulders, usually held so regally, I noticed for the first time the tiny freckles sprinkled on the white of her skin. They were such little-girl freckles.

Tears filled my eyes, and the love I'd first felt for her came flooding back, unsullied by jealousy or resentment. Oh, Sophie, I thought, what have I done to you? Why did I mention that miserable hatpin? Since I've forgotten everything else, seemingly forever, why couldn't the hatpin have remained forgotten too? Oh, Sophie, forgive me, forgive me!

What was said after that is a hazy dream. In my consternation I knew only that Sophie must not cope with Mr. Marcy alone. I heard Mr. Auerbach's voice booming out as he came up the stairs, "Where is she? Oh, Miss Weber! We're going to dance!"

I ran out of the room and was just about to appeal to him when I heard the front door close. It was Hugo, returning to get Daisy after having taken the children home to bed. Hugo was strong too, I thought, and he was a member of the family. Ignoring Mr. Auerbach, I leaned over the balcony rail and called down, "Hugo, help! Sophie needs you!"

My voice must have alarmed everyone who heard it. A minute later I was back in Sophie's bedroom with all the people who had come running when I had called—Hugo and Mr. Auerbach and those who'd been in the sitting room, Grandma and some of Leon's relatives. I was conscious of Mrs. Grenoble in the hall, hanging back, afraid to enter. Then there was a great deal of talk, but it was too fast, too confused, too repetitious to follow. Mr. Marcy seemed to be explaining and explaining, trying to answer all the excited questions uttered at once, one overlapping the other. When I looked in the hall again, Mrs. Grenoble had discreetly disappeared.

It was the word "murder," spoken by Mr. Marcy, and the sight of Grandma hitting him on the arm that shook away my cobwebs.

"Don't you dare say a thing like that about my daughter!" she cried.

"I'm not making any accusations, Mrs. Weber," said Mr. Marcy, retreating from her, "I'm only saying that the hatpin—"

"Don't you dare! I'll hit you!"

"You already have."

"I'll hit you again!"

I was right about Hugo. He was a tower of strength. He gently pulled tiny Grandma away from the policeman and held her hands securely in his while he tried to bring reason back to the discussion. His voice was low and calm. "Granted the hatpin is my sister's, how does it incriminate her? Couldn't someone else have found it wherever she lost it—in the hall, maybe—and taken it into the hotel room with him and used it there?"

"Of course, that's a possibility," Mr. Marcy said. "That's why I tell you I'm making no charges. Actually," he said, "when the hatpin was found, the department assumed it belonged to Mrs. Carlyle and that the man Miss Weber said she saw running away had picked it up from the bureau in a sudden homicidal rage. But even at that time the theory was worrisome to us. We felt funny about it. A hatpin just isn't a man's weapon."

In the momentary silence that followed I became aware of the fact that the music had stopped some time ago, and that the people from downstairs, one after another, drawn by the instinct of trouble seeping through the house, had come into the bedroom. My heart thumped. Max Hermansdorfer's eyes were on Sophie, and his brow furrowed with worry as he tried to understand what was happening. The glare of the electric light overhead shone on his glistening, rich brown hair and touched up the contours of his splendid mustache. The room seemed to me packed when the word "murder," was repeated by someone, and Sophie cried out, "But why would I have done such a thing? For what reason?"

Max's shocked face turned toward Mr. Marcy, who said uncomfortably, now that everyone was hanging on his words, "Perhaps to get the child."

"That's an insane thing to say!" Sophie gasped.

"You have her, don't you?" Mr. Marcy asked.

The faces were grave and grown up, and then there was a hubbub. I saw Max move forward and slip his arm around Sophie's waist protectively. He said something to her, I don't know what, but I caught the grateful glance she gave him. There was so much noise I couldn't even hear what Grandma was screaming at Mr. Marcy. Was it "My daughter is an angel, a saint"?

In the confusion I was forgotten and stood silently in the corner to which I had retreated. It was Sophie who suddenly called out, "Jane! Where's Jane?"

"Here I am," I said, emerging.

"I didn't know where you got to. Elise, take her out of here, will you?"

Elise reached for my hand. "I'm coming with you," Mr. Marcy said. He went into my room with us and kept every-

one else out but Sophie and Hugo. He turned to me when
he had closed the door. "Jane, listen to me. You remembered the hatpin. Doesn't anything else come back to you?"

"No," I murmured, conscious of the eyes upon me. I
started to cry.

"Try to think, Jane. When it happened, was there a man
in the room?"

I shook my head mutely, my throat too choked to speak.

"There wasn't a man in the room?" Mr. Marcy asked
gently. "A woman, then?"

"I mean I don't remember who was there," I managed
to say.

"Think back. Try."

"The child just doesn't remember!" Hugo exclaimed.
"Can't you understand that?"

Sophie put her hand on Mr. Marcy's arm, pleading.
"Please don't put this pressure on her. Leave her alone."

"As you say, Miss Weber. Still, she could clear you if
she wanted to."

"Were able to," Hugo amended it, "which is a different
thing."

"I don't even want Jane thinking along these lines,"
Sophie cried. "What do you want her to do," she asked of
Mr. Marcy, "make up some story out of whole cloth to
protect me?"

"Certainly not," Mr. Marcy said.

"In a minute she's not going to have any other choice."

"I merely asked a question."

"What right have you got," Hugo demanded of the
policeman, "to make her commit herself under stress like
this? She's said she's forgotten. Can't you let it go at that?"

Sophie said, "Elise, put her to bed."

Elise nodded, and the others went out. She tucked me
into bed without saying anything funny or satiric. If Elise
is this grim, I thought, my last hope for Sophie is gone.

She kissed me good night. Outside my door Mrs. Grenoble waylaid her. "Miss Weber, forgive me, but what on earth is going on?"

Elise told her as sketchily as she could.

"Oh, heavens, how terrible! But I don't understand. After all this time, you'd think . . . Well, why doesn't the little girl just tell them who did it?"

"Because she still can't remember."

"But I thought I heard them say she just recalled something."

"No," Elise said testily, "her mind is a closed book."

"Oh, how sad. I never heard of such a thing!"

"It happens every day," Elise said, and, noticing my door was open a crack, shut it firmly.

I don't know how long it was before the house settled into silence. Hours seemed to go by, while sporadic conversations broke out here and there, feet shuffled up and down the stairs, doors opened and closed. A clock struck somewhere, and there were exclamations—"Twelve o'clock! Happy New Year!"—but there was not much joy in them. The year 1909 was greeted at the Webers' without enthusiasm.

At last all was still. I tossed in my bed as sleep continued to elude me. I played an imaginary game of jacks in which I beat the invincible Pauline, going all the way, in one turn, from onesies through allsies. Suddenly I heard Hugo in the hall.

"Mrs. Grenoble! What are you doing here?"

"Oh, Mr. Weber, you frightened me! I didn't know you were in the house."

"I'm staying the night."

"Oh, I just wanted to see if the little girl was all right."

"Why shouldn't she be?"

"She told me she had a headache, and I was afraid all this excitement had made it worse."

Why, I had never told her I had a headache. It was a lie!

"I was going to get her something for it if she needed it.

If this is forward of me I'm sorry, but I do love children so, and I couldn't help thinking of her. Well, I suppose she's sound asleep, so I'll say good night to you, Mr. Weber."

"Good night."

Hugo opened my door gingerly and stuck his head into my room.

"Hello, Hugo," I said.

"So you're awake. Well, young lady, I want you to forget all your troubles and go to sleep. Tomorrow is another day, another year, in fact, and everything's going to be all right."

"Do you think so, Hugo?" I asked wistfully.

"Yes, I do. And, Jane . . ."

"Yes?"

"I'm going to lock your door and take the key away. When you get up in the morning, go out through Sophie's room."

"Why are you locking my door?"

"Because I'm crazy," Hugo said.

As he turned the key and withdrew it, he addressed someone else in the hall. "You still wandering around too?"

"*Ach*, I can't sleep. Such goings-on!"

"Mama," Hugo said, "I want you to get that woman out of here."

"What woman?" Grandma asked.

"Mrs. Grenoble."

"*Warum?*"

"Because we don't want a stranger in the house with all this happening, that's why!"

"You call a lady who was so much help with the wedding a stranger?"

"Yes, I do, Mama."

"We'll see."

"Out she goes tomorrow, Mama."

"On New Year's?"

"I don't care if it's her birthday!"

How odd it was that he had said that. For January first was *my* birthday. As sleep began to overtake me I thought: I'm not ten years old any more. I'm eleven. It's so late that today is tomorrow already.

8

New Year's Day

LONG AGO, when I had first come to Wilkins Avenue, I asked Sophie one day, "When is my birthday?"

"Oh, my darling, can you believe it? I don't know! I never thought to ask."

"Pauline's is in May. Trixie's is in December."

"I'll write a letter to ask your grandmother this very minute. I'm so sorry, Jane. How dreadful not to know when your own birthday is! I'm ashamed of myself for not inquiring."

"I hope it's soon," I said. "I want to hurry up and be eleven."

But when the reply came from my grandmother, I was told I was not to be eleven until January. I would have been disappointed but for the excitement of learning I had been born on January first, the very first day of the new year. Pauline was impressed and said, "Nobody I ever knew in my whole life had that for a birthday," and Trixie remarked, "You start out January with your birthday, then in February come Lincoln's and Washington's, and all of you are very famous."

I was flattered to be linked with such men until I found out Trixie thought me famous because my mother had been murdered and my name had been in the New York papers.

In spite of all that had happened on New Year's Eve, the family did not forget my birthday, and a stack of presents was on the dining-room table when I came down to breakfast the next morning. I had slept until ten o'clock because I'd gone to bed so late. Everyone else had already eaten, and the house echoed with the work that was being done to clean it up after the wedding—the chairs put back in their accustomed places, the silver restored to the sideboard, the china returned to the shelves, Tante Yohanna's plants moved to the conservatory, napkins and tablecloths set to soak for the washwoman when she came, stains removed from the carpets, water changed in the flower vases. Only Grandma was inactive. For once she sat with idle hands, unable to stir herself for the day's tasks. I asked Elise, "Is she sick?"

Elise shook her head. "No, she's worried. I don't know if she's afraid Sophie might be arrested or if she's just dreading telling Mrs. Grenoble to leave."

"Oh, Elise, is Sophie going to go to prison?"

"Not unless Mr. Marcy has bats in his belfry."

"If she does go, it's my fault."

"No, it isn't. Open your presents."

But I couldn't be consoled that easily. "I was the one who remembered the hatpin," I said.

"You couldn't help it. Now stop worrying—Mama's doing it for all of us."

When I went to the kitchen it was apparent Grandma had told our boarder nothing so far, for Mrs. Grenoble was cheerfully cleaning the stove, which she claimed had been left in a state by the caterers. She was, it seemed to me, the only cheerful person in the house that morning. She radiated good humor as she put away the blackening, fitted the stove lids back into their round holes, then rolled down her long sleeves, satisfied with a job well done. It was she who made my breakfast, brought it into the dining room, and tried to draw me into a conversation—but I felt tired and glum and would not talk. I could not eat, either, except for a gulp of milk and half a piece of bread. I left the rest untouched, and when I began to open my presents she stood at my side, exclaiming, "Oh, how lovely!" and "My, isn't that nice! You must be so pleased." But I was too unhappy to take any joy in being a birthday girl and looked sadly at my gifts and read the little cards that came with them.

Hugo came down the hall and, seeing me with Mrs. Grenoble, called to me to come upstairs with him.

"What will I do with my presents?" I asked.

He said we'd take them up to my room. He came into the dining room, nodded curtly to Mrs. Grenoble, and helped me gather my packages together.

"Thanks for yours and Daisy's," I told him, "and for Pauline's and Walter's and Ernest's and Trixie's."

"You're welcome. I went home a while ago to see how everybody was, and they all said to tell you 'Happy Birthday.'"

We went upstairs, but I hesitated outside my door. "It's still locked," I said. "I came out through Sophie's room."

He took the key out of his pocket and opened the door for me. We were putting my gifts on my bed when I asked, "Why did you spend the night here, Hugo?"

"Oh, I just thought I would. No reason."

I wanted to know what he was afraid of and why he had felt it necessary to lock me in my room, but before I got up the nerve to press him into answering he was gone. A few minutes later I went into the sitting room, where he was talking to Grandma.

"Do it right now, Mama," he was saying to her, "or I'm going to do it myself."

"I will pretty soon."

"Not pretty soon. Now!"

The opportunity to do what Hugo wanted her to presented itself immediately, for Mrs. Grenoble had just come upstairs and appeared in the doorway. "Now," Hugo whispered.

Grandma rose. "Mrs. Grenoble—" she began.

But she was spared the completion of her sentence, for the lady came forward and, taking Grandma's hands in her own, spoke warmly and rapidly. "Mrs. Weber, you've been so wonderful to me. And I like it here enormously. Were it not for what occurred last night, I would stay on forever and you would probably never be rid of me. But I know all of you are deeply troubled, and I feel I should not be here at this time."

Grandma clucked her tongue and, of course, said the unexpected. "You're more than welcome, and you just stay!"

"No, I'm only in the way. You have your problems, and an outsider doesn't belong in the midst of them. I'm going to pack and, with the best wishes in the world, take my departure."

"Not today!" Grandma exclaimed. Hugo glared at her, but she did not care. "It's New Year's! Where would you go?"

"There are always hotels."

"I won't let you," Grandma stated. "I won't let you spend hotel money."

"Oh, dear Mrs. Weber, it will only be until tomorrow, when I'm sure I can find other lodging."

"You stay right here till tomorrow. A hotel! They'll rob you!"

Mrs. Grenoble smiled. "While I'm not wealthy, it's true, I can still afford a night in a hotel."

Hugo nudged Grandma, but she ignored him. "I don't want to hear another word," she declared.

"Truly, I feel uncomfortable, knowing what has occurred."

"You don't want to be in a place the police came?"

"Oh, no, you misunderstand me! You don't believe for a minute I think any member of this household is guilty of anything, do you? No, I'm not concerned for myself, but for you. My presence at this time—"

"You'll stay till tomorrow," Grandma said flatly.

"But, dear Mrs. Weber—"

"Tomorrow! I won't let you be turned out in the cold on New Year's."

So that's the way it remained. Hugo threw up his hands and left the room. I followed him, but Grandma's expression, "turned out in the cold," stayed in my head, making me smile for the first time since I had awakened. For there was no cold to turn Mrs. Grenoble out into this New Year's Day. Ever since I had got out of bed and gone to close my window I had been conscious of a great thaw. Melted snow ran from the roof. Icicles dripped at the eaves and went crashing to the ground. Rainpipes and gutters gurgled. Water ran down telegraph poles, the trunks of trees, the sides of houses. Banks of snow had dwindled to patches on the grass, and the patches were turning to puddles. The outside air was warm, almost balmy, as on a spring day. Later, when visitors came, their shoes were damp, and the door mat on the front porch had to be used vigorously.

I don't know if there were always so many callers at the Webers' on New Year's Day, but on this one people came and went from noon onward. The house was in order by then, but Sophie and the others scarcely had time to wash their faces and put on fresh clothes before Daisy and the children arrived. Then the rush really began. The news of the policeman's visit had been spread by those who had stayed after the wedding. Though I kept out of the parlor, I heard repeated references to "the little girl," and it was hard to be lighthearted with Hugo's children when I was being whispered about. The very guests who started with "A Happy New Year to all of you!" and "Congratulations on the marriage!" were soon commiserating with the family

and giving advice and making Grandma tell over and over
what she knew of the murder, for Sophie refused to speak
of it.

In the afternoon Mr. Marcy came again, and Sophie went
up to the sitting room and had a long talk with him behind
closed doors. She came down looking grimmer than before,
and when he went there were new outbursts of questions and sympathetic protestations from the company. As
quickly as she could, Sophie left the parlor. Grandma ran
out after her and caught her at the foot of the stairs.

"What happened, Sophie? I thought that policeman was
going back to New York today."

"He was told to stay," Sophie replied vexatiously.

"Who told him?"

"He talked to New York, and those were his orders."

"How could he talk to New York? Crazy!"

"On the telephone, Mama. Long distance."

"All the way to New York on the telephone?"

"Yes, Mama."

"That's very good," Grandma said admiringly (whether
of Mr. Marcy or Alexander Graham Bell, I did not know),
before returning to the subject. "What did he want with
you?"

"Just to talk to me."

"What did he say?"

"Nothing."

"Now, Sophie!"

"Nothing, Mama! Nothing, nothing, nothing!" Her voice
broke on the last word. Anxiously Grandma and I watched
her as she turned away. Her foot was on the first step when
the rarely used knocker on the front door sounded out
loudly. Attuned as we all were to new dangers, we froze
where we were, unable to move.

It was Seymour who opened the door and took a telegram from the messenger who had brought it. He gave
the boy a dime from his pocket, closed the door, and came

to Sophie with the envelope. We watched her tear it open
and saw her fair skin grow even whiter when she had read
it. She raised her eyes from the paper at last, but she did
not look at us. Holding the telegram against her bosom, her
fingers widespread across it, she stared into space.

"Who's it from?" Seymour asked. "What does it say?"

It took her so long to answer that I thought she never
would. When she returned from the distant world to which
she'd flown, she spoke so quietly I could hardly hear the
words. "Seymour, I have to go some place at ten o'clock
tonight. Until then I want to stay in my room. Say 'Excuse
me' to the company, and please tell everyone to leave me
alone."

Then she fled up the stairs, and though Seymour followed her part way up, crying, "What's in the telegram?
Where do you have to go? What's the matter with you,
Sophie?" there was no answer, and when the door to her
room slammed he came down again, shaking his head.

"*Donner und Blitzen!*" he swore, passing me on the way
back to the parlor. "Why does she have to keep everything
to herself?"

Yes, why? Seymour was right. All along she had kept
things to herself. Until my playmate had cried out to me,
"Your father murdered your mother!" she had told me
nothing, and even then how much of the truth had she
concealed? Not once had she mentioned the letters from
my father, not to the family, not to me, not even to the
police, who were still making every effort to find him. And
now she would not say what was in the telegram and would
not answer Seymour's spoken questions or my tacit ones.
If I knew what she was hiding, or what reason she had to
hide it, I would know how to fight for her. But how could
I when I was so uninformed?

During the night I had had a wonderful reverie in which
I went to the police department, found Mr. Marcy, and
told him Sophie was innocent and that he must drop his

suspicions of her. I stood before his desk and spoke so eloquently that he cringed and cried out, "We would not dream of arresting her, Miss Carlyle, after what you have told us!"

But now, blinded by ignorance and perplexity, how could I deal with him? If I did not know her purposes, the dream could never become a reality.

If only I could remember what happened in New York I could still be her savior. If I could just picture the hotel room, my mother's face, myself standing on the bed in my nightgown, the man with the hatpin, anything! But try as I might, my mind's eye revealed nothing. I remained what I was, a helpless little girl standing in the hall of a house in Pittsburgh, and New York was lost in obscurity.

Sophie stayed in her room all the afternoon and would not come out for supper. When Grandma went up to argue with her, she found the door locked.

It was not until Max came, around eight o'clock, that she emerged, and then it was only because he wrote funny little notes and slipped them under her door that she was coaxed into making an appearance. "We are going to play the piano and make merry," he had written on one he showed me, "but we could not be merry without you." Another said, "It's New Year's Day. Time for fun and frolic. Please fun and frolic with us."

The door was unlocked, and when she came out of her room she was smiling. "Oh, Max, you're irresistible," she said.

"Then you must never try to resist me, because your struggles will be in vain. So take my arm and come downstairs."

"Well, for a while. I have to go some place at ten."

"Repeat that sentence, please. 'I have to go some place at ten *if Max Hermansdorfer gives his permission.*'"

Sophie laughed and repeated it.

Max changed the atmosphere of the house. He started

to play the piano, and each of us, pretending to the others we were not thinking of Mr. Marcy, crowded into the music room to listen.

Presently the rug was taken up in the parlor and some of the younger people began to dance. Grandma sent to the third floor for Mrs. Grenoble, who had kept away from the guests all day, to come and join the party. Grandma said she couldn't bear the thought of her alone in her room, missing such wonderful music.

She came down while Sophie was dancing with Mr. Auerbach. He had talked Sophie into trying, and after she got over her first awkwardness she began to enjoy it, and her skill improved with every passing minute. Sophie wanted to stop and introduce our boarder to those she had not met at the wedding, but Mrs. Grenoble said, "No, no, go on dancing. I just want to sit quietly and watch."

The guests drifted back and forth from the dining room, where coffee and cake had been set out, or helped themselves to wine and beer, while others stood around the piano, singing the words of "Come and Float Me, Freddie Dear" and "Message of the Violet." Grandma called for our favorite nickelodeon music, and when Max finished we applauded as loud as we could.

After that most of the older guests went home, and the other people showed off. Elise sang solo, out of key but rolling her eyes enchantingly, "I Just Can't Make My Eyes Behave." Mr. Auerbach said in some ways she was better than Anna Held. Seymour and Sylvester did a little dance to a hornpipe tune. Daisy whistled an entire song. Every time she caught her breath the bust ruffles under the bodice of her dress heaved up and down like an ocean wave. She was wonderful, trilling up and down the scale like a bird.

"My, my," Grandma said, "and I never even knew she could purse her lips."

Then Mr. Auerbach, who had a deep but surprisingly

good voice, sang the beautiful "Love Comes like a Summer Night." He looked at Sophie through the whole chorus steadily, but she did not lower her eyes as she might have done once. She gazed back at him confidently, a trace of a smile on her lips. She was enjoying herself. She knew both Mr. Auerbach and Max liked her, and she no longer acted like a woman who couldn't talk to men except about business. She talked about everything, unselfconsciously and with pleasure.

Why, with all that was hanging over waiting to engulf her, did she enter so willingly into the fun? Why was her color so high and why did she seem so excited? Hugo must have wondered too, for he took her aside and I heard him say, "You're having a good time, Sophie."

"Oh, yes!"

"What were you so upset about before? Why did you lock yourself in your room?"

Sophie sighed. "I'll tell you, and then I don't want you to mention it again. Mr. Marcy informed me this afternoon I'm restricted to Pittsburgh and Braddock for my activities until further word from New York. In other words, as I interpret it, I'm under surveillance."

"The fools *can't* be taking you that seriously!" Hugo gasped.

"Evidently the fools can. But I'm not going to let it concern me tonight." She reached out and looked at Hugo's watch, which hung from a chain over his vest. "Not until ten o'clock, anyhow, and I have over an hour."

Then she went into the parlor and was soon talking animatedly to Mr. Auerbach as though she intended to extract every bit of gaiety from each moment left to her. Where was she going at ten o'clock? She was confounding us all. She did whatever she made up her mind to do, and we were left on the fringe of her will, wondering always at her motives.

Hugo's eyes remained anxiously upon her, but I, a child, was easily distracted. I was soon drawn back to the music and laughter.

Sylvester and a girl danced a polka. Then, when someone cried, "Who next?" my eye was caught by Mrs. Grenoble leaning over to retrieve a handkerchief she had dropped, and I said to her, "Sing 'My Sweetheart's the Man in the Moon.'" She raised her head, and when her eyes met mine I observed them to have a peculiarly glazed appearance. She shrank back into her chair, and I requested the song again.

"I don't know it," I heard her say in a low, frightened tone over the sound of a Victor Herbert tune Max had begun.

"Yes, you do! You know it!" I screamed the words at Mrs. Grenoble. "'My sweetheart's the man in the moon, I'm going to marry him soon, 'Twould fill me with bliss, Just to give him one kiss, But I know that—'"

Mrs. Grenoble was shaking her head so violently that Elise, who stood next to me, gripped my arm, saying, "Stop it, Jane! She says she doesn't know it."

"Yes, she does! She does!" My voice, shrill and hysterical, carried to the music room, and Max broke off his playing abruptly.

In the ensuing silence, which seemed enormous, Sophie asked, alarmed, "What's the matter with you, Jane?"

Though I was aware everyone was listening to me, I cried out, "She says she doesn't know 'My Sweetheart's the Man in the Moon,' but she does! I know she does!" And then I started to sob.

"The poor child's overly tired," somebody said.

Hugo took my hand at once and tried to pull me out of the room. "Come on. Bed."

But I jerked myself away from him and, overcome by a compulsion I did not understand, pointed my finger at our terrified boarder. "You do know it, you do! I'll go up in

a great big balloon, And see my sweetheart in the moon,
Then behind some dark cloud, Where no one is allowed
—' "

Just as Hugo picked me up with his good arm, dangling
me from his waist, Mrs. Grenoble rose and ran from the
room.

Hugo might have carried me kicking and weeping all
the way upstairs, except that there was a loud knock on
the front door and he hesitated at the landing to see who
had come.

Sophie opened the door. Mr. Marcy was back for the
second time in one day. My tears ceased automatically.
Hugo and I, scarcely breathing, strained to hear what was
being said. Not a word carried to us, but when Sophie
turned her face in our direction she looked so stricken that
Hugo set me upon my feet, saying, "Go to bed, Jane." Then
he ran downstairs, crying, "Sophie, what's wrong?"

I did not go to bed. I remained on the landing. I had to
know what Mr. Marcy's second visit meant. My hand
gripped the rail so hard that my fingers hurt, but I did not
relinquish my grip. I clung to the substantial wood, waiting
for my world to fall apart. At first the voices in the hall
were low; then Hugo's rose with excitement, and I understood. Sophie was under arrest, and Mr. Marcy was going
to take her downtown!

It wasn't fair, Hugo protested. Until now there had been
no progress in the murder case. For nearly a year—nothing.
Now, at the first glimmer of light—the identification of the
murder weapon—the authorities were trying to make up
for lost time. They needed a culprit, but why Sophie? Because she was all they had?

There was no more music. Gradually Max and the other
people came out of the parlor and surrounded Mr. Marcy.
I nearly found it in my heart to be sorry for him as he
stared into so many hostile faces at once. He was polite and
patient while a storm of voices battered at him, and in the

end he won. He had convinced even that unreasonable gathering that it had no choice but to submit to watching Sophie being taken away in a hansom cab paid for by the police department.

The Webers looked stunned and glanced at one another, silently asking, What can we do? What can we do? Then Sophie raised her head and threw back her shoulders. She was resigned and calm. "Before I go I want to speak to my brother Hugo—speak to him alone."

Mr. Marcy hesitated, then granted her fifteen minutes.

I went up the rest of the steps to my room. Everyone was shouting again. The din floated up like a cloud, rising, rising. But all I made of it was that a lawyer must be found at once and that Max was going to attend to the matter.

I did not turn on my light. I sat down on my bed in the dark, deep in depression. I was the cause of everything that was happening. If Sophie had never met me, Mr. Marcy would not be taking her away now. Or if I had met her but had not screamed when the murder took place! Or if I had not thought of the hatpin! Oh, and why had I made such a scene with Mrs. Grenoble? What had got into me? What had forced me to make such a fool of myself. I had upset everyone, and at a time when Sophie had so much on her mind. And now what was it she wanted to tell Hugo? What was so imperative that it must be said before she went off with Mr. Marcy?

The minutes dragged on as I waited, expecting something to happen, I didn't know what, and at the same time fearing Sophie would go away without a word to me and that I would be left in ignorance.

But she didn't, after all. Sophie and Hugo came upstairs for their talk and moved directly toward my room. "I want her included in this," Sophie said softly as she pushed open the door.

The light from the hall fell upon me. "Why, she isn't even undressed," Hugo said.

"Are you all right now, Jane?" Sophie asked.

I told her I was. "I'm sorry about Mrs. Grenoble—"

"Never mind that now. I have a lot to tell both of you in a very short time. Jane, your father is arriving on the train tonight."

Hugo sounded stunned. "Her father—*what?*"

"He's coming from Denver."

"Denver! Is that where he's been all this time?" he cried.

"Yes."

"Oh," I said, "then he couldn't have been at the chrysanthemum show!" Sophie and Hugo looked at me. "Never mind," I said. "It isn't important."

"Between the two of you I'm losing my senses!" Hugo cried. "*How* do you know he's coming, Sophie?"

"I got a wire from him this afternoon, from Chicago. He wanted to be here for your birthday, Jane, but the train is nearly a day late."

"Well, what do you know!" Hugo said. "The lost is found—finally."

"Oh, Hugo," Sophie said, "I've known all along where he was."

He stared at her in astonishment. "Why didn't you say something? Why've you let them look for him all this time?"

"He's been a very sick man. Keep quiet and let me do the talking. We only have fifteen minutes."

"All right, all right."

"I've been in correspondence with him almost since the beginning. It said in the newspapers I took Jane home with me, and naturally he was deeply concerned about her, and about his mother, to whom he was afraid to write in case her mail was watched. As soon as I heard from him I wrote back, trying to put his mind at peace."

"His mother knew where he was too?"

"Of course. I told her."

"And neither of you said a word?"

"He had consumption, Hugo!"

"Consumption?"

"Yes, and you don't let a man who's suspected of murder rot in jail until he can prove he's innocent, when he has a sickness like that."

"You couldn't have told us, the family, you knew where he was?"

"We have a pretty talkative family, Hugo."

"You could have told me. You didn't have to keep this all to yourself."

"You were having troubles of your own. What's the difference about that now? The point is that tonight I was going to meet him at the station, and now I can't. And you've got to go instead."

"Oh, all so casually? I should be a delegation of welcome, while you're in jail? No, Miss Weber! The police can meet him!"

"You're going to meet him! Now listen to me, Hugo. This man has gone through hell. He'll be exhausted after a trip like this, and he's going to have one night of rest in a bed before he does anything. You understand that?"

"No, I don't. I have no intention of letting them take you when a better suspect is available."

"Hugo, it's Jane's father we're talking about."

"I'm sorry for Jane, but it's *my* sister *I'm* talking about, and I'm going to inform Mr. Marcy."

Hugo would have walked out of the room had not Sophie seized his arm. "Not tonight! And not until a doctor sees Mr. Carlyle and says he's fit to stand trial and all it entails."

"And in the meantime, *you're* fit? You're going to let them do what they like with you till this man chooses to declare his presence?"

"I know what he'll choose the second he hears what's happened to me. That's why I'm not going to let you tell him tonight, and you've got to promise me you won't."

"I'll do no such thing. Why should I protect him?

What's been going on in his mind all this time? Hasn't he
known the police have been looking for him?"

"Yes, he knew." She explained from the beginning how
my father had become ill in Baltimore. Finding out he had
consumption, he had left the vaudeville tour, taken my
mother and me to New York. His intention was to leave
us there while he was in Denver recovering in the Colorado
climate he needed. My mother was going to go back on the
stage. The three of us had spent a week in the hotel in
New York making arrangements, and he got on the train
the morning of the murder. He never knew it had taken
place until after he arrived in Denver.

"Oh," I cried out, "then he couldn't have committed it."

Sophie looked at me in amazement. "Did you ever think
he had?"

I turned my head away. "No," I lied.

But I had not fooled her. "Oh, Jane," she murmured,
shaking her head sadly. "Oh, Jane. I told you he hadn't.
But you didn't believe me, did you?"

Tears welled up in my eyes, and I blurted, "Sophie, what
did the letters mean?"

"The letters?"

"The ones he wrote you. He called you his dearest one
and his girl."

Sophie wrinkled up her brow in perplexity. "Me?"

The letter I had read in Braddock was as plain as though
the paper were still before me. I was able to recite it nearly
word for word. " 'Thank you with all my heart for the
packet of treasures from the hands of my dearest one. They
cannot help but lighten—' "

I could not go on, for Sophie looked so strange. She was
smiling, and at the same time tears began to stream down
her face. She put her arms around me and pressed her wet
cheek to mine. "Oh, Jane, *you* are his dearest one. The
packet of treasures was a sheaf of your test papers from
school, the ones with the best grades. I thought they might

cheer him up. His letter referred to you, his little girl."
Sophie pulled her head away and looked into my eyes. The
relief I felt must have shown there, for immediately Sophie
was overcome with guilt. "So you found the letters?" Her
tears got bigger, and her voice thickened. "What have I
done to you, Jane? What have you been thinking all this
time?"

Hugo exclaimed angrily, "This is what comes of refusing
to open your mouth! What have you let *me* think, and all
of us? This deception, all along, about adopting Jane when
you knew it was impossible because her father—"

"I didn't know it was impossible!" Sophie interrupted
sharply. "For a long time it was questionable whether or
not Mr. Carlyle would get well. And it was agreed that if
anything should happen to him, I would have her. But by
the time he began to recover I had so learned to respect him
—from his letters—that I knew Jane was luckier to have
him than me."

"Oh, very lucky—in either case," Hugo said bitterly. "A
foster mother who brings the law down on her head because of her obstinacy, or a father who knows he's being
sought and remains in hiding. Poor Jane."

"Hugo, he couldn't go back! Can't you understand? Do
you know how he found out what happened to his wife?
He'd gone straight to the doctor's office in Denver from
the train, and in the waiting room he picked up a newspaper
and there it was in black and white, the cruelest way in the
world he could have discovered it. He collapsed from the
shock and was put in the hospital, unconscious. When he
regained his senses and told the doctor his story, he received some stern advice. He was told he was physically
unable to go back to New York and go through what a man
suspected of murder would have to go through. He must
give himself a chance to get well by staying where he was,
the doctor said."

"I question that doctor's ethics," Hugo said. "Wouldn't you call his recommendation an obstruction of justice?"

"I'd call it a conspiracy of silence in the interest of the patient," Sophie said. "After all, no one else was in jeopardy because no one else was under suspicion. There was plenty of time for justice to take its course after Mr. Carlyle got well."

"Of course he agreed to this?"

"He did. He had Jane to think of! His mother, with me as a messenger, urged the same course." Her voice broke as she pleaded with her brother for approbation. "Please, Hugo, it wasn't as though anyone else was accused. He wasn't letting somebody else take the blame."

"Somebody else has been accused now."

Sophie raised her head and said firmly, "I'm *accused*, Hugo, not convicted."

"Not yet."

"Oh, for heaven's sake, what danger am I in?" Sophie cried impatiently.

"The danger of a continued conspiracy of silence," Hugo exclaimed fiercely, "on the part of Jane's father, her grandmother, the doctor in Denver, and, I suppose, a doctor in Baltimore, because somebody must have examined him there and there hasn't been a peep from him."

"Hugo, Mr. Carlyle is on his way back to New York to give himself up."

"Is he?"

"Yes! He left Denver the moment he was well enough. He only wanted to see Jane first, before the whole thing broke. Please, Hugo. This is a decent, kind man!"

Hugo shook his head in bewilderment. "You're innocent, I'm positive; he's innocent, you say. What I want to know is, who in the world committed the murder?"

"I don't know," Sophie said wearily.

Only I know, I thought, and I can't remember.

There was a knock on the door. "Yes, Mr. Marcy," Hugo called out. "In a minute."

Elise's voice said, "It's me, but he says time's up."

Sophie rose and put her hand on her brother's arm. "You'll treat Mr. Carlyle nicely when you meet him at the station? You'll do as I ask?"

Hugo sighed. "I'll be nice, but after I've talked to him you'll have to let me use my own judgment."

"But not tonight! Promise not to let him do anything until tomorrow, not even to tell him where I am till then."

"And what am I supposed to say?"

"That I'm ill—anything. Take him to a good hotel and meet him tomorrow. Then if you're convinced he's rested enough—"

"All right," Hugo said impatiently. "Don't keep repeating."

"Do you think Jane should go to the station with you?"

"You've decided everything else. Decide that."

"He won't be expecting a man to meet him. If Jane's there on the platform he'll recognize her and—"

"Either way! Whatever you want!"

"It's so late at night, but I suppose she'd better go." She leaned over and kissed me. "Good-by, Jane. Don't worry about me."

They went out of the room, and I was alone. I was so afraid. I wanted to see my father, but I was frightened of him. Or was I ashamed? Was my father really what Sophie thought he was, or would he let her shoulder the charges against her forever? Was he indeed arriving in Pittsburgh tonight, or was he on his way to the South Seas or some other faraway place? Was I the daughter of a coward who had only been waiting for the law to pounce upon somebody else, or of the gentle person Sophie had described? Well, I would soon find out.

I wanted desperately to get into bed and hide under the covers. I wanted to be a little girl. I didn't want to go downtown and face grown-up reality. But I sat still. I was so cold. Why was there no heat in the house?

In five or ten minutes I heard the front door slam. Sophie was gone. I went to my cupboard and took out my wraps. Soon afterward Hugo returned for me and helped me into my coat. We went down the back stairs and out the back door to avoid people who were still standing in the hall talking about Sophie's arrest. Before we'd walked a block, Max's Reo pulled up at the curb beside us.

"Wherever you two are going at this hour," he said, "I think you'd better let me drive you there."

Hugo hesitated only a moment before taking my hand and helping me onto the seat beside Max. Then he slid in next to me. "Did you get a lawyer, Max?"

"I did. He's on his way downtown. Where are you going?"

Hugo told him which depot, and the automobile picked up momentum. Neither of the men spoke. There was only the sound of the motor and of the tires hissing against the wet street. I tilted my head one way, then the other, noticing, when we passed a street lamp, how grave were the profiles of my companions. And Hugo cradled his broken arm as though it pained him. I closed my eyes, letting an uncontrollable sadness wash over me.

"I think the thaw is over," Max said.

"Yes," Hugo agreed. "It's getting cold again."

"The street is slippery already. In an hour everything will be frozen solid. The water running down the gutters will turn to ice. The trees will be stiff as monuments."

"Yes, the weather's certainly changing."

"Well, Hugo," Max said after a pause, "are you going to tell me why you're going to the station?"

Even before he started to talk, I knew Hugo would tell everything. I wanted to stay awake to hear the whole story again, how my father had left my mother and me in New York and had gone to Denver for his health's sake, how he had found out about the murder, and all the rest. But weariness dissolved me, and I slumped against Hugo. I couldn't hold sleep back.

When I opened my eyes again we were nearly downtown. We were driving along a river, and the great blast furnaces of the steel mills thrust their fire dramatically into the night skies. I had never been in this part of Pittsburgh after dark, and so I was astonished at the sight that spread before me—gigantic exploding rubies, carmine reflections in the river, the tortured night stabbed and bleeding.

Hugo was watching it too. "I always think hell must look like this," he said.

"Perhaps," said Max. "It's terrible, but beautiful too. Both. I'm going to describe it in a symphony some day."

"I didn't know you composed."

"I've just started."

I sensed rather than heard the sounds from across the river, a throbbing, the shouts of the men, the hiss of molten ore. "Why are they working at night?" I asked. "And on New Year's too?"

Max said, "Once they start the furnaces, they can't stop them. They must go on and on, fed constantly, like ever-hungry dragons."

"Put that in your symphony," Hugo said.

We reached the station. The train had not yet come in, and while we waited I lay on a bench, my head in Hugo's lap. I went to sleep again and dreamed a hungry dragon was advancing toward me, snorting and roaring, closer and closer. But before it could eat me I opened my eyes and knew the dragon was only the train coming into the station. I sat up and rubbed my drowsy eyes. Soon we were on the platform, the dragon was breathing quietly, and Hugo nervously watched the people getting off the train, wondering how he would recognize my father.

Suddenly I was no longer tired. My hopes rose, and I knew my father was everything Sophie believed him to be.

I stood beside Hugo, my hand in his, waiting for something wonderful to occur, for someone I had known and loved all my life to give me back my lost days gone by, to make me whole again so that the past and present would be fused and I could save Sophie.

I did not even notice the tall, thin man until he stopped beside us and cried, "Jane!" He bent over me and held me close. "Happy birthday, my darling. I'm sorry I'm so late, the day is nearly gone." When he released me, I pulled back my head and peered into my father's face. He was a stranger to me.

Mute with disappointment, I listened to Hugo introduce himself and Max and explain that Sophie had been unable to come. My father appeared worried about her absence at first, or perhaps only apprehensive at being met by two strange men, but after a few minutes my presence seemed to give him confidence and he began to relax. I knew, because Sophie had told me, that he was thirty-eight years old, but, though there were touches of gray at his temples, he looked to me much younger. He stood tall and erect, and even though he had been on the train for days he had managed to keep himself clean-shaven and his appearance was meticulous. His collar was white and neat, his overcoat without a crease. As he talked, expressing his gratitude at being met so late at night, I tried to read his expression. His features were finely chiseled, his face sensitive, but it touched no chord in my heart, brought back no memories. Was he gentle and kind, as Sophie had said he would be, or was he a murderer? Should I feel sorry for him because he had left a little girl in New York who loved him and when he came back to her she felt nothing at all? Could he tell?

"How do you feel?" Max said.

"I'm fine," my father replied, but his words were belied by the dark rings under his eyes. "A little tired, perhaps. The train was snowbound for eighteen hours in the

West." He clung to my hand as if for strength. "Now that I've seen Jane, I think I should go directly on to New York."

"If you mean to report to the police," Hugo said, "it can be done as well here."

"Good."

"But it can wait until tomorrow. Don't you think you should have a night's sleep first?" Hugo asked it so freely that any question he had had in his mind concerning my father must have been dissipated by the sight of him. For Hugo there was certainty. Why was there none for me?

"No, I'm all right. And it will be a relief to get it over with."

Max picked up his suitcase, and as we were leaving the station a man hurrying in, perhaps late to meet the train already arrived, struck against my father, making him stagger. There was only a curt "Sorry" from the man, and he was gone, but the wind had been knocked out of my father, and he was forced to sit down for a minute on one of the benches.

When he rose again we walked slowly for his sake. Passing under a street lamp, we noticed how pallid his face had become, and Hugo said, "It's nonsense turning yourself in tonight. Let's take him to a hotel, Max. What do you say, Mr. Carlyle?"

My father was tempted. "I think if I could have long enough to take a bath, just long enough for a bath, I'd feel better."

We drove to the Fort Pitt Hotel and let him out. He said good night to us, and we watched him walk away under the canvas canopy, his shoulders sagging. Hugo glanced worriedly at Max.

Suddenly he opened the automobile door again. "I'm going with him." He jumped out of the car. "Max, take Jane home. And stay the night in the house, would you?" He called back some explanation, but we could not hear what he said because he hurried so swiftly after my father. We drove off.

It was apparent that my father was not yet entirely recovered. No wonder Sophie had wanted to spare him. No wonder she went with Mr. Marcy without saying, "I can tell you where to find the man you're looking for, so let me be."

On the way downtown, more asleep than awake, I had heard Max say of Sophie's decision, "Only she would have done this. Only Sophie would have had the courage." She had only his letters to go by, but she had had the faith to postpone my father's ordeal as long as she could. And for a few more hours Hugo and Max and I would continue to protect him. After that it would be up to him to bear the burden of accusation.

The family was still up when we got home, and frantic. Where had I been? Where was Hugo? Why had we left the house? I did not care how Max explained it. Too tired for anything but bed, I went upstairs.

I looked into Sophie's room, where everything was tidy and lovely, the white bedspread without a ripple on its surface, the flowered carpet well swept, the dresser-top neatly arranged, from buttonhook to pincushion. But oh, the room was so empty without Sophie.

I got undressed and crawled into my bed. I thought of the man I had seen at the Phipps Conservatory. If he was not my father, who could he be? Only a reporter, as he had told Pauline? Or the real murderer? I shivered and pulled the blankets closer about me.

At last I heard everyone coming upstairs. "Do you know why Hugo wants me to stay all night?" Max was asking.

"He doesn't trust Mrs. Grenoble," Elise replied. "Last night he locked Jane's door."

"Then I'll do the same."

"Hugo *ist verrückt*," Grandma said. "Crazy, crazy. And my daughter is a jailbird. I won't sleep a wink all night."

For no reason at all their voices comforted me.

Max came and locked my door. I called out a good night to him, and he shouted back that he would be in the sitting room if I wanted him.

The house is a fortress, I reminded myself between sleep and semiconsciousness. Grandma is not going to sleep a wink all night, and maybe none of the others will, either. All my friends are awake, guarding me, guarding me against harm.

My confidence was ill-founded.

I awoke with a start at about three in the morning, knowing someone was in the room. I could see nothing until the figure of a man, outlined against the dull light made by the winter moon, passed between my bed and the window. He was coming toward me slowly, slowly, from Sophie's room. I screamed and at the same time rolled over the side of my bed onto the floor and plunged under the bed as fast as I could scramble. It flashed through my mind that, after all, the man might be my father. I kept on screaming.

The man's hand was on my shoulder when I heard Max hurtle himself against my door. I knew his attempt was futile, that the door would not give, and that he must use the key or enter through Sophie's room. Would there be time? I was being pulled out from under my bed with inevitability, even though I clung with all the strength of my hands to the wooden slats above me. I wondered who was panting so loud in the room. Was it I, or was it my assailant?

My hands were wrenched from their grasp, and I felt the carpet's nap scrape harshly against my stomach. I don't know what would have happened then had not Max, like a great primeval winged beast, come flying through the air, crashing against the man and tumbling him to the floor. For a few minutes they thrashed about. Then there was a sud-

den cry of pain, and one of them, I could not tell which at
first, went racing out of the room.

I lay where I was, without moving. It seemed a long
time, though it probably took no more than twenty beats of
my heart, before I heard someone else coming and the electric light blazed on. It was not until then that I knew Max
was lying in the corner like a crumpled and abandoned doll.

Seymour, in his nightshirt, barefoot and his hair tousled,
gaped at us. I sat up. He drew in his breath, then ran to
Max and bent over him. I thought Max might be dead, but
he opened his eyes, looking first at Seymour, then at me.

"It's all right, Jane," he said weakly and tried to stand up.

Then Sylvester and Elise were in the room, awakened
by my screams. "Get a doctor, somebody," Seymour said.
Sylvester hurried out without a word.

Max's hand went to his chest, and when Elise tore open
his shirt blood was flowing from a tiny wound. "I don't
think it's too bad," she said.

Max stood erect. "Neither do I. I'm just scared to death,
that's all."

"What happened?"

"A man tried to get me," I said, "but Max saved me."

Seymour grasped my arm. "Who was the man?"

There was no need to answer, for all of us, at nearly the
same second, saw the hatpin lying in the middle of the
floor. It was one of Sophie's with a round head, garnet-
studded this time. We stared at it, then at one another.
Everyone is so pale, I thought.

By the time Dr. Reichart came, Grandma had appeared
in her dressing gown, her braid hanging down her neck.
Apprised of the situation, she had gone down to the kitchen
to make coffee, her panacea for everything. It was she who
let the doctor into the house and brought him upstairs. Max
was lying on Sophie's bed. The color had returned to his
face, and he smiled when Grandma said to me on entering

the room, "Shame on you in front of the doctor! Put something on over your nightgown!"

I slipped into my room and put on my kimono while Dr. Reichart examined the patient. The wound, he said as I returned, was not very deep and nothing much would come of it unless it became infected. "Hardly worth getting me out of bed for."

"You were asleep?" Grandma asked. "Not playing pinochle?"

Dr. Reichart glared at her. "No, Mrs. Weber, and if this" —pointing to Max—"were you instead of a stranger, I would charge you three dollars instead of two."

"If it was me it would be worth it."

"If it was you I'd be pretty sure I'd stabbed you myself. So I wouldn't charge you anything!"

"Don't do me any favors," Grandma told him.

His hands trembled with rage as he applied the dressing to Max's chest, but before he could think of a retort Grandma suddenly cried, "*Ach Gott,* my coffee is boiling over!" and hastened downstairs.

After summoning the doctor, Sylvester had remained at his house to use the telephone. He had called Mr. Marcy to inform him that the same man who had killed my mother had made an attempt on my life. He came back just as Dr. Reichart was leaving, and told us Mr. Marcy was on the way.

We did not have to wait long. As fast as a hansom could bring him, Mr. Marcy arrived to learn the details of the stabbing. While he listened to us he held the hatpin in his hand, twisting it around and around as though he expected it too to talk to him. When he could think of no more to say he inquired, "And none of you have any idea how the man got into the house? Nobody heard anything?"

"Not unless Mrs. Grenoble did," Grandma said.

"Who's she?"

"Our boarder."

"I didn't know you had a boarder."

"You met her New Year's Eve when you were here."

"I must have thought she was one of the guests. Where is she now?"

"In her room."

All of us but Max and Sylvester trooped up to the third floor with him. He knocked on the door, but there was no answer. He went into her room, and we followed. He turned on the light and nobody was there. The bed had not been slept in; the candlewick spread which covered it was without a crease. The chair, however, looked recently sat upon, its cushions still crushed from the weight of a body. Mr. Marcy felt them to see if they were still warm, but they were not. He opened the cupboard, revealing a few wooden hangers, from which hung Mrs. Grenoble's cape and the only two dresses we'd ever seen her wear. The bureau drawers, when he opened them, were nearly empty, and so was her valise, which stood in the corner.

"She certainly doesn't own much," Mr. Marcy said. "How long has she lived here?"

"Only a couple of days."

"Is that so!"

"She spoke about a trunk," Elise said, "but it didn't come."

"I wonder what happened to her, such a nice woman," Grandma said, staring, bewildered, at the immaculate bed.

"Your 'such a nice woman,'" Elise said, "was probably only here for the purpose of letting the man in the house."

Grandma was outraged. "I don't believe it! A lady who was so good with helping with the wedding!"

"How did she happen to come here?" Mr. Marcy asked.

"I had an ad in the paper," Grandma said tartly. "So there!"

"How did she answer the ad? By mail? By—"

"She came to the house and knocked on the door," Grandma began. "And I—"

"No, she didn't." I corrected her. "She was in front of the house with Trixie and me, and you came outside and started to talk to her."

"And mentioned you had an ad in the paper for a boarder, Mrs. Weber?"

When Grandma nodded, Mr. Marcy went on, "So she found a convenient way to get into the house. Grenoble? Grenoble? It makes me think of something. Isn't there a town by that name on the way into Pittsburgh by train? If someone needed to make up a name on the spur of the moment, might she not think of a name she had just heard called out by the conductor on a train? When did you see this so-called Mrs. Grenoble last?"

Seymour said, "Last night," and then Elise brought up the subject of the song, telling how I'd suddenly insisted Mrs. Grenoble knew it, how she'd denied it, and, when I'd grown hysterical, how she'd run out of the room.

Mr. Marcy looked at me. "What was the name of the song?"

I told him.

"Why did you think she could sing it?"

"I don't know. I just did."

" 'My Sweetheart's the Man in the Moon,' " he repeated. "Where have I heard it? It sounds vaguely familiar, but I'm not very good about songs. Is it identified with anyone?"

"Like 'Roley Boley Eyes' is with Eddie Leonard?" Elise asked.

"That's exactly what I mean."

"Ask Max. He's a musician. Maybe he knows."

We gathered around the bed on which Max lay, and looked at him anxiously, but all he could say was that the song was very popular and dozens of people might sing it.

He plucked at the tufts on the bedspread a moment. "I see what you mean. Whom did Jane know in the past? Who were her parents' friends? Vaudevilleans. If the song reminded her of an actor, and the actor were the murderer, then . . ."

"Yes," Mr. Marcy said. "Go on."

But Max hesitated. Was he thinking that my father was downtown with Hugo this very minute and that we might ask him whose song it was? If Max wouldn't mention this, did I dare? No! What if the song were in my father's act!

"Come on," Mr. Marcy said. "There must be a reason why Jane thought of that particular song and why it disturbed her so much."

But Max shook his head. "I don't know who in particular is identified with it."

"But it could be with an actor?"

"Well, of course, something that well known."

"All right," Mr. Marcy said. "I must get to a telephone."

"Why? What are you going to do?"

"Some research on the theater."

Before he left, Mr. Marcy gave Seymour a gun. I wondered how he could have carried it on his person without any of us knowing.

He did not come back that night.

It was after ten in the morning when I awoke. I went to the window and saw that the snow had been falling heavily. The tree boughs sagged with the weight of it, the street was a thick white blanket marred only by ruts carved by passing vehicles. The policeman on our beat was standing in front of the house, kicking his feet against the lamppost to keep them warm. It had just stopped snowing. There was white upon his bucket helmet and upon the stand-up collar of his brass-buttoned uniform. How funny the weather had been—first a thaw, then a freeze during the night, and in the morning all this snow.

I watched the policeman a little while. He did not go away. Perhaps Mr. Marcy had sent him to guard us.

I dressed, and when I went into Sophie's room Max was still asleep on her bed. I tiptoed past him.

The house was quiet. I found Elise dusting in the parlor. "Where's everyone?" I asked.

"Mama's in the kitchen, Sophie's in jail, and Seymour and Sylvester went to the store."

"Today?"

"It's Saturday, isn't it?"

"Oh. Where's Hugo? And Mr. Marcy?"

"Neither of them heard from."

Grandma, in an apron, appeared in the doorway. "So you're awake, ten-o'clock scholar? And Max?"

"Still sleeping," I said.

"*Ach*, that such a good nickelodeon player should be stabbed in my house! Who would have imagined it? Let him sleep, poor man."

Yes, poor Max, I thought. And poor Sophie. And poor Hugo. And poor everybody. What troubles I had brought for them all when I had arrived that Saint Valentine's Day. And never, not once, had there been a word of reproach. Why did not Grandma, or Elise, turn upon me now and point out that it was my coming that had eventually led Sophie to prison, Hugo into an agony of worry, Max to feel the point of a weapon in his chest and yet keep silent for my father's sake? Instead, Grandma said she would fix me a nice breakfast with cocoa, my favorite, and Elise said she would play dominoes with me later. Tears of gratitude forced themselves into my eyes, and I turned my head away lest they be misunderstood and anyone think I was sorry for myself.

After breakfast I did not know what to do. I washed my few dishes and then decided to go out into the snow. I heard Max in the bathroom splashing at the wash bowl as

I went to my room to get my coat and overshoes. I came out again, pulling a tassel cap over my head.

Nobody saw me, nobody stopped me. If it came into my mind at all that it might be dangerous for me to leave the house, I must have shoved the thought aside. I went out the back door, not because the policeman was in front, but because I wanted to wander near the tennis court, along the paths where I had played during other days. To say good-by?

Did I know that, whatever happened to Sophie, to my father, I would not have much time here any more? It was strange that while I was still at Wilkins Avenue I had such nostalgia for it. I loved every creaking board of the back porch, the slanting cellar doors, the wash line stiff with winter. I missed them all even while I walked and looked at them.

My feet crunched the snow underfoot as I passed through the garden, remembering the spot where the hollyhocks had stood in summer, where the bleeding hearts and the lilies-of-the-valley grew among the ferns in the shade. I wandered among the familiar places. Here by the spring Trixie and I had made mudpies. There on the bower the honeysuckle vine had filled the air with scent. I passed the place we had jumped rope when the boy had yelled at me. I roved over the tennis court, leaving a curious trail of footprints in the snow, remembering Sophie in her white dress with the big pearl buttons and her racket in her hand. Gone were the net, the tennis balls, the players calling to each other, "Good shot," "Thirty love," "Your serve." The trees in the field were bare, but I saw them again as they had been when the locusts were in bloom and the chestnuts had yielded so plentifully their rich brown smooth buckeyes which Pauline and I strung into heavy necklaces to wear all of an afternoon. Gone were the butterflies, the smell of clover, the little breezes of summer. I would never lie in the grass in this place again, watching clouds drifting by and swallows winging past.

Sadly I moved to the little grove of trees where Sophie used to lie in the hammock on Sunday, reading. I went into the hidden secret place. I had never put the hammock away as I had been supposed to, I recalled. It was still there, heavy and full as though someone were lying in it mantled with snow.

I nearly turned away, leaving it to the elements once more, but I noticed the shoes and stood rooted to the spot. There *was* somebody in the hammock. A pair of feet in men's black brogans, from which the snow had fallen away, protruded at one end. All else was covered white.

I felt no fear at first, only wonder. How long had the man lain suspended, motionless while the snow fell upon him until nothing of him was visible but those ghastly shoes? Who was he and why was he here?

I advanced and reached out to brush his face clear. The snow fell away in chunks, revealing a visage frozen solid, looking like a wax dummy's, eyelashes iced, and only a faint trace of color in its lips to tell me this had once been a living man.

As I stared at the chill face, all that I had strained to remember for so long came flooding back. I saw the room in the hotel. I see it still.

There is blue carpeting on the floor, a mirror in a gilt frame on the wall. I see myself in bed with Nancy Myrtle May beside me, but her name is Diane. There is a bouquet of hothouse roses in a vase on a bedside table. I see my mother in a gray silk dress, opening the door to let in Ray Beaumont. He shakes hands with her and comes over to the bed to say hello to me. I tell him I have a cold and he says, "Well, I see you still have the doll I gave you." I touch his hand because I like him, and because so many times he has let me stand in the wings to watch him on the stage dancing and singing.

My mother invites him to sit down and tells him my father is ill and has gone to Denver. She has sent for Ray, she says, because she wants him to pay her the money he owes her. She can put it to good use now.

He denies, pleasantly at first, but growing testy as he continues, that he owes her anything at all.

"You know very well what you agreed to," my mother says, reminding him that when she sold him her act upon her retirement from vaudeville he had given her three hundred dollars with the understanding he was to pay her a hundred dollars a year in the future. He had made two payments and stopped.

Of course he has stopped, Ray cries, because the act no longer bears any resemblance to what he bought. He has eliminated all the comedy and added a whole new element —high fashion. He has changed the act gradually but entirely, using six chorus girls to back him up, and there is no longer one song from my mother's act that he uses any more.

"We still have an agreement," my mother says quietly.

Ray stands up, dancing with rage. He could not pay her even if he wanted to! His voice grows wilder and more frenzied. He has spent a fortune on new material; all he makes goes into the act to improve it, to make it shine until the name of Ray Beaumont, the Mayfair Fashion Plate, is one that provokes ecstasy in a booker's heart!

I sit up in bed, wondering why he is so angry, picturing him as he is on the stage, a beautiful lady who sings and dances. I think of the great moment at the end of the act when he whips off his wig and he is a man! I see it—the tug of the hair, the flourish, the bow.

"I buy my gowns at Worth," he shrills at my mother. "And where did you buy yours? I pay in the hundreds, as much as a thousand!"

"Control your dreadful temper, Ray," my mother pleads. "You'll have a heart attack again."

He ignores her. "I'm the greatest female impersonator in the world! I buy at Worth! At Worth!"

He picks up the hatpin from the dresser, Sophie's hatpin, which I had taken and brought to our room. He raises his arm, and as he steps toward my mother he brings it down again. My mother falls to the floor. He throws away the hatpin, flings it with all his strength, and hurries from the room. He does not give a backward glance, but he is weeping. "I buy at Worth! At Worth!"

I stand up on the bed and begin to scream.

That was how it had been.

I turned my back on Ray Beaumont, dead and frosty in the hammock, and walked slowly back to the house.

Grandma sat in the kitchen, stirring something in a bowl. "Oh, Grandma!" I choked and put my head into her warm white apron.

She listened to what I remembered, her hand on my head smoothing my hair, her little body tense with excitement and compassion. When I came to the end she kissed me and said, "You must tell Mr. Marcy what you told me. I wonder where he is."

It was an hour before Elise found him and brought him back to Wilkins Avenue. He listened to me quietly and respectfully and thanked me when I finished. Though he was surprised Ray Beaumont was dead, my identification of him as the killer did not startle him at all. Mr. Marcy said he had been talking long distance on the phone ever since he had left the house in the middle of the night. He had awakened theater managers and bookers, spoken to newspapermen and police departments in other cities. At last he had learned of a theater in Erie that had burned down a few days after Christmas. Ray Beaumont, the Mayfair Fashion Plate, had been on the bill.

The fire explained everything. Ray Beaumont, with time on his hands, attempted again to find out if my memory had

come back. Twice before he had tried, disguising himself
with a patch over his eye; twice he had not been sure. This
time he had been sure—until I had mentioned "The Man
in the Moon."

The *Pittsburgh Gazette* told it all the next day. The
famous actor, dressed as a woman, had come to Pittsburgh
on a train. He hung around the house until Trixie and I
came along, got into a conversation with us. Though
Grandma invited him inside for coffee, he had been unable
to learn anything about me. So when the room was offered
he rented it and, finally convinced that my amnesia had
lasted and that he was safe, tried to leave on New Year's
Day—but Grandma had talked him out of it. That very
evening I connected him with the song from his act. Fearing I would soon recall everything, he had tried to kill me.
When Max interfered, he fought him off and ran out of
the house the back way. The exertion had probably
brought on the fatal heart attack, for he was known to have
had a slight one years ago. Evidently he began to feel pain
in the garden, staggered down toward the tennis court
and, finding the little stand of trees, wanted to hide himself in it. There he had seen the hammock, crawled into it,
and died.

Sophie Weber, who had spent a night being futilely questioned by the police, and my father, who had turned himself over to them after a few hours' rest upon reaching
Pittsburgh, were released.

When all of us, even Grandma, were tired of talking
about the big happenings at our house, we thought of other
things—my father's continuing recovery in a rest home,
the dances Sophie went to with Max, her investment in
Mr. Auerbach's new motion-picture company. All three
men, it seemed to Grandma, were in love with Sophie, and
the only question was which one she would choose to
marry.

"Oh, Mama, stop it!" Sophie would cry. "I think I'd prefer to go back and talk about the murder again."

Toward the end of February my father told us he was well enough to return to the theater, that he had accepted an engagement in New York in an operetta. The next day Sophie and Max announced their engagement.

The celebration was nearly as good as when Sylvester was going to propose to Hilda Klopstock. "My Sophie to be married!" Grandma kept exclaiming. "I'm so surprised!"

"You are not," Sophie retorted. "You're the only one who always expected it."

"To someone or other," Elise said, "no matter who."

"I'm glad it's Max," Grandma said, kissing him. "Play me some nickelodeon music."

And he did: boy-girl music; now a sinister tune for the bad man; train music; the heroine is in danger; True Blue Harold to the rescue; love-kiss music. How much it told!

I said good-by to Trixie and Walter and Ernest and Pauline, and to all the Webers. Then, nearly a year to the day after I had come, I left the house on Wilkins Avenue.

Though my father's career soon took me to Europe, Grandma and Sophie wrote to me often. I treasured their letters, rejoicing when Hugo's editorials were published in a book that sold well and made him something of a pundit in time to come, when Mr. Auerbach built a studio in Hollywood (Sophie's two hundred dollars eventually became nearly a hundred thousand), and when he married Elise. Seymour and Sylvester never married at all. They kept the store going until they retired in their fifties, still spoken of as "the boys." I saw Sophie a number of times. On one occasion she and Max visited me in Paris where they had come for the introduction of his *Three River Symphony*. They were very happy and had a little girl of their own. Sometime later I had a marvelous reunion with Pauline and Trixie in New York. I sorrowed when Grandma's letters ceased.

She died at eighty of a stroke in the lobby of a motion-picture palace.

I have had a good life, traveling much, living in many places. I have enjoyed them all, but as a vacationist does. I have always felt a long way from home.